CHASING THE
MOON

PENNY CHAMBERLAIN

 **sono**nis PRESS WINLAW, BRITISH COLUMBIA

Library and Archives Canada Cataloguing in Publication

Chamberlain, Penny, 1958-
   Chasing the moon / Penny Chamberlain.

ISBN 1-55039-157-7

   1. Smuggling—British Columbia—Vancouver Island—
History—20th century—Juvenile fiction. I. Title.

PS8555.H289C43 2006   jC813'.6   C2006-904025-7

Sono Nis Press most gratefully acknowledges support for our
publishing program provided by the Government of Canada
through the Book Publishing Industry Development Program
(BPIDP) and the Canada Council for the Arts, and by the
Province of British Columbia through the British Columbia
Arts Council and the Book Publishing Tax Credit, Ministry of
Provincial Revenue.

Edited by Laura Peetoom and Dawn Loewen
Cover photo (figure) by Mike Donnelly
Cover and interior design by Jim Brennan

Published by   Distributed in the U.S. by
Sono Nis Press   Orca Book Publishers
Box 160   Box 468
Winlaw, BC V0G 2J0   Custer, WA 98240-0468
1-800-370-5228   1-800-210-5277

books@sononis.com
www.sononis.com

Printed and bound in Canada by Friesens Printing
Printed on acid-free paper that is forest friendly
(100% post-consumer recycled paper) and has
been processed chlorine free.   The Canada Council | Le Conseil des Arts
                                                     for the Arts | du Canada

For my parents,
Albert (Hap) and Joan Keel

1 The Station

Kit set her suitcase on the station stairs and sat down beside it. All the other passengers from the train had gone. Ages ago, it seemed. She was the only one left. There wasn't much at this stop—she could see the general store, the post office, the butcher's, the blacksmith's and, set at some distance from the other buildings, the Prairie Inn. There had been very little change since the last time she'd been here, several years ago. In one direction the road disappeared into a dusty wall of fir trees. In the other direction the road rose and fell gently between farmlands. Waves of heat shimmered off the land. Somewhere in the long yellow grass by the station, a cricket chirped a sad and solitary song.

She had been travelling since early that morning. Her neighbour, Mrs. Bolton, had bundled her onto the first train in Nanaimo.

"When you get to the end of the line you only have to walk a short way. Cross the Johnson Street bridge into downtown Victoria. Go to the corner of Douglas and Pandora and catch the next train, the Interurban, out to the Saanich Peninsula," Mrs. Bolton had said hurriedly as the train puffed and the whistle blew. "Here's the money for your ticket. Make sure you get off at the Saanichton station. That's your stop. And mind you don't talk to strangers. Your mother would never have that. She made me promise I'd remind you."

Kit didn't need to be reminded. She'd heard it many times before. Kit had never ridden a train by herself before, let alone two in one day. She had never been alone in downtown Victoria either. She'd followed a group of other train passengers across the bridge and found herself on a busy street corner. Taverns and rundown rooming houses lined the street. A group of workmen in dirty overalls had gathered in the doorway of a nearby tavern. They'd been smoking cigarettes and talking in loud voices. One of them had called out to her, "You lost, missy? I'll show you the way." The other men had laughed as Kit hurried by, careful not to look in their direction.

The city had seemed bigger than she'd remembered, the buildings taller. Noisy motor cars crowded the streets and she kept bumping into people with her suitcase. She wasn't sure which way she was supposed to go to catch the next train. Finally she reasoned it was better to ask directions of a stranger than be lost in a big city. Surely her mother would understand. But it was not without a twinge of guilt that she approached a respectable-looking woman on the sidewalk. The woman pointed her in the correct direction. "Two blocks that way…and you better hurry." Kit ran all the way. The train was already there, waiting and ready to go. She climbed aboard, paid her fare and sat down by the window, out of breath.

Now here she was. She twisted around to check the sign on the station. *Saanichton,* it read. Yes, she was definitely in the right place. The station clock showed five minutes to four. Her father was supposed to have been there to meet her train at three.

She stretched out her legs, smoothing her starched dress firmly over her knees and studying the pattern on the fabric. It was a light cotton, a simple green and orange plaid, and, when she turned the edge over, she could see the fine stitches her mother had made underneath where she had let the hem down. That had been months ago, before she'd become sick. Kit traced a finger along the tiny, careful stitches and straightened the dress again.

Then, far in the distance, bumping down the road between the farms, a truck appeared, trailed by a plume of dust, like the tail on a rooster. Kit could see the truck crest each hill and then disappear into the next dip of the road. The engine hiccuped and the doors and windows rattled as it approached the station. Kit stood up eagerly and picked up her suitcase.

But the truck passed by without even slowing down. Kit had only a second to see that the driver was an old man in a battered straw hat—not her father at all. The truck passed the station, the noise gradually subsiding as it rattled farther and farther away. All that was left behind was a slow settling of dust.

Kit sat down with a sigh. It was very hot. The cricket had stopped singing. She checked the clock. Only five minutes had passed. It was four o'clock now; she could wait no longer. She stood up again, grabbed her tan leather suitcase and marched down the steps.

She decided to check the blacksmith shop first. She could feel the heat as she approached. Inside the flames roared and raged as the blacksmith fanned them with an enormous pair of bellows. Her father wasn't there. Nor was he at the post office. The inn, with a row of cars pulled up outside, seemed more promising. It was a noisy place with gales of laughter and clinking of glasses. She put her suitcase down and looked in the window. But her father was nowhere to be found.

As she walked back toward the station, she noticed the shopkeeper standing in the door of the general store. He wore a long white apron and a visor that cast a greenish shadow over his face. "You looking for someone?" he called.

Kit shook her head mutely. Not only was she forbidden to talk to strangers, she didn't want to admit her own father had forgotten her.

"You sure?" He had a kindly face.

She shook her head again. She was going to have to walk, she decided. That was all there was to it. She set her shoulders squarely and set off down the side of the road, well aware that the shopkeeper was watching her go. One thing Kit hated was someone feeling sorry for her. She made herself swing the suitcase a little to show she didn't care. The long road stretched ahead of her through the farmlands. On one side were green rows of corn, and on the other side was a field of freshly cut hay scenting the air with a warm, sweet aroma.

Kit trudged along the edge of the road, whispers of dust billowing up around her feet. Before long her socks and shoes were thick with dust. When she shifted her suitcase from hand to hand she could see the ridges the handle had left on her fingers. It banged awkwardly against her leg, growing heavier, it seemed, with every step. She passed field after field. The sun beat down. There were few signs of people, and only a couple of cars went by as she trudged along. Kit was careful to always step onto the shoulder of the road as they passed. Once a brand new gasoline tractor rumbled by. Occasionally she'd come across a mailbox and, at the far end of each lane, she'd see a farmhouse or a barn. Sometimes a curious dog would stir itself, come halfway down the driveway and stare at her.

Just when the backs of her heels were beginning to sting from the rubbing of her shoes, she crested another hill and the ocean came into view. It was still a good distance away, but there it was, Haro Strait. And there were the islands, rounded like the backs of whales. The names of the closest ones came quickly to mind: Sidney Island, James Island. And there was D'Arcy Island, where the leper colony was. Then, farther away, the San Juan Islands. She knew the San Juans were American islands, and that somewhere in that expanse of blue was an invisible line that marked the border between Canada and the United States. Farther away still, past the islands, rose the mountains of the mainland. She could see Mount Baker, the tallest one of all, snowcapped even in summer. The blues and greens before her mixed together like a watercolour painting, the colours softened and blurred where they met. Kit took in a deep breath. The air was fresher and cooler than at the dusty train station. And it held the sharp, invigorating tang of salt water.

She was almost there. Her steps quickened. The farms gave way to fir trees. First one or two trees appeared, and then a few clusters, and finally a stretch of forest. Then she saw the mailbox at the side of the road, a tin box on a crooked post with their name, AVERY, marked in peeling red letters. Beneath, in smaller letters, was printed HOME AGAIN BAY. Kit felt a smile play at her lips. She was home again. The red flag on the mailbox was not standing upright but Kit lifted the squeaky door and peered in anyway. No mail. She let the door clang shut. Maybe tomorrow there would be a letter from her mother.

The driveway edged into the tall maple trees and firs, two rutted paths with a thin swath of grass in the middle. It was darker and cooler now that she was out of the sun. Kit followed the meandering curve of the road first one way and then the other. And then she was out into the light again and there before her was the house.

It sat halfway down the slope to the water. It was square and squat, with red shingle siding and white trim around the windows. The pitch of the roof was low with a dormer window facing the ocean. Kit felt her breath catch at the sight of it. Her old room. She could remember how she would open her eyes in the morning and look out that window, over the berry field, the little orchard—two apple trees, two pear and two cherry—and out over the roof of the barn towards the sun-glinted water.

She scanned the yard but there was no sign of the truck or anyone around. The grass had grown tall. An old, rusted bike leaned against the barn, pitched forward where it was missing the front wheel. The two farm horses that used to pull the plow were not there. There were no chickens clucking and pecking at the ground. The orchard had not been pruned, and the branches spread wildly. The saddest sight of all, though, was the strawberry field. It had gone to weeds. The ground was hard and dry. There was no protective layer of straw and the plants had withered. Some of the leaves were red and curled in on themselves. It was the beginning of July, the tail end of the season for strawberries, but, still, the plants should have been yielding a scattering of white flowers and a few berries. As far as she could see there was not a single flower. Kit bent to look closer, lifting a drooping stem and smoothing out the three stunted leaves it held. She ran her fingers through the leaves of plant after plant until she found a sad cluster of fruit—tiny, hardened, malformed nubs where the berries had dried up and turned brown.

This was not at all the way Kit had remembered the farm. She mounted the stairs to the long veranda that fronted the house, and she could see that the house, too, had been neglected. The paint was peeling. A crumbling wicker rocking chair sat idle in the corner, its cushion in tatters. She pressed her face up to the torn screen of the door and knocked.

"Hello? Is anyone there?" She could see through the screen that the main door stood open, but beyond that it was difficult to make out the interior of the house. Everything inside was dark compared to the white-brightness outside.

"Hello? Dad?" she called, louder this time.

Still no answer.

Kit pulled open the screen door and set her suitcase down beside a pile of dirty shoes tossed in the corner. She walked slowly down the hall, looking left and right into each room. Piles of old newspapers and mail-order catalogues littered the floor. A thick layer of dust coated the bell of the gramophone. There was clutter everywhere. The clock above the mantel read a quarter to twelve, at least five hours slow. Could that have been why her father hadn't been at the station to pick her up?

She stopped in the kitchen doorway and her stomach recoiled at the mess of greasy dishes and dirty glasses. A long, brown, twisted flypaper hung from the ceiling in the centre of the room, studded with dead flies. She stepped tentatively into the room. The floor felt sticky under her feet. In the dismal silence she gazed at the stack of dirty dishes in the dishpan. The top plate held a thin puddle of water with floating lumps of greyish material. The only sound was a persistent fly that buzzed and bumped up against the dirty kitchen window trying to get out.

Kit turned back into the hallway and climbed the stairs to her old room. The ceiling sloped down on either side, just as she remembered, and the window still held the same view; but an elaborate web had established itself in the corner above the window. The spider in the centre was as big as a quarter. The mattress was bare, the blue-and-white-striped ticking had faded, and big, fuzzy grey dustballs had gathered under the bed. She sat down on the mattress and the springs creaked a pitiful welcome.

How long had it been since she had last been here? How long since her mother had left her father? Three, perhaps four, years. In some ways it seemed like forever and in other ways it was just like yesterday. She had clear memories of her mother and grandfather running the farm while her father was away in Europe fighting the war. Her mother would check the mail each morning to see if there was a letter from him. She worked long hours on the farm and in the quiet evenings she'd knit socks for the troops. Then, finally, the day came when Kit's father had come home again, tall in his uniform. He'd lifted Kit up, up high in the sky and twirled around and around until she felt she was flying. For that moment everything was perfect.

But it didn't last. Not long afterwards influenza had swept through the country and her grandfather became ill.

For days everyone in the house spoke in hushed tones. One night she woke to hear her mother crying down the hall. That was the night he had died. After that her mother and father ran the farm themselves. They worked in the fields and they told her everything would be fine. But somehow Kit knew they were smiling only for her. Something was wrong between them.

For the most part, the tension was under the surface, percolating. Their conversation was strained, almost formal, with each other. Kit rarely witnessed an outright argument—she suspected they made an effort to conceal these from her—but there were a few occasions she could recall.

Kit's father drove the truck at high speeds, barely braking to take the corners.

"Slow down," her mother would urge him over and over. "You're scaring me."

One day her mother made him stop the truck. She got out and told Kit to get out as well. She straightened her hat and announced she wasn't going to risk her life for one more minute. They were going to walk home instead.

Another time, Kit's mother confronted him when he came home from gambling on horses at the Willows Race Track.

"You're wasting our money," her mother had said. "Before you know it there'll be nothing left."

She tried to make him promise he would stop going, that he wouldn't gamble anymore. But he would not make such a promise.

She said the war had changed him, that he never used to be so reckless. She said he was a different man than the one she had married.

Not long after that she told Kit to pack her things into

a trunk. They were going to Nanaimo. She'd found a job as a teacher there. They were leaving the farm and they were leaving her father.

Kit hated to think about that awful day. Her mind slipped sideways instead, to something else, anything else. She stood up and straightened her skirt. She would make her bed up, that's what she would do. Downstairs, she rummaged through the shelves of the linen closet for sheets and a pillow slip and a couple of blankets. They smelled of must and mothballs so she shook each one vigorously outside, making them snap. Then she carried them upstairs to her bedroom, propped open the window to let in some fresh air, and made up her bed.

She knew she had a lot of dirty work ahead of her so she pulled on a pair of overalls from the bottom of her suitcase and tied a kerchief tightly around her head. Then she found a mop in the broom closet and poked it under the bed to collect the dustballs. She had to shake it out several times, but finally the wood of the floor gleamed darkly. She shoved the mop high up into the corner above the window and swirled it around to catch the sticky web. The spider pulled itself up into a black ball and stuck onto the end of the mop. Very carefully she carried it outside and eased the spider into a clump of dandelions.

Then she took a dusting rag and cleaned off the top of the chest of drawers and the mirror above it. Her reflection in the mirror showed pale skin, a narrow, pointed chin and a chunk of flat, straight hair that poked out, strawlike, from under the kerchief. She didn't think she was very pretty. In fact, in her overalls and with most of her hair pushed back, she looked almost like a boy.

Kit unpacked the rest of her suitcase, laying her things

in the drawers and hanging up the dresses in the closet. The last thing she did was take a framed photograph out from the side pocket of the suitcase, her favourite picture of her mother, her mother before she got sick. The eyes were dark and lively and there was a gentle turn to the mouth. Kit studied the photograph and then set it down on the top of the chest of drawers. She closed her eyes. "Please…," she whispered. "Please get better."

2 A Night on the Town

Kit wound up the clock, moved the hands to six o'clock, and put it back on the mantel. She only guessed it was six o'clock; she didn't know for sure. But it felt as if three hours had passed since her father was supposed to pick her up at the station. And still there was no sign of him.

She took a determined breath and entered the kitchen. She found kindling and split wood in the box in the corner and stuffed them into the firebox of the cookstove. She lit it with a match and opened the damper to make the fire burn well.

Then she took two galvanized buckets from the back porch out to the well in the trees behind the house. A solid platform had been built over the top of the well, and in the centre a wooden lid covered the hole. Kit grasped the lid's handle with two hands and pulled it aside. Then she hooked a bucket onto the rope. She turned the crank of the windlass and lowered the bucket down into the well. When she cranked it back up again it was full to the brim with cool, clear water. There was a foul smell to it, though, sulphurous like rotten eggs. It made her stomach turn. Kit had almost forgotten how the farm's well water smelled. In Nanaimo she and her mother had running water—both hot and cold—whenever they wanted it. All they had to do was turn on the faucet. It didn't smell of rotten eggs, either. They'd had an indoor toilet, not an outhouse like on the farm, and electricity and a telephone as well. She knew it was going to seem strange living back on the farm again without the modern conveniences she was used to. She filled the second bucket and then replaced the lid over the well.

The buckets were heavy and they slopped against her legs as she walked. The warm smell of woodsmoke greeted her at the back door. She poured some water into a big kettle and set it on the stove. The rest of the water went in the stove reservoir so she would have hot water later when she wanted it.

Soon the kettle was hot and steaming. She emptied it carefully into the white enamelled dishpan and swished in some soap. One by one, Kit took the plates and scraped cold clumps of food, eggshells and tea leaves into the compost pail. She soaked the dishes in the hot, soapy water, scrubbed them with a brush, dried them and put them away in the cupboard. Then she wiped the table, swept the floor and mopped it clean. She stood in the centre of the room with her hands on her hips and looked around with satisfaction. At least this part of the house was tidy now.

Through the kitchen window she could see the rose garden her mother used to keep. The plants had long, spindly tendrils and only a few tightly furled buds. Kit carried the dishpan full of dirty water outside and poured it slowly onto the thirsty earth at the base of the roses. It was gratifying to see how eagerly the ground sucked it up.

Then she set the dishpan down on the back stairs and

walked down the path to the outhouse. She could see it leaned a little to one side. The door creaked when she opened it. The air was stale and heavy and rank. She held her breath as she pulled the door closed and latched the hook. Inside, the wooden seat had an uneven oval hole cut in the middle. A few ribbons of sunlight crept between the boards in the walls, piercing the shadows. Kit ripped a page from the old Sears catalogue in the corner, used it hastily and dropped it down the hole. Then she rushed out into the fresh air where she could breathe deeply again.

As she was walking down the path back to the house she saw a flock of crows descend into the cherry trees. They squabbled and squawked, picking through the foliage looking for fruit.

"Shoo!" she yelled, running through the berry field with her arms waving. "Get away!"

Up they rose, all at that exact moment, as if they were part of a single being, and away they flew. There were hardly any cherries left. The birds had ravished them.

She walked listlessly past the house and up the path to the top of the ridge. The second field came into view. It was the larger one, the one they had used for corn, potatoes, carrots and onions. It should have been planted long ago, with everything now thriving in straight, neat rows, but all she saw was grass and weeds.

Kit scuffed through the long grass on the way back to the house, feeling her stomach rumble. She hadn't eaten since lunch. The icebox on the back porch did not feel very cold. In fact, there was no ice inside. It held only a bottle of milk. She took a whiff, screwed up her face and dumped it out. Clotted, sour curds plopped thickly from the bottom of the bottle. There was half a loaf of bread in the breadbox but it felt dry as sandpaper. She tossed it into the compost pail. The pantry looked more promising. Dusty jars of preserves were lined up in rows. Lots of strawberry jam. *Applesauce 1919, Pears 1920, Pickled beets 1920,* the labels all in her mother's fading handwriting. Kit selected a jar of applesauce and brushed off the dust. But when she tried to open the lid, it would not give. She rapped it sharply with a knife, and gripped it firmly with a dishtowel as she tried to twist the lid open with all her might. But it refused to budge. It had rusted shut.

A noise outside! Kit stood absolutely still, listening to the purring sound—faint at first—getting louder as it approached. The sound of a motor car, no doubt about it. She raced out the screen door. A new Model T Ford, black with gleaming brass trim, pulled up to the house and then the door opened. Her father stepped out. His pale linen suit was well cut with cuffed trousers, and he wore a sharp-brimmed fedora hat.

"Dad?" Kit said from the veranda. When she spoke, he jerked upright as if he'd been poked by a pin. He looked towards the door, holding his hand up to block the sun and squinting. "Who's there?" he said.

"Dad, it's me. Kit."

"Kit? Kit! What are you doing here?"

"You were supposed to pick me up at the station. I had to walk all the way." Kit came to the edge of the veranda and looked down the stairs to where he stood at the bottom. He'd taken off his hat and held it in front of him. Now she was closer she could see that a day's growth of beard darkened his lower face and that his suit was rumpled.

"Today! I thought you were coming Thursday. That's what Jeannie said in her letter. Thursday. I'm sure of it.

Pretty sure, that is…But look at you, Kit. You're practically all grown up."

He jumped up the stairs two at a time, spun her around and gave her a bear hug. Kit hugged him back, smelling tobacco on his clothes.

"How old are you now?" Her dad stepped back and surveyed her. "Ten? Eleven?"

"I'm twelve, Dad. Almost thirteen."

"Almost thirteen." He shook his head in disbelief, as if she had just told him she lived on the moon. "Almost thirteen. Imagine that. And you walked all the way here from the station?"

Kit nodded.

"Well, I'll be. That would have taken you close to an hour, I'd say." He swept open the screen door. "Come in. Come in and sit down." He whisked the newspapers off the couch for Kit to sit down and took the chair across from her. "I haven't had time to tidy up," he apologized. "The place is a bit of a pigsty, not like when your mother was here. How is she doing? Feeling better?"

"I hope so. They say the hospital's supposed to be a good place for her."

"Have you eaten yet? I'll fix you something. What do you like? Eggs? Toast?" He retreated into the kitchen, and Kit could hear the cupboard doors banging. Then he reappeared in the doorway wearing a sheepish look. "Seems like we're a bit low in the food department," he admitted, but then his face brightened. "How about if I take you out for dinner? How would that be? A nice dinner for our first night together? And then we'll pick up some groceries on the way back."

"Sure." Kit jumped to her feet.

"Just give me a few minutes, then. I'd better shave and get a fresh shirt. Can't disappoint my best girl." He winked and flashed a white smile, looking as handsome as a screen idol.

Kit ran up the stairs and whipped the kerchief off her head. The overalls came off next and then she slipped the green and orange plaid dress back on. Her white socks were too dusty to wear again. Even after she shook them out the window, they were as grey as thunderclouds. She used them to wipe off her shoes and then poked around in the drawer for a clean white pair. She took a pass at her hair with the comb to make it lie straight. Ready. Then she was bounding down the stairs again.

Her dad was shaving at the washstand in the bathroom. He'd taken off his shirt and was in his undervest. A froth of white shaving suds covered his lower face. He leaned forward with his chin tilted up and ran the razor carefully along the skin. Kit sat down cross-legged at the door and watched. Every stroke of the razor made a rasping sound and then came the swish of the razor in the water.

"Dad? Did you notice anything about the kitchen?"

He cocked an eye in her direction. "The kitchen. You mean besides not having any food in it?"

She waited expectantly. He had to have seen the dishes had been cleaned and put away, the floor mopped and everything wiped clean.

He took a final pass with the razor and then splashed water on his face and wiped it with a towel. "What about the kitchen?"

"Nothing." She made a pretense of tying her shoes even though they were already tied.

Her dad patted on some aftershave and buttoned up a

clean, pressed shirt, fresh from the launderer. "Okay, Kit. Are you ready for a night on the town?"

"Saanichton?"

"I'll take you all the way to Sidney." He took her by the hand and waltzed her down the hall until she was laughing and dizzy.

The leather seats in the car felt smooth and warm from the sun as Kit climbed in. She watched her dad switch on the ignition, pull out the choke knob and adjust the spark and the gas levers. Then he hopped out of the car and, with a practised flourish, turned the engine crank at the front. The engine started with a sputter. He jumped back in beside her.

"Listen to that," he grinned, readjusting the choke and the levers until the engine idled smoothly. "Purrs just like a kitten."

They bumped down the driveway and then they were out on the open road. How wonderful the air felt against her face and blowing through her hair. The sun was lower now, casting a soft, golden light over the hills. In only a matter of minutes they had reached the main road. Saanichton was straight ahead, Victoria south. But they turned north, travelling up the peninsula, through a long, shady tunnel where evergreen boughs formed a roof overhead. The noise of the engine, louder in this enclosed place, echoed off the massive tree trunks. The car raced through the tunnel with exhilarating speed; in no time they were out the other end. They glided between the wide open fields with the ease of a swallow swooping through the sky. They passed a farmer with his horse and wagon. Kit turned in her seat. Already the farmer was left far behind. She turned back, stealing a sideways look at her dad's profile. His hair was slicked back like Rudolph Valentino's in the movies. He had a bump in the centre of his nose—it had been broken once in a fight, he used to say. It didn't detract from his looks; if anything, it made him seem more intriguing, more like a rogue, a rascal, a bandit king.

They were at the outskirts of Sidney now: small, plain houses, barefooted children playing hopscotch in the dust, a boy dancing on stilts, stray dogs. Then came the tree-lined streets with the sidewalks and bigger houses, the children here with neat hair ribbons and shiny new bikes. The car turned onto the main street downtown and pulled up to the curb.

Kit's dad escorted her across the street to the café and they sat in a booth at the window. Kit had a ginger soda in a tall glass with ice cubes and a straw—how thirsty she was— and chicken with biscuits. She liked sitting by the window. Not only could she watch people as they passed by, but they could see her too, sitting with her dad, having dinner in a restaurant. She liked the way the waitress knew her dad by name and brought her another soda on the house.

Kit's dad left the waitress two whole dollars for a tip, and they stepped out into the warm evening air. The sidewalk still held some of the afternoon's heat. The sky had turned indigo with a blush of rose where the sun was beginning to set. A flock of crows swooped overhead, their wings a swoosh of fluttering. She looked up and saw them, black against the sky. They were circling each other, cawing and bickering like schoolyard bullies. A terrible noise. Down they swooped again, closer still. Kit ducked her head, feeling the rush of air and feathers. Then, as if on some secret signal, they flew off.

"Darn crows," her father said, and took her arm as they

crossed the street. The birds reminded Kit of the ones she had shooed away from the cherries. She pushed the thought from her mind. It was too nice an evening to be thinking about the problems on the farm.

"How about some ice cream?" her father said. They had stopped in front of Stacey's ice cream parlour, where the red door stood open and welcoming.

There was no question of which flavour. Chocolate for both of them, always their favourite. They strolled up and down the block with their cones, studying the movie posters at the theatre, admiring the store windows.

Then it was back to the car with one stop at Critchley's general store for milk and bread and eggs. "I'll get the milkman to start delivering milk again regularly to the house now that you're here," Kit's father assured her as he picked up a newspaper.

"We need some ice delivered, too," Kit reminded him. "There's none left in the icebox."

"Right..." He was studying the front page intently.

Kit peeked over his arm. There was the date, July 9, 1924. Underneath, the headline in large print: *U.S. Prohibition Threatened*. She started to read the smaller print below, *Clandestine activities challenge Coast Guard...*, just before the newspaper was folded up.

"What's Prohibition, Dad?"

"Prohibition?" he repeated, absentmindedly, as he stuck the paper in the bag of groceries and gave the cashier an extra dime.

"Yes. Prohibition. What is it?"

He shot her a sideways look before he answered. "A few years ago the United States government passed a law. They don't allow any alcohol in their country. The prohibiting of alcohol—that's what Prohibition means."

"So alcohol is against the law…"

"That's right. Down in the United States it is. But that's their country and their law. Here in British Columbia we don't have Prohibition anymore. We tried it, a few years back, but it didn't last. It's a thing of the past now. Doesn't affect us anymore." He ruffled her hair and then opened the car door with a flourish. "I'd say it was about time to head home."

Kit held the bag of groceries on her lap as they drove home again over the country roads. The twilight hour was deepening; long shadows crept across the fields on either side. The air was sweet with the smell of hay. She laid her head back against the seat, looked up into the plum-coloured sky and smiled a wide, satisfied smile.

~

That night, Kit had the first strange dream. *A man was sleeping under an apple tree. At first she thought he was her father but then he woke, opened his eyes and turned to look at her. She saw, then, that he was not her father. He was a stranger. There was something unsettling about the way he smiled at her, and, when his lips parted, a swarm of bees flew out.*

3 *Vivian*

Kit was getting ready to have a bath in the tin tub in the bathroom. She'd intended to ladle out all the hot water from the stove reservoir with the dipper, and heat up the kettle and a big pan of water as well. But when she went out to the well the first bucket came up only half full. The water still smelled of rotten eggs, but it was no longer clear. It was muddy and there was something floating in it. Kit jumped back. The bucket tipped over, spilling dirty water everywhere. There it was on the grass—slippery, slimy and revolting. A dead snake! It must have been dead for some time; its flesh was beginning to decompose. Kit's nose wrinkled in disgust as she made herself flick it aside with a stick. Then she picked up the bucket and lowered it down into the well again. This time it came up with only a bit of sludge in the bottom.

Kit ran back to the house and stuck her head in the back door. "Dad? What happened to the water? I'm only getting sludge up from the well."

She heard him curse under his breath somewhere inside the house.

"Dad?"

He marched out to the well without saying a word and lowered the bucket. When he cranked it back up again it was empty. He slumped back on his heels. "Looks like the well's run dry again."

"Run dry?" She couldn't remember the well running dry before. "But what are we going to do for water?"

He offered her a weak smile. "Wait it out until some rain comes, I guess. In the meantime I'll take some two-gallon bottles into town and fill them with water. We can swim in the ocean to get clean."

Kit took this in. Even though he was trying to appear positive it was obvious he was irritated by the inconvenience. Kit was starting to feel irritated too. It had been hard enough hauling all their water from the well. Now there was no water at all. "Everything about this farm is falling to pieces," she said. "Nothing's been kept up."

Her dad took in a deep breath and blew it out. "I know. I know," he said, shaking his head.

"It looks like you had a terrible crop of berries this year, and the top field for the other crops…it hasn't even been plowed, let alone planted. And now the well's gone and dried up."

"It's not very good, I know. The well has been running dry every summer for the last few years—usually sometime towards the end of summer. I can't say I've ever seen it happen this early before. But then we've had a long stretch of dry weather. That'll do it."

Kit regarded the muddy bucket. "We used to have so much water before. It was always such a good well."

"Well, Kit, it's different now. It has something to do with McCauley's new well across the road. After he put that one in, things haven't been the same."

"Mr. McCauley?" Kit remembered him as an old man with a tuft of white hair who lived alone in a house hidden from the road. "Maybe you can get some water from him."

Kit's father made a noise that sounded like a snort. "That old coot." Then he stood up and patted her on the shoulder. "Don't you go worrying yourself about the farm, Kit. I've been looking at getting into another line of work—something I'm better at. I can't think of too many people who got rich selling berries and potatoes."

Kit looked him up and down in a glance. It was true. Even though he had lived in this house all his life he never did seem like a farmer. His tastes ran to nice clothes and shiny new cars. There was something about him that seemed more at home in town than in the country.

"You go down and have a swim, Kit. I'll load up some bottles and go into town for water. How's that?"

A swim would be just the thing, Kit thought as she changed into her bathing suit. It would be something fun after spending the entire day yesterday washing the windows, scrubbing the bathroom and generally getting the house in order. She took a towel from the bathroom and walked through the prickly yellow grass down the slope towards the bay. It had been two days since she'd arrived at the farm and this was the first chance she'd had to go down to the beach. Sunlight shimmered off the water, and high overhead a seagull whirled and squawked in the fresh morning breezes.

When she reached the top of the bank and looked down into the bay, she saw the boat. Where had that come from? It was quite large, long and narrow and low to the water. And it was tied up to a wharf. Kit blinked her eyes. There had never been a wharf there before. The wood of the wharf was still light coloured. It could not have seen many winter storms, she thought. When she'd lived here before they'd had only a small rowboat, pulled high up the bank, turned upside down over the logs and tied to a tree.

The path, too, had changed. It used to be steep and dusty. But now the path led to a ramp. Kit held the railing and placed her feet carefully on the treads where the ramp angled down at a steep pitch. The boat was a dark grey, the cabin small and squat, with hardly room for a person to stand up straight. She pressed her nose up to the cabin window, taking note of the steering wheel, the compass and a few rolled-up maps. Behind the cabin was a great square box where she guessed the engine was and, behind that, a large, open deck.

Kit walked to the stern of the boat. *Nighthawk, Victoria, BC*, it read in square, black letters. She paced off the distance from stern to bow. Ten giant steps. That made it about thirty feet, she figured. Why would her father have such a big boat? As she climbed back up the ramp she decided to ask him about it as soon as he got back with the water bottles.

Beside the ramp a series of steps had been cut into the bank like a staircase leading down to the curve of the beach. She hopped down each step. Home Again Bay was not large, more of a cove than a bay. Sun-bleached logs lay nestled up against the bank. She crossed them nimbly and jumped down to the beach. The stones were small, rounded and every shade of grey. They shifted under her feet as she walked towards the water. Where the water lapped the stones, they became dark and glossy, suddenly infused with colour. Scattered amongst them were bits of shell—pink clamshells no bigger than a fingernail, tiny snail-like peri-winkles and gleaming dark blue mussels. Bright green seaweed washed over them like ribbons.

Kit stuck one tentative toe in the water. Freezing cold. She took a deep breath and plunged straight in. It was so cold it made her gasp and her bones ache. A second later, she rushed out, her teeth chattering, her skin goosebumped, threw a towel over her shoulders and sprinted back to the house.

After Kit had dressed in dry clothes and combed the knots out of her hair she went outside to hang her bathing suit and towel on the clothesline. Her father's car was still gone. She tried to think how long it would take to drive into Sidney, fill the bottles with water and then drive back. About an hour? He should be coming back any time now, she thought.

She trudged down the dusty driveway to put out the empty milk bottles, pick up the fresh milk and check the mail. There was a handful of letters for Jack Avery, and, from amongst them, one small square envelope slipped out. It was a pale blue envelope with a pretty flowered border along the flap at the back. Kit turned it over to see the writing on the front. *Miss Kit Avery*, it read, *Home Again Bay, Saanichton, British Columbia*. The writing was neat, the familiar hand Kit knew so well. Her mother's. Hastily she ripped open the envelope.

July 9, 1924

My dearest Kitty,

I am writing this letter on the day you leave but I know you will be at the farm and settled in by the time you get this.

Please don't be sad. Things will turn out just fine. I know it.

This will be a chance for you to get to know your father better. I'm sure you will have a wonderful time there just like you used to when you were a little girl.

Your father has written to say how happy he is that you are coming to live with him. He says he has wanted you to come for a long time. I know he hasn't always been good at writing or visiting but try not to judge him too harshly. He has a kind heart and he means well.

You're going to be a big help for your father coming now at the end of the berry-picking season and looking after the other crops. It's a busy time of the year for him. I suppose some things just turn out the way they're meant to, after all.

Kit bit her lip at this point. What would her mother say if she knew that he had let the farm go—that there hadn't been enough berries this year for even one afternoon's jam making? She smoothed out the letter and continued reading.

And you mustn't worry about me. They are taking wonderful care of me in the Tuberculosis Pavilion, here at the Royal Jubilee Hospital in Victoria. I can sit out in the fresh air on the sun porch and read and look out over the grounds. Sometimes I even feel well enough to try a crossword puzzle. It is a comfort for me to think that you are not so very far away, up on the Saanich Peninsula.

The only thing I regret is not being able to see you. But we must follow the rules and do as the doctor says. We cannot run the risk of you getting sick as well. Each day I thank the Lord that you have been spared and that you have your health. I promise to let you know as soon as the doctor says visitors are permitted.

31

I have made friends with some of the other patients. In the next room there is a young lady called Ada and, across the hall, an older lady called Lily. I have told them all about you and shown them your picture. They say you look like a fine young girl, which, of course, you are. I told them how you looked after me when I got sick and how you kept the house up and how brave you've been through all of this.

Kit, you must forgive me but I do worry about you. Promise me you will remember to eat lots of vegetables and drink milk every day. Try not to go to bed too late. Do as your father tells you, and don't talk to strangers. I want you to stay healthy and safe.

Do you remember that day last summer when we packed a picnic lunch and rode our bikes all the way to the Millstone River? It was such a hot afternoon we took off our shoes and waded in and the rocks were so smooth and slippery. You almost slipped in trying to catch a water skeeter. And then we had our picnic on the bank. Wasn't that a lovely afternoon? Memories of days like that help me pass the time.

The words shot straight to Kit's heart. She closed her eyes and felt her body sway one way and back again. An image of that afternoon—the slow-moving water, the dappled light, her mother's face—floated lightly across her eyelids. Oh, how she wished her mother would get better. She would get better, wouldn't she? She wouldn't die. She was in good care. Everything would be all right. Kit opened her eyes and read the end of the letter.

I will do my best to get better as fast as I can, dear Kitty. We will be together again before you know it. I promise.

Take heart.

Lots of love,
Mum
P.S. Did you remember to pack enough socks?

Kit slid the letter back into the blue envelope and tucked it into the pocket of her overalls. Then she took a deep breath, steadied herself and walked back to the house.

Lunchtime came and went. Maybe her father had decided to drive all the way to Victoria. Perhaps he'd had other business to take care of. The afternoon stretched out, long and hot and still. The only movement came from a white cabbage butterfly flitting over the berry fields. Kit lounged, restlessly, in the wicker rocking chair on the veranda and tried to read a book. Broken fragments of wicker poked mercilessly into her back. She adjusted the cushion to make it more comfortable. The chair creaked as it rocked back and forth, back and forth, a lonesome sound, it seemed to her. Finally, late in the afternoon, she heard a car in the driveway.

There was someone sitting in the passenger seat—someone with bobbed, dark brown hair and kiss-curls. A squeal of laughter came from the car as it bumped over the rough ground and then came to a stop in front of the house. Kit watched as her father leapt out of the car and ran around to open the passenger door. Out stepped a woman in a bright, flowery dress. It was the latest fashion, with the waistline dropped to the hip. The woman's lips were red as cherries.

"Honey," the woman said, looking up into Kit's father's eyes, "I'm just dying of thirst. Why don't you make me a cool drink while I freshen up?"

"Whatever my sweetie wants." Then he caught sight of Kit standing at the top of the stairs. "Oh…Kit."

The woman's head pivoted around quickly and her sharp, dark eyes fixed Kit like a pair of tacks. "Who's this?"

Kit felt her mouth form a polite smile.

"Kit. My daughter, Kit. Didn't I tell you my daughter was coming to stay? And Kit…this is Vivian."

The woman called Vivian arched a well-shaped eyebrow, taking in Kit's overalls and hair tucked back under a kerchief. "But, honey, you don't mean she's going to be *living* with you?"

Kit's father nodded. "Well…yes. At least until her mother gets better."

Vivian pouted. Then she straightened her dress and tottered up the stairs. She put her cheek next to Kit's—her perfume too strong, too sweet—and pretended to kiss her. "I just know we're going to be the best of friends," she said as she opened the door. Then she called over her shoulder, "I've got to run through to the outhouse, Jack. I can't wait a second longer." And in she went.

Kit stared after her as the door banged shut.

"I'm sorry, Kit," her father said, coming up the stairs. "I guess I should have told you about Vivian. You'll like her when you get to know her." He held the screen door open and gestured, with a tilt of his head, for her to go in.

Earlier in the day Kit had been intent on finding out about the strange boat moored in the bay, but it no longer seemed important. Now, instead, Kit wanted to know who this Vivian was. This woman who waltzed into the house as if she owned it—she didn't even have to ask where the outhouse was. Kit stood in the living room doorway, watching her father as he took some fancy glasses from the china cabinet, humming a lighthearted song.

"Dad?"

He took one look at her face and his expression fell. "Come on now, Kit. Don't go looking like that."

Kit opened her mouth to speak, but just then the back door opened and Vivian's high heels came tapping through the kitchen and down the hallway.

"Honestly, Jack! I don't know how you can live out here without indoor plumbing. I swear by my silk knickers, I really don't."

Knickers! Kit had never heard a lady say that word in front of a man before. She looked from Vivian to her father to gauge his reaction.

He didn't seem to notice. "I know. And to make matters worse, the well's dried up," was all he said.

Vivian clicked her tongue in annoyance. "Well, that won't do, will it? Living out here is no better than the way our grandparents used to live. You should move into town. Electricity, water, telephone—everything's modern and up-to-date. Besides...," she smiled coyly. "Wouldn't you rather live closer to me?"

Kit's father took her hand. "Of course I would. You know that."

Kit was horrified. She looked from her father to Vivian and back again. What about the farm? What about her mother? What about her? But before she could say one word of protest, Vivian had thrown herself down on the couch, tossed off her shoes and put her feet up. "Have you got my drink ready?" she asked. "I could soak it up like a sponge."·

"Coming right up," Kit's father said as he went into the kitchen.

Kit and Vivian were left alone in the room. Vivian lit up a cigarette. She inhaled deeply and exhaled a puff of smoke.

Her hand turned to the side, the cigarette smouldering in a long, narrow holder, the soft, smooth whiteness of her inner arm revealed. She studied Kit, and then said, "How long's your mum going to be sick?"

Kit swallowed. She wished she knew. She felt a twist of sadness when she thought about how much she missed her mother. "The doctor didn't say."

Kit could see Vivian's fingers tapping impatiently on the arm of the couch. Just then Kit's father came into the room with two drinks. "A whisky for you and a whisky for me."

Vivian flashed him a bright smile. "Thanks, lovey. Come and sit by me." She swung her feet around, patting the cushion beside her. Then she took a long drink. "My, that's good."

Kit's father sat down. "I'm sorry, Kit. I got drinks for us but I forgot about you. Did you want something? There's some iced tea."

Kit knew very well there was iced tea. She'd made it herself earlier. She'd been able to keep things cold in the icebox ever since the ice truck had delivered a big fifty-pound block of ice. But Kit shook her head. "I'm not thirsty." Her eyes were still on Vivian. Never could she imagine her mother drinking whisky and smoking cigarettes.

"Well, how about if we all go into town tonight for dinner? Would you like that?" he asked.

Kit nodded but she didn't feel very enthusiastic about the idea. She knew it wouldn't be the same with Vivian tagging along.

Vivian tossed her head and giggled. "Ohhh. That's a wonderful idea. You know I'm terrible in the kitchen. Can't even boil an egg. Let's go out for dinner and maybe the picture show afterwards. There's a new Charlie Chaplin playing." She squeezed Kit's dad's arm playfully, then turned to Kit. "Why don't you run along and change into something nice?"

Kit dragged herself upstairs to her room and plunked herself gloomily down on the bed. She could hear Vivian's laughter from downstairs and she made a sour face in the mirror.

Then she looked at her mother's picture on the dresser. The expression was gentle and patient. Kit gave a big sigh. Then she straightened her shoulders and stood up. She would try to be gentle and patient like her mother, she decided, even though she didn't feel like it.

She opened the closet door and looked at her dresses— all four of them. There was the one she used to wear to church, with a lace collar. There was the green and orange plaid she'd worn on the train. The third was a robin's egg blue with white rickrack in two zigzagging lines down the front. And the fourth was her favourite. It wasn't the fanciest and she had almost outgrown it—but it was the one that reminded her of a day back in Nanaimo not long before her mother got sick.

Kit took the dress from the closet and the memory floated, dreamlike, to the surface of her mind. They were on the porch swing by the house they rented in Nanaimo. Kit had just opened her eyes. She'd been asleep. Her mother was reading beside her. She could feel the sway of the swing and her mother's arm across her back, warm and comforting. Sounds of birds twittering in the tall maple tree beside the house had woken her. She could see the fine stripe of her skirt fabric draped across her legs, only now the stripes were not straight as they were when she was standing. Now they wandered and curved like roads crossing a mountain.

She lay, swaying back and forth, looking at the wandering stripes, feeling warm and happy. She wished she could keep that moment forever.

Kit hugged the dress to her. That day had been before her mother's cough had started—a cold they had thought, nothing more. But the coughing had continued and then came the fevers and night sweats. Her mother was always tired. She couldn't go to work. Climbing the stairs to go to bed exhausted her so much she began sleeping on the couch downstairs.

Kit remembered seeing her huddled there under a blanket. How thin and depleted she looked, like a lifeless bird. Coughing took all her energy. Kit's mother had once been able to climb to the top of Mount Benson and back in a day. She used to pack her wooden case of paints and brushes and canvas and hike miles and miles through the forest searching for perfect spots to paint. She had been a woman who led her school class on long, rambling nature hikes, identifying native plants along the way, by both common and Latin names. It was hard for Kit to believe such a robust woman could have turned into something so fragile.

One day, through sheer determination, Kit's mother ventured out of the house for the first time in weeks. She went to the polling station to cast her vote in the provincial election. "Women have struggled for so long to get the vote. I am not going to miss this," she had insisted. But when she returned, drawn and exhausted, she'd reached for a white handkerchief and spat out a mouthful of bright red blood. They were both shocked. But neither of them could bring themselves to say what they had both begun to suspect. The doctor came. He closed the door to the living room and Kit, her ear pressed to the door, could hear their quiet, murmuring voices and then her mother's tears. Kit's heart sank. That's when she knew for sure, when she heard her mother's weeping through the door. And then everything happened so quickly. There was the packing up to go to the hospital in Victoria and the hurried arrangements for Kit.

Kit's nose turned snuffly and her eyes welled up as the memories flooded back. Her face in the mirror looked red and splotchy.

"I'm not going to feel sorry for myself, no matter what," she told her reflection. Then she squeezed her eyes shut, willing herself not to cry. She wiped her nose with the back of her hand and slipped the striped dress over her head. She whipped off the kerchief and ran a comb through her hair.

Downstairs, as she approached the living room, she heard Vivian's pleading voice. "But can't she stay with some-one else?"

Kit stopped and listened.

Her father's response was low and quiet. "Well, it isn't the best situation for me either. I can't just drop everything now that she's here."

Kit felt herself stiffen.

Her father's voice continued. "It will just be for a short time. I promise."

Kit made her feet stomp heavily along the floorboard to announce her arrival. As she entered the doorway her father and Vivian straightened up.

"You look nice, Kit." Her father smiled. "Ready to go?"

Kit glanced at Vivian, busy lighting up another cigarette. Obviously the two of them would be happier on their own. "I don't feel so well. I've got a stomach ache," she said.

Her father looked concerned. "What's wrong? Was it something you ate?"

Kit blushed and hung her head. She didn't want to be caught in a lie.

Vivian piped up then. "Oh, Jack, don't be such a silly goose. It's probably just her time of the month."

Kit stared at Vivian. She could not believe those words had come out of Vivian's mouth—and in front of her father, too. "No, it isn't," Kit rushed to say. "I just don't feel well, that's all."

Vivian drank up the rest of her drink in one gulp and set the glass down. "No. I suppose not. She hasn't got much of a figure yet—even in a dress."

Kit felt her mouth gape open. Whether she had a figure or not was none of Vivian's business.

Her father stood up. For a moment Kit thought he was going to put Vivian in her place, but instead he put on his jacket and simply said, "Well, I'm hungry. Who's coming?"

"Count me in," said Vivian.

Suddenly Kit didn't want to be left behind. She didn't want to let Vivian win so easily. "I'll come," she said. And she noticed with some satisfaction that a hint of disappointment crossed Vivian's face.

This time Kit had to sit in the back seat. She could see the way Vivian's wavy hair bounced as she tossed her head. At the restaurant Vivian did most of the talking. Kit sat quietly, barely eating and thinking how much the woman reminded her of a parrot in her bright, showy dress.

"Still not feeling well?" her father asked, noticing how she toyed listlessly with her peas.

"I'll be okay." She made an effort to smile.

"Let's get you home, then. We can go to the movies another time."

On the way home Kit looked up at the stars, the familiar

constellations she knew so well. There was the North Star shining bright, always constant. If only other things had stayed the same as well.

Her father turned around in his seat. "I'm going to drop you off first and then I'll take Vivian home."

Kit considered this for a moment. "But, Dad…then you'll have to backtrack."

Vivian twisted around. "It's late," she said. "You should be getting to bed if you're not feeling well."

Kit was silent the rest of the way. She could feel her fingernails digging into the flesh of her palm.

They dropped her off at the end of the driveway.

"See you soon, Dad," she said.

"Good night, Kit. Have an early night and you'll feel better in the morning."

The car turned around and the red tail lights headed back down the road.

Suddenly the night seemed very dark. Huge trees crowded menacingly up to the lane like fearsome giants, their branches blocking out the night sky. She could hear rustling of leaves in the bushes. Was it the wind? No, there was no wind tonight. Maybe animals stirring. A raccoon perhaps.

Something swooped down from overhead, skimming by so closely she could hear the whispering of wings. As it flew off again Kit could just make out the dark shape of a bat.

A twig snapped behind her. Kit froze with alarm. Then her feet began to move, faster and faster, until she was running. Finally, up ahead, she could see the looming, shadowy shape of the house. She was almost there. Her toe caught in a root and she stumbled, headlong, to the ground.

She got to her feet again, rubbing the dirt off her hands.

What a relief to run up the stairs and yank open the door. She slammed it shut behind her and turned the lock. Her heart was pounding in her chest and her fingers were shaking as she lit the kerosene lamp. Silly, she told herself. There was nothing out there.

Kit got ready for bed, emptied the pan of melted ice water from under the icebox, then steeled her nerves and ran out to the outhouse and back again. She didn't want to go to sleep before her father got home so she took a blanket down to the couch and curled up to wait. The clock on the mantel was the only sound. She checked the time. An hour had passed. How long could it take to drop Vivian off and come home? The sound of the clock ticked on and on. Kit closed her eyes…

~

Kit's eyes blinked open. Her heart was beating hard. Something had awakened her. A sound outside. Was it the car door slamming shut? Her eyes flew to the clock. So late, it was after one in the morning. She ran to the door and pressed her face to the window.

At first she could see only the blackness of the night. The lamplight did not extend past the bottom porch stair—not far enough to see if the car was outside. Two dark moths danced up against the window and she drew her face back from the glass to watch them. They flickered across the glass and then came to rest with their wings, each swirled in intricate patterns, slowly opening and closing. She was about to turn away when she caught sight of another flickering, farther away, out in the darkness. A light—a light at the barn door. It lasted only a moment and then it was gone again.

Had it been just her imagination? Or was someone out there in the dark? Kit gathered the blanket around her and tiptoed down the hall past her father's room. The bedspread was drawn smoothly across the top. There was no sign it had been disturbed.

Upstairs, she crawled into bed and huddled, shivering, under the covers.

4 *The Charity Picnic*

First thing the next morning Kit went downstairs and checked her father's room. There he was, fast asleep. His mouth hung slightly open and a faint snore sounded with every breath. Kit quietly closed the door.

Across the hall, in the bathroom, she noticed a gold tube of lipstick on the washstand. Vivian must have left it, she thought. Kit approached the lipstick cautiously, as if it might suddenly leap up and bite her. She poked it with a finger and it rolled slightly one way and then the other. Then she pulled the lid off and looked inside. Bright cherry red. It had a faint smell to it—both waxy and perfumed. Kit twisted the bottom of the tube until the red lipstick emerged. She looked at her reflection in the mirror. Her lips were a pale fleshy colour, if it could be called a colour at all. She leaned towards the mirror and applied the lipstick, first to her top lip and then the bottom. Although she tried to be careful it was hard to keep it from going past the edges. Then she smacked her lips together and stood back to consider the effect. The smear of red was garish, unnaturally bright, like clown's makeup. Quickly she grabbed a cloth and rubbed it off the best she could. A stain of red remained on her lips and no amount of scrubbing could remove it.

She made breakfast for herself, put on a pair of overalls and then stepped outside. The morning was clear and brisk and a salty wind blew up from the sea. The tops of the tall fir trees tossed back and forth. She crossed the yard to the barn, remembering how she'd seen the light there the night before. The barn was a tumbledown building that listed to one side. But on the door was a brand new padlock. It was bright and shiny—not a speck of rust. Kit gave it a yank but it wouldn't budge. She walked down the side of the building, past the broken-down bike, around the back—with its makeshift lean-to stacked with wood, a wagon and an assortment of tools—and up through the tall, tangled grass on the other side. There was no other way to gain entry. Up high, well above her head, was a dusty four-paned window. Kit cast her eye about and spotted an old wheelbarrow under one of the apple trees. She pushed it into position under the window and then carefully climbed up into it. Her hands reached up to the windowsill and she steadied herself as she stood up straight.

It was dark and shadowy inside the barn, difficult to make out anything at all. She pressed her hands to either side of her face and peered in again. Gradually she could make out stacks of boxes along the wall. They'd be the boxes for berries and potatoes and carrots, she thought. Not that there was going to be a harvest this year. She turned and jumped down to the grass.

A gust of wind whipped her hair across her face and she pushed it back out of the way as she walked down to the water. There were whitecaps in the sun-washed bay and the waves rushed, wind-driven, against the rocks. The boat tossed and pulled against its moorings. The water was too rough for a swim this morning.

As she turned back to the house she noticed something, far back in a thicket of trees—a small, ramshackle building, so overgrown with brambles she almost didn't see it. The pickers' shack. She'd almost forgotten it was there.

When she had lived here years ago, they'd hired one or two pickers for the berries every June. They were usually men travelling through, looking for a bit of work. They all worked hard when the berries were ripe: Kit's mother, her father, the pickers and Kit, herself, after school and on the weekends. They would tie old jam or honey buckets to their belts and pick berries in the hot sun. At the end of each row they'd dump the buckets into boxes. The boxes fit into wooden crates, twenty-four to a crate. Each crate was stamped *Home Again Bay.* They were loaded into the truck, taken into town and sold to the jam factory. In the evening her mother would make a big meal and they'd all sit down together at a long makeshift table of boards and sawhorses, set under the trees. The pickers slept in the shack at night. When the berry season wound down, they'd be on their way again.

Now the shack had a big hole in the roof and one of the windowpanes was broken. Brambles choked the path, making it almost impossible to get any closer. It had probably been years since anyone had used the place.

Kit wandered up to the house. Maybe her father was awake now. She could make some breakfast for him. She went back inside and cracked open his door. But he was still in the same position and still snoring. She closed the door again with a sigh.

46

At noon, her father's door finally opened and he shuffled out with his hair sticking up at all angles.

"Hi, Dad," Kit said brightly.

He looked at her, bleary-eyed, and rubbed his head. "Hi, yourself," he said eventually. His voice sounded thick and groggy.

"You must have got in late last night. What time did you go to bed?"

He swung his head slowly towards her and considered the question. "Late." Obviously he was in no mood to talk.

Kit watched him as he went out to the back porch, opened the door of the icebox and stood looking inside for a minute as if he'd forgotten what he was doing there. "Why don't you sit down," she said. "I'll make you some tea and toast."

She heaved up one of the bottles of water from the floor, poured a generous amount into the kettle and set it on the stove. Then she rummaged about for the tea and bread. As she was waiting for the kettle to boil, she tried to catch his eye. But he was sitting at the kitchen table with his head in his hands. He didn't look up once.

She took the teacup and the plate of toast to the table and sat across from him. Even though she had a lot of questions she wanted to ask, she made herself wait until he had sipped some tea and was sitting up straighter.

"Dad? How come you were out so late last night?" An image of the lipstick in the bathroom sprang into her mind as she asked the question.

Her dad chewed on some toast and swallowed. "Vivian doesn't like to go into a dark house by herself. She scares easily."

What about me? Kit wanted to say, thinking how scared she had been last night. Besides, how long would it take to check the house and make sure it was safe? But instead she said, "Were you doing something out at the barn last night when you got home? I saw a light out there."

For a second he stopped stirring the milk in his tea. Then he gave it a few more stirs and put down the teaspoon. "Just making sure everything was locked up for the night."

"Why do you keep it locked up, anyway? What do you keep in there?"

He was looking right at her now. "Nothing. It's an old building and it's starting to rot. It's dangerous now. The roof could cave in at any time. I don't want you poking around there. You hear?"

She was surprised by his intensity. "Okay." Then, deciding to change her tack, she said, "Do you think Mum is going to get better?"

"I'm sure she will."

Kit studied his face. Was he just saying that so she wouldn't worry? "She says she's not allowed any visitors yet. Do you think that means she's worse? Maybe we should go and see her, anyway. They wouldn't stop us from seeing her if we drove all the way into Victoria, would they?" she ventured.

"Come on now, Kit. We have to do what the doctor says. She needs to rest now."

"Dad…?"

"Mmmm?"

"What happened between you and Mum? Why didn't you get along with each other?"

He put down his tea. "When we were young we were very much in love." He started haltingly, but then the words began to flow. "Not long after we were married, the Great War started. I joined up right at the beginning. I never imagined it would be almost four years until I'd come home again. That war lasted far longer than anyone thought possible. It was a terrible thing—the Great War—even for those of us lucky enough to live through it. My friends all around me were killed or wounded. And I changed, I guess. That's what happened." His voice trailed off for a moment and then he continued. "When I came home from the war it was hard to settle back into farming life again. I felt restless all the time. It was as if I didn't fit in my own skin anymore. I took a risk or two, I don't deny it. I liked the thrill of it. I bet on the horses. I made a few bad business deals. I lost a little money. And I let your mother down. Finally we decided that, even though we still cared for each other very much, it would be better to live apart."

"But you didn't get divorced. You're still married, right? Maybe you can get back together."

He took another sip of tea before he answered. "I'm not so sure she'd want to take an old rascal like me back." He shrugged his shoulders as he said this, and laughed as if it was a joke.

But Kit did not want to laugh. "You still love her, don't you?"

His grin faded. He looked up at the ceiling for a moment and then directly at her. A softness had come over his face. "I'll always love your mother…as long as I live. But Kit, believe me, things are not the same as they used to be."

Perhaps it was only her imagination, but Kit thought there was a wistfulness, almost a sadness, about the way he said this. Did he wish they could all be together again too, just as she did?

But then his expression changed. He was studying her in an oddly curious way. "What happened to your mouth?" he asked.

Kit's hand flew to cover her lips. They must still be stained from the lipstick, she realized. "Oh…nothing. Probably berries. I found a few tail-end ones."

Her dad kept looking at her and she felt acutely uncomfortable. She rushed to think of something to change the subject. "Have you thought about getting one of those new gasoline tractors for the farm?" she asked. "I noticed a lot of the farmers are getting them now."

"A gasoline tractor?"

"It would be so much easier on the farm with a tractor. Easier to plow than when you had the horses. Or paying for one of those big steam tractors to come around."

"I don't know, Kit. I haven't given it much thought."

Kit waited, but he seemed to show no interest in pursuing the topic. Then she said, "I saw the boat down in the bay. Are you taking up fishing?"

He downed the last of the tea in one quick motion and stood up. "I might be. I'm thinking of doing a little night fishing. Have to keep all my options open."

"Night fishing? What do you mean, night fishing?" She'd never heard of such a thing. That wasn't the only thing she was curious about, either. She wanted to ask how he could afford a boat, and a new car as well, with the farm doing so poorly.

But her father ruffled her hair and said, "Enough questions. I better get dressed before the day's half over."

"It *is* half over," said Kit, but he'd already left the kitchen.

~

A few days later Kit sat at her bedroom window and wrote a letter to her mother.

July 15, 1924

Dear Mum,

Are you feeling better yet? When can you have visitors? Does the doctor say anything about when you might be able to come home?

I've been getting settled in at the farm. Things are fine. Well, not exactly fine. To be honest it hasn't been a good year for the crops—not much in the way of berries and the well's dried up. We have to take our big water bottles in to Sidney to get them filled. We try to use the water sparingly but, even so, you'd be surprised how quickly we go through the bottles. I take a swim most days to get clean and we've been taking our laundry into town to save water. But there's still the water we need for the dishes, and making tea and washing vegetables. I figure we must go through two bottles a day.

Dad's not really much of a cook so I've been trying to make the suppers. So far, I can do scrambled eggs and potatoes and peas and sausages. I guess you can say we're eating well enough, but it's nothing like the suppers you make.

Kit put down her pen and read what she'd written so far. Should she say anything about Vivian? No. That would only worry her mother. She probably shouldn't mention anything about how rundown the farm was looking, either. She picked up her pen and wrote instead,

You'd be very proud of how I was able to mend a torn buttonhole on my overalls. I searched upstairs and downstairs until I found a spool of thread and a needle. I made the stitches very small, just like you showed me. I think that if the thread hadn't been red, and the overalls blue, you would hardly be able to see the stitches at all.

The farm seems very quiet after living in Nanaimo. Dad says old Mr. McCauley is still living across the road. I never see him though. He likes to keep to himself, I guess. It would be so much better if there was a family living there, with someone my own age.

Dad's got a fishing boat now, called the NIGHTHAWK, and he's put in a wharf down at the bay. Did you know about this? He says fishing is where the money is these days. He must be right because he has a new model car and wears very smart clothes. This afternoon Dad came home with a big surprise. It's a brand new RCA radio that runs on batteries. We put it in the kitchen on the shelf next to the plate rack. Tonight when I was washing the dishes I heard a baseball game broadcast at the exact time it was happening, all the way from Seattle. There are all sorts of other programs as well—funny ones and radio dramas. I heard Duke Ellington playing and it was as if his band was right there in the kitchen just for me. All of that out of a little box. Can you believe it?

Mum, please hurry up and get better. I miss you.
All my love,
Kitty

~

The days passed by and then one morning Kit woke up, a strange dream still fresh in her memory.

A boy was riding a unicycle. He was wearing a harlequin outfit, a wide crimson sash around his waist and an odd, peaked hat. But his feet were bare. He rode in circles, each circle becoming smaller. In the centre lay a thickly coiled serpent. The serpent's tongue darted in and out. The boy's feet swept by, tantalizingly close to the snake. And the skin of his feet was pale white, thin and delicate as a petal.

Kit could feel her own feet prickle as if they'd been bitten by the dream snake. She blinked her eyes open, and pulled back the covers. For just a moment—just as the last traces of the dream were disappearing—she wondered if she would see a mark on her feet. But they looked as they always did. Nothing out of the ordinary. She wiggled her toes and stretched. Then she dressed quickly and ran out to check the mailbox. The red flag was raised. There was a letter in the mailbox. She ripped open the envelope and read it eagerly.

July 21, 1924

Dear Kitty,

I was very happy to get your letter and hear about life back on the farm. I have read it over so many times I think I know it almost by heart. Kitty, do make sure you are getting enough greens and that you have at least two big glasses of milk every day. I am glad to hear you are becoming handy in the kitchen. What a blessing you must be for your father.

It's a shame about the well. I can't recall when it's run dry before. Perhaps if we get a few days of rain it will fill up again. We don't realize how much we depend on something as simple as water, do we?

I didn't know about your father's boat and that he had

53

taken an interest in fishing. He must have forgotten to mention it. I must say I find it hard to imagine your father taking up fishing, but there you go. It just shows how people can surprise you.

I know you are anxious for me to get better and, believe me, that is my dearest wish as well. But the doctor says it will take time and we must be patient. Some days I do think I feel much better. Today I had such a nice afternoon. Ada and Lily and I all sat on the sun porch for several hours. It was lovely and warm. One of the nurses brought us a deck of cards and we all played hearts. Although Lily is getting on in years and appears terribly feeble (the nurses push her bed out to the sun porch), she is actually very sharp and an excellent player. She told me she can speak five languages and that she has travelled as far as Constantinople. Ada has not played as much but she has a good sense of humour and a lovely infectious laugh. We all love Ada. She tells funny stories about when she used to work as a telephone operator before she got sick. She's overheard the most amazing conversations. I sometimes wonder if they can all be true. Ada is engaged to be married and when she is well again she is going to have a big wedding with a three-tiered cake and a white silk dress. There is nothing Ada likes better than to talk about her wedding plans. She hardly pays any attention to the cards and has to be reminded when it's her turn. It was not surprising that Lily handily won the game. Afterwards we all had a go at a crossword puzzle. It was a very pleasant way to spend the afternoon. I think perhaps it was one of my best days since I've been here.

It reminded me a little of those Saturday mornings we used to have. Do you remember? We'd make pancakes for breakfast and then stay in our dressing gowns until noon, just because we felt like it.

I miss you more than I can say. Please take good care of yourself.

All my love,

Mum

P.S. You didn't say whether you'd packed enough socks.

Kit folded the letter up and slid it into her overalls pocket. When she got back to the house her father was awake, making himself a pot of coffee in the kitchen. "I've got an idea," he said. "How'd you like to go to the hospital charity picnic up at the fairgrounds?"

"What's that?"

"It's a big fundraiser to raise money for the Royal Jubilee Hospital."

Kit's heart flip-flopped. "You mean the hospital where Mum is?"

"That's right. Everyone brings a picnic lunch. There's going to be a carnival this year with shows and rides...even a Ferris wheel. All the proceeds go to the hospital."

"Oh! Can we? That would be swell." Kit was excited, not only because it sounded fun, but also because it would raise money to help her mother.

"Sure we can. We can do anything your heart desires."

A short time later, the car bumped over the grassy field and came to a stop beside a row of other cars. Kit jumped out and grabbed the picnic basket from the back seat. At the far side of the field she could see the top of the Ferris wheel over the tents, and she could hear the rollicking music from the carousel. Although it was not yet noon, heat waves were already shimmering in the air.

Kit insisted they go on the Ferris wheel first. Up they went, high, high and higher. Kit looked down at the crowds of tiny people below, the booths selling hot dogs and the field where the cars were parked. Farther away, the land stretched out in gigantic patches of farms and trees, out to the blue water and the hazy horizon where faraway mountains hid themselves in a mist. Kit gripped the iron bar in front of her and then they were going down. Her stomach leapt up to her throat.

"Are you scared?" her father asked.

She shook her head and sat staring straight ahead. Her knuckles had turned white from hanging on to the bar so tightly.

When Kit stepped down from the Ferris wheel the ground felt wonderful under her feet. The cotton candy booth was next. Kit leaned forward and looked down into the whirling bins. The man took a thin paper cone and twirled it around and around. The strands of shiny pink floss collected quickly on the cone. It looked like fairy gossamer, so delicate and light. The first sweet bite melted on her tongue. It had been many years since she'd tasted cotton candy. She took another bite and closed her eyes to savour the taste.

When she opened her eyes again, she couldn't believe who it was she saw. Vivian was heading through the crowd straight towards them. Kit's first impulse was to duck away between the tents.

"Let's go over to the games." She started to pull her dad sideways.

He took a few steps but then he stopped. "Look, there's Vivian!" he said.

Kit's heart sank. Vivian tottered up to her father and gave him a big kiss on the cheek. It left a red mark like a mosquito bite. "What a coincidence seeing you two here," she winked, then giggled and snuggled up to his arm.

From the way she said it, Kit wondered if the two had planned to meet. She took another bite of the cotton candy but it was hard to enjoy it anymore. Now that Vivian had arrived, her father seemed to forget all about her. Kit was left to lug the picnic basket, studying Vivian's high-heeled, pointy-toed shoes as she tagged along behind them. Each shoe sported a flimsy ankle strap held in place by one tiny, cloth-covered button. Such impractical shoes to wear to a picnic—they made her teeter as she walked and she kept leaning up against Kit's father for balance.

They passed rows of tents where, for a small amount of money, it was possible to see a ventriloquist, a contortionist, a Punch and Judy show or the World's Daintiest Lady—only thirty-five inches tall. But Vivian and Kit's father walked by all of these. They stopped in front of a stall that sold brightly coloured scarves instead.

"Look at this one," Vivian said as she held it up in front of her. "Does it suit me?" It was a vibrant red silk, embroidered with a splash of flowers and finished with a luxuriously long fringe. It looked like something a flamenco dancer might wear. "Or how about this one?" Vivian took another scarf down from the rack.

Kit watched glumly as Vivian looked at every scarf and asked her father's opinion. Finally she selected the first one, the flashy red scarf. The clerk wrapped it and Vivian looked very satisfied with herself as she came out of the stall.

Then Kit's father looked from Vivian to Kit, noticing her as if for the first time. "Would you like a scarf, too?"

Kit hesitated. She didn't want to appear greedy, like Vivian. It wasn't so much that she wanted the scarf for herself, but it might be something she could put in the mail for her mother. A small gift.

Then Vivian piped up. "There was a green one that would suit your colouring. It would be just right with your gorgeous blonde hair. I'll show you."

Kit's eyes narrowed as Vivian once again flitted through the racks. Was she just putting on an act, pretending to be nice because Kit's father was there?

"Here it is." Vivian pulled out a silky swath of fabric, lovely and airy. The colour fluctuated as it moved, lighter and darker, like summer leaves shifting in a breeze. "Look. It's perfect for you." Vivian held it gently up against Kit's cheek. It felt so soft and light it was hardly there at all. "Do you like it?"

Yes, Kit thought—in fact, she couldn't imagine a scarf more beautiful. Vivian and her father were both nodding their heads, waiting expectantly for her response. Kit could see they wanted her to like it. They wanted her to be happy, after all. She felt the weight of the foul mood lift. She would take it. She would accept Vivian's peace offering.

Just as she opened her mouth to reply, Vivian suddenly snatched the scarf back. "No. I suppose not. You're more of the tomboy type, aren't you?"

"But…," Kit started to protest. Vivian was returning the scarf to the rack, her manner almost gleeful. Kit pressed her lips together and then she said, "It's too hot for a scarf. I don't really want it."

Vivian shrugged her shoulders, took Kit's father by the arm and neatly steered him away. Kit picked up the picnic basket and trudged along behind them, fuming. She had a strong suspicion Vivian knew exactly how much she'd wanted the scarf—and that she'd taken a nasty delight in calling her a tomboy. Which wasn't even true. Hadn't she worn a dress to dinner the first night they'd met? She took a bite of her cotton candy but it had become sticky and coarse. Dark red beads had formed in clumps and a persistent wasp circled close, attracted by the sweetness. Kit dumped the cotton candy in the garbage can. She wiped her hands on the legs of her overalls and scuffed through the dusty grass as she followed the pair at a distance.

When it came time for the picnic lunch, Kit's father pointed out a shady spot under a tree. He spread out the blanket on the grass and they all sat down. Even out of the sun's fierce glare, the air was still blistering hot.

"The hottest day of the year," her father said. "That's what they're saying."

They opened the picnic basket but Kit could hardly eat a bite. Now that Vivian was there, she felt impatient for the day to be over. But Vivian and her father took their time, lingering over the lunch.

A small group of women had gathered in the shade of some nearby trees. A middle-aged woman took her place on a stand. She put on a pair of spectacles and looked steadily out at the crowd. "The Woman's Christian Temperance Union is a sisterhood—a union of women like you and me—working to make our lives and our families' lives better." Her voice was strong and commanding. "The Union has fought the war against the evils of drink, battled the demon rum. It has convinced our government to try Prohibition..." A scattering of applause rippled through the crowd.

Then a man joined the back of the crowd. He cupped his hands around his mouth and taunted, "Didn't work here, though, did it?"

The speaker addressed the man. "It was a noble effort, a

valiant effort. Prohibition was meant to improve the lives of many—to ban drunkenness from our streets and from our homes."

The man in the back yelled, "A man has a right to his drink…"

The woman ignored him and continued. "Prohibition was a fight worth fighting. We have no regrets. And we support our sisters in the United States who continue with the effort. The Woman's Christian Temperance Union continues to fight on many other fronts. It has fought to win women the right to vote…" The crowd erupted in more applause and cheers. "And we will fight for more social welfare improvements. United, we have a strong voice. Join us, sisters, and we will make a difference."

Kit was interested in what the woman was saying. She could remember her mother talking about the Woman's Christian Temperance Union. She stood up and took a few steps closer. Behind her, her father stirred himself and began to load up the picnic basket. "Let's go see some of the other tents," he suggested.

But Kit was curious to hear more of the speech. "Can't I just stay for a few more minutes?" she asked. But he had already set off towards the tents with Vivian on his arm. Once again Kit was left with the picnic basket. She glowered darkly as she grabbed the handle. It was lighter now, which at that particular moment was the only thing she was grateful for. She took one last look at the group of women under the trees and then trudged out into the glaring heat after her father and Vivian. They'd stopped in front of a tent and her father was leaning forward to read the sign. Then he straightened up and looked around until he caught sight of Kit. He beckoned her over.

"Look at this. The Great Orsini and his World of Magic."

Kit looked at the photograph on the sign. The Great Orsini glared out at her with dark eyes under heavy eyebrows. He had a thin pencil moustache, and he was wearing a turban decorated with stars and moons. Kit took a step to the left and his eyes followed her.

"What do you think? Should we go in? It's just about to start." Her father checked his watch.

A man was closing the door flap of the tent. "One minute to showtime," he called.

"Is there room for three more?" Kit's father asked him.

"You bet, mister." He pocketed the money Kit's father offered to him and pointed to the bench at the back.

It was dark inside the tent, the afternoon heat made more intense by the enclosed space. There was a fluttering of fans as women tried to cool themselves. Kit followed Vivian and her father as they stepped over feet to reach a space on the bench. Just as they sat down, the man who had taken their tickets picked up a bugle and blared a fanfare. The audience fell silent.

"Ladies and gentlemen, boys and girls," his voice boomed over the crowd. "Prepare to be transported to the strange world of the magical arts. You will be astounded. You will be mystified. From Kalamazoo to Prince Albert, Saskatchewan, audiences have been flummoxed and bewildered. What you are about to witness is not mere trickery. Oh, no. This afternoon you will experience true magic…the unknown, the unexplained, and—I assure you—it is not for the faint of heart. Now…ladies and gentlemen…boys and girls…I present to you…the one…the only…The Great Orsini!"

The curtain parted and there was The Great Orsini right before them with his arms outstretched and his head thrown back. The crowd gasped at the sight. He was not as big a man as Kit had been expecting. Quite short, in fact, even standing on a stage and wearing a turban—the same one he'd worn in the picture. He had dark brown makeup smeared on his face and dramatic black lines emphasizing his eyes. Then a sudden puff of smoke flew up from near his feet and he was completely enveloped in the haze. As it cleared away, the crowd gasped again. He had disappeared.

Vivian let out a little shriek.

Then a deep, baritone laugh rumbled from the back of the tent. The crowd turned. The tent flap burst open and in strode The Great Orsini. He marched up the centre aisle to the stage, his long purple cape sweeping behind him. The crowd burst into applause as he made an elaborate bow.

He produced a bunch of flowers and made them disappear into a series of knotted handkerchiefs. Then he made them reappear again. He took several enormous gold hoops, linked them together into a chain, and then shook them apart. He had one of the audience members come up on stage and inspect each hoop to testify it was solid, free from any cuts or openings.

Kit glanced over at Vivian and her father. Vivian's eyes looked as big as doughnuts.

"Now, for my final feat of magic," The Great Orsini announced, "I will call on my assistant."

A slim, dark-haired boy joined him on the stage. He had a fluid way of moving, supple at the joints. His eyes were deep set and black as ink. He was maybe fifteen or sixteen years old, with an open shirt and a wide crimson sash around his waist.

Something about the boy stirred a memory in Kit's mind. There was something familiar…

Then The Great Orsini bellowed, "I will need a volunteer from the audience." He held his hand to shield his eyes and scanned the audience. He stopped, looking in Kit's direction, and pointed a finger.

But he was not pointing to Kit. He was pointing to Vivian.

Vivian clapped a hand to her mouth and then tottered up to the stage. The magician took her hand as she climbed up the steps.

"Such a beautiful lady," he commented smoothly. "What is your name?"

"Vivian."

He led her to the centre of the stage, still holding her hand. With an elaborate flourish, he directed the boy assistant to turn away and cover his eyes with a purple scarf. Then The Great Orsini set three tall glasses on a table. One glass was half filled with water. The other two were empty. "Vivian, I would like you to arrange these glasses in any order you choose."

Vivian set the glass with the water in the centre, the two empty glasses flanking it. The Great Orsini took a black cloth, shook it and laid it over the glasses. "Now, I ask you to observe the table and the cloth covering the glasses. Tell me, are the glasses entirely covered?"

"Yes."

"Can you see any drops of water anywhere on the cloth or on the table?"

"No."

"Is there any way you can tell which glass has the water in it?"

"No."

"Fine." He clapped his hands sharply. "Assistant, you

may approach the table."

The boy assistant untied the scarf covering his eyes, turned around and stepped up to the table.

"Now, I will communicate telepathically to my assistant and he will tell us which glass contains the water." The Great Orsini pressed his fingers to his temples.

The assistant put one hand over the first glass. It hovered briefly in the air above the glass. Then he passed his hand to the centre glass.

Kit held her breath. She could see his hand begin to tremble until it was shaking violently.

"The water is in this glass," he announced.

The Great Orsini whipped off the cloth, revealing the centre glass with the water in it.

The crowd clapped. Someone from the back of the tent yelled, "Make him do it again."

The magician made a slight bow of acknowledgement. "Assistant, I will ask you to turn your back again."

Once again his assistant turned around.

"Now I will ask the lovely Vivian to rearrange the glasses."

This time Vivian set the glasses with the water-filled one last in line. The black cloth fluttered down to cover them again and the assistant approached the table. His hand held steadily over the first glass and the second glass but when he came to the third the shaking began.

Once again he was correct. Twice more the glass was repositioned and twice more the magician's assistant easily selected the correct glass.

The magician and his assistant bowed repeatedly before the applauding crowd. And Vivian stood proudly next to them, all flushed, with a wide smile and glittering eyes.

5 The Dance

Kit sat, cross-legged, on the grass in a corner of the biggest tent at the charity picnic. Before her was a row of chairs and, in front of that, a collage of bobbing, weaving and swinging legs. It was the dance at the end of the day. Fairy lights were festooned in great swags all along the top of the tent. On the stage on the far side a three-piece band played a bouncy, jazzy beat.

The sun had set, but the day's heat still lingered in the tent, and there was a closeness in the air. Kit liked the music and her foot tapped along. But she didn't know how to dance very well. She hadn't had much practice, either. Her father had taken her by the arm when they'd first arrived. He'd spun her around, making her laugh. Then he'd led her to the centre of the dance floor, Kit stumbling to follow his lead. They'd made a complete circle around the tent and Kit had just started to fall into the rhythm of the dance.

Then it was Vivian's turn. That had been more than an hour ago and they'd been dancing ever since. Kit could see them now through the crowd. They were up near the front of the stage. Her father's hand lay in the middle of Vivian's back. She was snuggling up close to him and looking up into his face. Their legs moved together in perfect unison. The skirt of Vivian's dress swirled gracefully as she moved, and the new red scarf swung against her back.

Kit looked down at her denim overalls. She would have worn a dress, too, if she'd known there was going to be a dance. The pant legs rode up to reveal her ankles and she could see several angry-looking mosquito bites. She broke off a long yellow piece of grass and scratched it up and down against the itchiest ones.

The song finished and Kit looked across the dance floor hopefully. Maybe her father would dance with her now. But no, another song started up and he remained with Vivian. They didn't even glance in her direction. It was as if they'd forgotten all about her.

Kit stretched out. It was getting late and she was starting to feel tired. She laid her face down, grass pressing into the side of her cheek, and gazed sleepily at all the legs— chair legs, spectators' legs and dancers' legs. Then she turned to face the other way. The canvas of the tent was thick and heavy. She poked up the edge and fresh, cool night air eased in, brushing her face like a powder puff. It was dark outside. She could make out the shapes of other, smaller tents, a scattering of lights and the huge presence of the Ferris wheel in the background. Far away, just over the horizon, there was a shimmer of pale green in the night sky where the sunset had faded.

She closed her eyes, breathing in the soft smell of the grass, and drifted into a warm, dark half-sleep. Each song was like a wave, gathering to take shape and then washing up on the beach as it finished. And as each one finished, another one rose right behind it. Kit dozed on…

~

Her eyes sprang open. There was no music. She sat straight up. It felt late. There were only a few people left in the tent and the band members were packing up their instruments. Kit's eyes flew across the dance floor. There was no sign of Vivian or her father. She jumped to her feet. How could they have left without her?

Maybe they hadn't. Maybe they were outside looking for her right now. Kit grabbed the picnic basket and rushed past the men stacking the chairs.

It was inky black outside. Everything looked different now. The tents loomed like dark, menacing giants. Kit picked her way between them, careful not to trip on any of the posts and ropes. Two men, all in shadow, emerged from around a corner and she almost walked straight into them. They passed by and disappeared into the darkness. Something ran scurrying ahead of her, across the path. A small cat? A rat?

It was much cooler now. She rubbed her arms briskly as she glanced furtively into the shadows where the animal had gone. Would it jump out again? But she could not see anything there and she hurried past.

The fairgrounds seemed deserted. She decided she'd look in the field past the Ferris wheel where the cars were parked. She would see whether her dad's car was there.

Some of the tents glowed inside, a soft, diffuse light. She skirted along their edges, and past the booth that had sold the scarves. It was all locked up now. Then she was at the magic show tent. The sign was still in front, declaring The Great Orsini. Someone had forgotten to bring it in. From the back of the tent she could hear voices. She stepped a little closer. Shadows of two figures inside were cast in silhouette against the canvas of the tent.

"Don't be ridiculous. If you want to be paid, you'll hafta start helping me with more of the tricks." The words were slightly slurred.

"But that's not fair. I shouldn't have to work for free." It was a softer, gentler voice.

"Free? Who clothes you and feeds you and puts a roof over your head? You get all of that for free and you're still complaining."

"I'm not complaining. I just want what's fair. A dollar or two, that's all I'm asking."

The shadows of the figures against the tent were large and distorted. Kit could see every movement they made as they argued.

"You're ungrateful, that's what you are. Stupid and ungrateful. Do I get one word of thanks for everything I do for you? There isn't a father that's done more for his son, I tell you. But that's not enough for you. You just keep wanting more, don't you?"

"I don't. I don't want anything from you except my pay. Just give me my money and I'll go."

There was a moment of silence. Then the harsh, older voice came again. "You can't leave me. You wouldn't dare. You're part of the act."

"You can get someone else."

There was a snort of exasperation. "I can't just get someone off the street. You know that." The voice became more pleading. "Come on. Be reasonable. You don't have anywhere to go. And who would hire you...just a boy? Think about it. You're better off staying with me. This is the life you know. This is where you belong."

"But, Dad. That's what I'm trying to tell you. I want a

different kind of life."

A second of silence, something ominous in that moment. Then one shadow raised an arm. It came down hard. The sharp sound of a slap. "This isn't good enough for you, huh? Is that what you're saying?" Another slap. "You think you can do better for yourself. Fine. How do you like that?" Slap! "And that?" Slap! "Come on, boy. What do you have to say for yourself now?"

Kit's muscles cringed with each sound as if the shadowy hand were meeting her own flesh. Her heart raced and her breath came in quick, short gasps. She wanted to shout out, to tell them to stop. But at the same time every inch of her longed to get away. She could not be there a second longer. She wheeled around, feeling ashamed of her cowardice, and in her haste stumbled over a tent peg. She scrambled to right herself, all arms and legs. Then, back on her feet again, she made a swift retreat.

She ran as far as the cotton candy booth before she allowed herself to stop and catch her breath. She looked hastily back over her shoulder—nothing to see but darkness and shadows—before she continued on towards the field.

If the fairground was dark, the field where the cars were parked was even darker. The moon was no more than a sliver—a boat tossed in a sea of stars. The grass formed a lumpy, uneven surface. Only a few cars remained. Kit tried to remember where they'd parked. It was along the far road, near a row of tall trees. She stumbled across the grassy field until she could make out the blackness of the trees against the sky.

Then she saw a light flash, and burn out. There were low voices and the red end of a cigarette glowed in the night.

Kit froze. She was close enough that she could smell a whiff of the smoke. They were men's voices, talking quietly. Kit was going to continue on, giving them a wide berth, but then she saw their outline. Two men leaning up against the dark shape of a car. Her father's car.

Kit crept closer. What were these men doing loitering around her father's car?

Loud laughter from the men came then, and Kit recognized one laugh—her father's. She would have known it anywhere.

She was going to run up to him but then she heard the other man say, "I've got another batch ready. I'll bring it over in the next couple of days."

Kit paused.

"All right. I'm running a bit low and I've got another run tonight." That was her father.

"Don't take any chances, hear?"

"Don't worry, Lou. I know the route like the back of my hand."

"That will be two runs in two nights. Are you sure you want to do it?"

"It's good now, not much moonlight. The less light, the better."

The man tossed his cigarette down on the ground and stepped on it. "I better get going. You have a good night, then."

"I will. It will go smooth as clockwork. You'll see."

"Good night."

"Night."

The man walked back towards the fairgrounds.

Kit took ten deep breaths, then she called out, "Dad, here I am." She approached the car.

"Kit! I was just coming to look for you. How long have you been there?"

"I just got here." She wondered if he would say anything about the man with the cigarette or why he had left her in the dance tent. But he just opened the car door for her and said, "Hop in. Let's go home and get you to bed."

The car bumped across the field and up onto the road. Then they were gliding through the night. Her father hummed a little under his breath, the sound adding to the hum of the motor like a chord. Kit waited, but still her father did not offer any explanation of what he'd been doing.

"Where's Vivian?" she asked by way of a start.

Her father tapped the steering wheel with a couple of fingers as he drove. "Vivian drove herself home. She had her own car."

"Who was that man you were talking to?"

His fingers stopped drumming. He glanced over at her and then looked back at the road. "Just a friend."

Kit waited but he didn't say anything more.

"Why did you leave me at the dance?"

He reached over and patted her knee. "Kit, I wouldn't leave you. You know that. I was out looking for you. I thought you might have gone back to the car."

Kit looked steadily ahead out the window. They were approaching a gas station. The light over the pumps was still on, even though it was late. A figure was walking down the side of the road. Kit felt the car swerve to avoid him. She turned her head just in time to see a boy—dark pants, dark jacket and a crimson sash at his waist. He was directly under the light, eerily lit from above. Then, in the next instant, as if some magic switch had been flipped, the light was extinguished. A sudden shock of blackness flooded in and the boy vanished like an apparition. It was as if he had never been there.

Strange, Kit thought as she turned her gaze forward once again. Strange that the streetlight would go out at that exact moment. She stared at the car's headlights casting two yellow pools in the darkness only a moment ahead of them. Hypnotizing to watch. Everything else was black, an expanse of the unknown. And the car rushed forward like an act of faith.

6   *The Knight of Cups*

Kit felt the sun on her face making the insides of her eyelids glow red. She didn't have to open her eyes. She knew it was early. The sun would be just coming up over the tops of the trees and slanting in her window. She turned to face the wall, snuggling deeper under the covers and hoping she could slip back into sleep.

Last night her father had told her to go straight to bed as soon as they'd got home from the charity picnic. It was late, he'd said. Too late for kids to be up. And so she had, but she could not fall asleep. She lay, staring up at the ceiling, listening to the house settle and thinking about the man with the cigarette. What kind of business could he possibly have with her father? And why didn't her father want to talk about it? She could hear her father moving around downstairs for a while and then the sound of the door opening and then closing again. She continued to listen but all was quiet. Had he locked the door and then gone to bed? Or had he gone outside?

Kit had crept to the window and looked out. There was a light in the barn—a faint glow from the window and the cracks between the boards. The barn door opened. The area outside the door was briefly illuminated. The shape of a man, tall like her father, slipped out, pulling a wagon loaded with boxes. He closed the door again, and disappeared into the shadows of the night.

Kit had kept watching. She saw him return to the barn several times and emerge again, each time with another load. Then the light in the barn went out. Maybe, she'd thought, he would come back into the house now. Kit had hopped back into bed and listened for the door to open again. She had waited and waited but all she could hear was the *tick tick tick* of the clock on the dresser; then a muffled sound outside like the hoot of an owl. She had wanted to stay awake until she heard him come in again. But the clock ticked on and there was no sound at the door. Her eyes began to feel heavy and she struggled against closing them. But sleep overcame her and she felt herself sink down into its soft, dark depths.

Now it was morning. Kit opened her eyes. The early light played across the flowered wallpaper. She stretched and then sat up, threw back the covers and padded over to the window. It was a clear summer morning. The water glinted in the sunlight and the dew lay white across the grass. In the morning light the barn looked as ordinary as a barn could look.

Kit shook out her overalls, pushed her legs into them and did up the buttons. She ran her fingers through her hair, tiptoed downstairs and stole a peek into her father's room. There he was, asleep. It had to have been very late when he'd got in.

Kit opened the icebox, poured herself a glass of milk and drank it all in one gulp. She cut a thick slice of bread and covered it in strawberry jam. Then she hopped down the back porch steps. The morning air was cool and fresh, the grass still wet with dew.

The barn door was padlocked shut. She tried to peer in through the narrow crack but it was difficult to see much of anything. Then she went down to the wharf. There was the *Nighthawk*, bobbing gently up and down, straining against its moorings, just as it always was.

She was going to go back into the house when she noticed a thin vapour of smoke creeping up through the trees by the pickers' shack. One by one she pushed the snarly brambles aside and approached the rundown building. Her first thought was that it had somehow caught on fire. But then she saw the ring of rocks surrounding a small campfire about a dozen feet from the door of the shack. Kit froze. If there was a campfire, that had to mean someone was there. Someone who shouldn't be there.

Kit stood as still as a statue. Her legs and arms began to feel stiff from not moving. Finally she took a couple of steps closer, and then a few more. Then she was at the broken window. She looked inside. Nobody was in sight, but there was a jacket slung over the back of a chair, and on the small rickety table in the corner, she could see something square about the size of a fist.

Kit edged along the side of the shack to the door and went inside. There was a clutter of debris over the floorboards. The only furniture was the chair, the table and, on the far side, a wooden platform holding a bare mattress with a wad of stuffing seeping out a hole.

She tiptoed closer to the jacket. It was black and threadbare at the cuffs, and one of the buttons hung from a thread. She eyeballed the width of the shoulders. Bigger than hers, but smaller than her father's. There was something in the pocket, a corner of crimson fabric showing. A handkerchief, perhaps. Or a scarf. She thought of pulling it out, going through the pockets, but decided against it, at least for the time being.

She turned her attention instead to the object on the table, a slim cardboard box. Its surface felt smooth and waxy against her fingers as she picked it up. She pulled back the flap at one end. It was well worn—it had been opened many times. She tipped the box and the contents slid out into her hand as smoothly as an opening drawer. A deck of cards. They seemed slightly bigger than usual, and they were adorned with a gold and blue geometric pattern. She took the top card from the deck and turned it over. It featured a full moon and, within it, a second crescent moon. She turned the next card. Crossed swords in the centre and on each side a heart. One of the hearts was the usual valentine heart but the other heart was different. It looked like a real human heart, an irregular shape sprouting blue and red veins and arteries. Kit felt a prickling in her own heart. What kind of cards were these? She turned the next card. A woman with long flowing hair was leaning forward at the edge of a pond. She held her hair out of the water with one hand and supported herself with the other as she gazed at her reflection in the water. Above her head the night sky was studded with stars.

Kit was so fascinated by the cards she did not notice the figure darkening the doorway of the shack. The figure stood absolutely still. Then he spoke.

"What card do you hold?"

Startled, Kit jerked her hand back, dropping the cards. They fell to the floor at her feet—a fluttering sound like the rustle of bird wings.

The stranger looked at her calmly, giving no indication that he was surprised to discover her looking through his things. Kit was annoyed with herself for feeling so flustered. Wasn't he the one trespassing on her father's property?

The boy was taller than she was, and looked to be several years older. His hair was dark and longer than most boys'. A lock of it fell over his forehead and down to a set of eyes so black and riveting Kit found it difficult to look away.

And then she realized who he was. He was the boy from the magic show.

Kit found her voice. "What are you doing here?"

The boy shrugged his shoulders nonchalantly. "Just passing through. I needed a place to sleep last night, that's all."

Kit glanced towards the bare mattress and then back again. "Does my father know you're here?"

He shook his head and his lips formed a lazy smile.

Kit suddenly felt frightened. He could be a criminal, a murderer even. He was standing in the doorway, blocking her only escape. The window, perhaps? She eyed the jagged edges of the broken glass doubtfully.

But then the boy rearranged his features in a contrite expression and said, "I'm sorry. I know I should have asked permission but it was so late last night I didn't want to disturb anyone. Don't be afraid. I won't hurt you. You can leave if you want to."

It was as if he had read her thoughts. He stood back from the doorway, making a graceful gesture with his hand indicating she was free to leave. There was something courtly in his manner.

Kit studied him. Her gaze shifted slowly to the scattered cards on the floor. "I'll pick these up first. I'm sorry."

She dropped to her knees and he came to help her gather them up. Most of the cards had fallen face down, their gold and blue backs showing. But several strange images stared up at them.

"What's your name?" he asked.

"Kit. What's yours?"

He knocked the edges of the cards down against the floorboards to even them out. Then he looked up at her. "Caleb."

"Are you...travelling somewhere?" She wanted to ask if he was running away.

He shrugged and sat back on his heels. "Maybe. I'm not sure yet." His face clouded over momentarily, but then he grinned. "Do you want to see a trick?"

"Sure."

Caleb sat down at the table, shuffled the deck of cards and asked her to cut the deck. "Now take the top card but don't let me see it."

Kit looked at it. It was the same card she'd had in her hand when Caleb had surprised her at the door—the woman with the long hair gazing into a pond at night. Kit felt a tightness in her chest.

She looked from the card to Caleb. He was watching her thoughtfully. "That is the card you were holding when I first saw you, isn't it? It's the Star card."

Kit felt her mouth gape open.

"It is, isn't it?" He smiled knowingly, reached forward and plucked it from her hand. Then he placed it, face down, on the table. He had not turned it over to see it himself.

"Yes," Kit said. Her voice sounded small. How did he know which card it was without looking? And how did he know it was the same one she'd held earlier?

He looked up at her. His eyes were calm and dark and steady. "I'll tell your fortune," he said.

One by one he placed a circle of seven cards around the centre card, the one that he had called the Star. Then he put the deck aside. He leaned over the cards and dropped his head. He held his hand over one of the cards, not touching it, but just hovering above. He moved his hand from one card to the next. His hand appeared to be trembling, a very fine movement, almost imperceptible. He made the complete circle, then he turned over one card. It was the card with the full moon and the crescent moon within.

The next card he turned was the swords and the two hearts.

The boy raised his head and smiled an enigmatic smile. He did not make any comment. Kit did not say anything, either—but her mind was racing. How was it possible that this boy knew the exact three cards she had looked at? He had to have been at the doorway longer than she had realized.

Quickly, he turned over all of the remaining cards in the circle, but left the centre one untouched. He considered the cards for several minutes without a word. Kit began to feel restless, but then he spoke.

"This one is the Knight of Cups." He paused, considering the strange man with the body of a fish instead of legs. "It means that a young man...a sensitive man...comes into your life."

Was he talking about himself? Was he the young man the card suggested? Kit felt her eyes narrow. He was having fun with her. Teasing her.

"It also has to do with travel on water," he added. Then he pointed to the next card, a dancing man in a black and silver jester's costume and a little dog at his feet. "Adventure and change. A new beginning."

Kit shifted nervously. Certainly, coming to stay with her father was a change and a new beginning. Stop, she told herself. It was silly superstition. She knew that. Anyone could read their own life into what the cards said.

Caleb continued. Next came a figure with one arm raised skyward. At the wrist, a tiny wing. One leg, also, rose from the ground and at the ankle was another tiny wing. "The Magician. It means you have all you need to create whatever you want in life."

Kit chewed her lip as she stared at it. That was exactly what she believed. She was responsible for her own fate. Whatever happened in her life was because she made it so, not because the planets lined up a certain way, or the lines of her palm crossed or did not cross. And certainly not because of a handful of cards.

He moved to the next card. "Hard work and perseverance. Physical work.

"The next is upside down. Do you see?" The card, indeed, lay reversed—a dark green dragon breathing fire and a woman holding a branch rising from the flames. "If it appears upside down it changes the meaning," he explained. "The Queen of Wands reversed. It means a jealous woman. Someone unstable and demanding."

Kit immediately thought of Vivian. Despite herself, she leaned forward to hear what he would say next.

It was the card with the crossed swords and the two hearts. His finger hovered over it and then came to rest directly upon the human heart. All around his finger Kit could see the protruding veins and arteries.

"Heartache," he said.

Kit felt as if something had touched her own heart. It was true. Her heart did ache, whenever she thought of her mother. But what if the card meant more than that? What if her worst fear—that her mother would not get better—was about to come true?

Nonsense, she told herself firmly. These cards were nothing but nonsense. Now Kit was sorry she'd ever agreed to this silly game.

"The Moon." Caleb pressed on to the next card. "Tricks and lies. Deception."

Kit's palms prickled with sweat.

There was only one card left, the one in the middle. His hand took the edge of the card and turned it.

And Kit gasped. The long-haired woman was no longer gazing into the water. She was reaching up to pluck a star from the sky. Kit blinked her eyes rapidly. Did her eyes deceive her?

But before she could look more closely, Caleb turned the card face downward again.

"Let me see that card." She reached for it, but he whisked it away.

"Let me see."

He slowly held out his hand and she took the card. But now the woman was looking into the water again. So it had just been an illusion, what she had seen before. A trick of the light.

She looked up at him. "What does this card tell you?"

He regarded her thoughtfully. He opened his mouth to speak.

"Kit?" It was her father's voice calling from across the yard. He was awake.

Kit leapt to her feet, shot Caleb a warning look and

pressed a finger to her lips.

"It's my father," she whispered. "Stay here." Then she turned and ran from the shack, through the snagging brambles and all the way up to the house.

7 The Witching

"I'm going to take the boat over to the marina at Canoe Cove to get gassed up," Kit's father said. "You okay here?"

Kit nodded. All she wanted to do at that moment was get back to the pickers' shack. She could have opened her mouth right then and there and told her father about Caleb. But she didn't. Something made her stop. It wasn't that she was being deceitful, she told herself. Not really. It was simply that she wanted to find out more about the strange young man for herself before anyone else got involved.

After her father had gone she took some food from the icebox and hurried across the grass to the shack in the trees.

"Here, have this." She handed Caleb a bottle of milk and half a loaf of bread.

"Thanks. Did your dad say anything?"

"No. He had to get some gas. I'll talk to him later." She watched him chew on the loaf of bread and take a long swig straight from the bottle. When he swallowed, his Adam's apple bobbed up in his throat and dipped back down again.

Kit put her hands in her overall pockets and then pulled them out again. "I saw you at the charity picnic yesterday," she blurted out.

He stopped chewing.

"I saw you at the magic show. You did the water trick. I recognize you."

Caleb wiped his mouth with the back of his hand. "Yeah," he admitted. "That was me."

"Well, are you going to go back?"

He shook his head. "Nope. I'm never going back."

Kit was silent for a moment, considering this. "Well, what about your family? Do they know where you are?"

Caleb scoffed, "There's just my dad. My mum died years ago. No brothers. No sisters. Just my dad and me." He winced slightly. "My dad and I don't get along." He put down the bottle of milk, and as he leaned forward the lock of hair on his forehead shifted forward as well.

Kit stared at the skin on his temple. It was mottled red and purple. At the centre of the discoloration a thin cut extended back into the hairline. "Did he do that to you?"

Caleb covered it quickly with his hand. He did not reply.

"Did he? Tell me, Caleb. He did, didn't he?"

Caleb turned to look at her. His cavalier manner had vanished. Now there was something wounded and soft in the dark of his eyes. She knew the answer before he spoke. "Yes. He did." His voice was hardly more than a whisper.

She put out her hand and he flinched away. "Let me look," she insisted. Carefully she pushed the hair aside again. "Does it hurt?"

"Just a little."

"I should get you some disinfectant from the house.

And a plaster."

"No. I cleaned it last night. It'll heal on its own. They always do."

"You mean he's done it before?"

"Look at this." He pulled his pant leg up above the ankle, revealing a nasty yellow bruise that spread upward farther than she could see. "He kicked me there. But it doesn't hurt anymore. I'd say that one is probably a week old."

"Does he hit you a lot?"

Caleb shrugged. "Depends what you mean by a lot. When he gets to drinking, though, I can pretty well count on it." He pushed his pant leg down again and glanced over at her. "I could fight back. I could probably knock him to the ground if I wanted to. I'm taller than he is now. But I guess I'm not much of a fighter." He took another bite of the bread and chewed it steadily.

Kit tried to imagine what it must be like living with someone like Caleb's father. She thought about her own father. Sure, there were things that frustrated her about him, she thought, but at least he didn't hit her.

Caleb dusted the bread crumbs off his shirt and looked at her. "I guess you might call me a sissy—running away instead of standing up to him. But I'm old enough now to go my own way and that's what I'm going to do."

"Where're you going? Do you have someplace in mind?"

"Nope." He grinned and swung his arms wide. "Wherever I end up, that's where I'm going. I'm used to travelling, you see. I've been up and down the coast and across the prairies. That's what life in the carnival is all about."

"Don't you go to school?"

"Nope. My mum taught me what I need to know... before she died. I can read and I can do sums in my head better than most. Some people say I have a natural head for figures."

"How did your mum die?"

"Car accident."

Kit wanted to ask more about it. She wanted to know how he felt about losing a mother. But one look at him, at the way his jaw had tensed, made her stop. She chewed the end of her thumbnail slowly as she thought. She wondered what life would be like alone on the road, always moving from one spot to another, never settling down. "Maybe I'll ask my dad if you could stay with us for a while."

"Don't worry about me. I can look after myself." Even though he tried to sound sure of himself, Kit thought she heard a waver in his voice.

"There's plenty of room in the house."

"No." He shook his head firmly. "I wouldn't want to impose."

"Well, what about this shack? I'm sure I could find you a blanket and sheets and a pillow. We could sweep it up and cover the broken window and fix the hole in the roof so it wouldn't get wet inside if it rains."

Caleb didn't say anything immediately and Kit hoped he was considering the offer. Finally he shrugged his shoulders. "It might be a good idea. My dad will be out on the roads looking for me. He's going to be pretty darn mad, I can tell you that. I probably should lie low for a couple of days."

"What do you think he'd do if he found you?"

Caleb shrugged and his lips twisted into a wry smile. "Let's just say it would be better if he didn't."

Kit stared at him. She could just make out the angry red blotch on his temple through the strands of dark hair.

"But I'll only stay if your dad doesn't mind," he added.

"He won't." She was sure her dad would want to help him out. "I'll go get some things to fix this place up. I'll be right back."

Kit ran back to the house. She went through the linen closet quickly, gathering up sheets, a woollen blanket, a towel and a pillow. She tucked the broom under her arm on the way out.

"Here," she said as she handed Caleb the broom. "You start sweeping. I'll go get some more stuff."

She picked up a few tools from the lean-to at the back of the barn, and then rushed from room to room in the house, finding a bowl for washing up in and taking one of the jugs of water from the pantry. Then her eyes caught on her mother's jars of preserves. Slowly, she traced her finger across the feathery script on one of the labels. Her mother had been so healthy when she'd written this. The three of them had been all together, living on the farm. They'd been a family. And, now, only a few years later, it had all changed. It didn't seem fair.

Kit took a long, steadying breath and set her shoulders squarely. She wasn't going to feel sorry for herself. At least she had a mother, unlike Caleb. She promised herself she would write her mother a letter and have it ready for the mailman by tomorrow morning.

But first she needed to get back to the business at hand, finding something to cover the broken window. She rummaged through the clutter on the floor under the bottom shelf. Empty jars, a box of Christmas decorations and there—perfect!—an old cutting board. It took two trips to carry everything to the shack. On the last load she heaved up the heavy water bottle with one arm and balanced the rest in a wobbly pile with the other arm.

She staggered to the shack and dumped the bottle down at the door with a thud. "Look at all this stuff," she said. "Water, a bowl, a comb and some soap. Oh, and the outhouse is down the path through the trees at the back of the house."

They snipped the worst of the brambles back from the path with a rusty pair of gardening shears. Then they turned over the mattress. It was in better shape on the other side and they smoothed down the sheets and blanket and tucked them into place. The small room was starting to look quite livable.

"Look at this," Kit said, holding up the cutting board. "We can use this to cover the hole in the window."

"Great. How are we going to keep it in place?"

"I brought a hammer and..." She dug in her overalls pocket. "Here are some nails." She held the board in place and Caleb hammered a few nails on each side to secure it. Then she stepped back and looked up through the hole in the roof to the sky above. "Now, what are we going to do about that?"

"Leave it. I like it that way. I can look up at the stars at night."

"But what if it rains?"

Caleb laughed. "A little water never hurt anyone."

Just then they heard the *put-put-put* sound of the boat chugging up to the dock. "Wait here," she told Caleb quickly.

Kit hustled down the ramp just as her father tied up.

"Was that hammering I heard up there?" he asked. "What were you up to while I was away?"

"Oh...um...nothing much." Suddenly she wondered if

she'd made a mistake, saying Caleb could stay in the shack before checking with her father. She tried desperately to think of something else to say. "The birdhouse had fallen down. I was just putting it back up." She pretended to fiddle with the button on her overalls as she said this, shooting a quick sidelong glance in his direction. She was relieved to see that he appeared to accept her explanation.

"It's another scorcher today, isn't it?" he said, wiping his forehead. "Hotter than blazes."

"Let's go up to the house and sit in the shade on the veranda," Kit suggested. "It'll be nice and cool there." She didn't want him to catch sight of Caleb before she had a chance to explain.

They walked up the grassy slope to the house. Kit's father took the wicker rocking chair and she sat on the steps at his feet.

"Dad, if you met someone who was trying to make a fresh start in life but needed a little help, you would help them, wouldn't you?"

He was rocking gently back and forth. "Sure."

"And if someone needed food, you'd give them something to eat…?"

He eyed her curiously. "I suppose so."

Kit pressed on. "And if someone needed a place to stay, you'd let them stay here, right, Dad?"

He stopped rocking. "What's going on, Kit?"

"Nothing…I mean nothing much. I mean, don't you think it would be good to help a person who needed a place to stay? Just for a short time. Not long. A few days maybe."

There was a long silence. "Kit…?"

"What?"

"Did you tell someone they could stay here?"

Kit shifted her feet nervously, but before she had a chance to reply her father continued. "Because if you have, you can just turn around and tell them no. I'm not going to have someone else in this house. Just having you around is more than enough."

Kit felt her mouth drop open. Was he saying he didn't even like having her in the house? His usual easygoing personality had vanished and now his lips were pressed together into a thin, straight line.

"But…" She didn't know what to say.

Her father's expression softened. "I'm sorry. I didn't mean to sound that way. You know I love having you here, don't you?" He ruffled the hair on the top of her head. "Now what's all this about giving someone a place to stay?"

"Don't worry," she said quickly. "I was just wondering, that's all." But all she could think about was Caleb out in the pickers' shack. What was she going to do now?

~

Hours later Kit's father loaded up the empty glass bottles into the car. "I've got to get some more water. Do you want to come into Sidney with me?" he asked.

Normally Kit would have jumped at the chance but today she was anxious to see the car pulling out of the driveway. She had been edgy ever since her father said he didn't want anyone staying with them. She had not yet had a chance to talk to Caleb. At one point when she had been washing the dishes she'd seen the top of Caleb's head pass by outside the window. Luckily her father was shaving in the bathroom—if he'd been in the room he would have surely seen him too. Kit had watched Caleb take the path down to the outhouse and several minutes later pass by the kitchen window again on his way back to the pickers' shack. Half a minute later her father had come out of the bathroom and walked straight into the kitchen. Kit felt almost dizzy when she thought how close she had come to having her secret discovered.

Now her father was finally getting into the car. "Do you want me to pick up anything for you in town?"

"No...oh, I mean yes." She'd almost forgotten. "A toothbrush."

"One toothbrush it is. I shouldn't be long."

"Take your time. Bye."

She waved as the car took the turn of the driveway and disappeared into the trees. Then she turned around. From where she stood the pickers' shack could not be seen but she knew it was there, on the other side of the field, nestled far back in the trees. Even though the sun was still shining brightly overhead, the moon had risen, strange and foreign in the blue late afternoon sky. It hovered over the exact spot where the pickers' shack stood.

The moon made her think of the fortune card with the moons, and a tingle of goosebumps rose on her arms. She took a deep breath and then ran to the pickers' shack. She was going to tell Caleb he would have to go. But when she looked in the doorway and saw how homey the shack was starting to look, she hesitated. Caleb was carefully washing the remaining intact section of the window with a damp rag. All the dust and cobwebs had been removed and now the glass sparkled.

She knew she should just come straight out and tell him now. There was no point in putting it off. Then Caleb turned to her and the light from the window fell on the bruise at his temple. It made her wince to see it, and all her

91

resolve vanished. How could she turn him out, someone who'd been through so much already? And he'd only just got himself settled. It didn't seem right to tell him to go.

"You can stay overnight," she said. But as she spoke she realized that it didn't seem much of an offer. "Two nights maybe," she added. "Will that be all right?"

"That would be swell. Do you think I should go up to the house and meet your dad? I should thank him for letting me stay."

"Oh," Kit said quickly. "He's just gone into town to get some more water." Immediately she regretted her decision to let Caleb stay. How could she possibly manage to keep Caleb and her father apart?

Caleb nodded. "That must have been his car I heard pulling out of the yard." He paused and then nodded towards the cards still laid out on the table. "We haven't finished telling your fortune…"

Kit shivered. Tricks and lies. Deception. Almost immediately one part of her fortune was coming true. She was lying to her father and lying to Caleb. She sat down shakily and fixed her eyes on the centre card, the last card in her fortune: the card with the long-haired woman. The card that had made her doubt her own eyes.

"No." Kit looked away and shook her head. "I don't want to play anymore."

"Sure?"

"Sure."

Caleb scooped up the cards and slid them into the box with a shrug. "You said your father went into town to get water? Why does he need water?"

"Our well's run dry." She went on to explain about the water problems since Mr. McCauley had put in his well.

"Have you tried witching another well?"

"Witching?" she repeated. "What do you mean?"

"You know. Finding water. Divining, some people call it. Or dousing. It sounds like your neighbour's done something that's changed the underground water route. You need to find another location that will tap into where the water is now."

She thought about how her father seemed to have lost all interest in the farm. "I doubt my dad has done much about it."

"You need a witcher, then."

"I do?"

"Sure. And I'm just the person for the job. Looks like this is your lucky day."

Kit stared. "You mean you can witch water? You're a witch?"

He laughed. "A *witcher*. I can divine water."

She remembered what he had done with the water glasses at the magic show. "But isn't it just a trick?"

Caleb smiled a crooked grin. "See for yourself." He walked into the woods, casting an eye over the trees and bushes. "I need a young green sapling. Willow would be good. Alder in a pinch."

"How about this one?" Kit reached up, grabbed a branch and pulled it down to eye level.

Caleb glanced at it and shook his head. "Too thin."

They went a few more steps.

"This one?"

"Too old. It has to be young."

Kit spotted a young tree about twice her height, deeper in the woods. "There. That one."

Caleb nodded. "That will do nicely." He considered

each branch carefully before selecting one and bending and twisting it until it finally broke free. Then he pulled a pocket knife from his pocket and sliced off the twigs and leaves, leaving a Y shape. He checked the suppleness of the branch, bowing it easily one way and then the other. "Nice and green," he said approvingly. "It's a good one."

"Now what?" Kit asked.

"Now we try it out. Where's your well?"

"I'll show you." Kit led him up through the orchard, past the house and into the trees near the driveway. They stood on the wooden platform covering the well. Kit pulled the lid off. It was completely black below. She found a small pebble and dropped it in. They both listened. A moment passed, and then came the sound of a distant clatter.

"Sounds dry as a bone," Caleb commented.

"We haven't had water for weeks. We're hoping it will rain sometime."

"Well, let's try this out." Caleb wrapped his hands around the witching stick, holding the split top branches in each hand with the base branch pointing straight ahead. He walked away from the well and Kit followed. The branch seemed to tremble now and again. Caleb stood still each time as if he was testing the quality of the branch's movement.

"Are you doing that?" Kit asked. It reminded her of the way Caleb's hand had trembled over the cards.

"No. I'm just feeling the attraction of the water through the branch."

"Can anyone feel it?"

"Some people just have the gift."

"Can I try?"

Caleb handed her the branch. She held it out over the same spot and closed her eyes. Maybe it was just her imagination, but she felt a tingle race up her arms. When she opened her eyes again and looked at the branch it was completely still. She handed the branch back, feeling a little skeptical. "It didn't move."

"No…but did you feel anything?"

"I thought I felt my arms tingling, but I'm not sure."

"You did?" His eyes caught hers. "How did it feel?"

"Like I said…tingly. In my arms." Why was he looking at her like that?

"Maybe you do have the gift. You just have to learn how to use it."

Kit rubbed her arms uncertainly. She didn't know what to think. "Come on," she said. "See if you can find any water."

Caleb continued walking forward, holding the branch in front of him. He was out in the field now, crossing the width of it back and forth as if he was pacing. In several spots the branch shook, but Caleb still wasn't satisfied. He walked back past the well again and moved even deeper into the trees. Kit was starting to wonder when her father would be coming back. It would never do to have Caleb out wandering around the property when her father drove down the driveway. Then, suddenly, Caleb let out a shout. The branch was jerking violently, now angled towards the ground. Caleb was shaking so much that he dropped the branch.

"This is the spot," he said with certainty. "If you dig a well here you'd have more water than you'd ever need."

Kit stared doubtfully at the dry earth. "Are you sure?"

"Positive."

Slowly Kit bent and picked up the witching stick. Sure enough the branch began to twitch in her hands as if it were alive. Kit could not believe her eyes. The movement was not as strong as when Caleb had held it but it was definitely moving.

"Look at that, Kit. There's no doubt about it. It's the gift!" Caleb said.

Kit stuck the branch into the ground to mark the spot. Even when she stood up again she could still feel her arms trembling. Then she began to doubt herself. Maybe she had just been excited. Maybe that's all it was. Nothing to do with the witching stick. The only way they would know if water was there for sure was if they dug down into the earth.

"Let's get a shovel and start digging." Any worries Kit had about her father coming back had flown from her head. She raced out of the trees to the lean-to at the back of the barn. She rummaged through a pile of wood and tools…an axe, buckets, long-handled pruning shears for the orchard and—oh, just what she was looking for—a couple of shovels and a pick. She grabbed the shovels, the pick and a bucket, and lurched back into the trees.

The blade of the shovel sliced through the mat of brittle brown maple leaves and pine needles into the dry, sandy soil. The first few minutes were easy and they worked quickly, piling the dirt to one side. But then, a few inches down, the soil became darker, richer, heavier. Their shovels grated against stones. They came upon tough and knotted roots as thick as Kit's arm. She had to fetch the axe to chop through them. As they laboured on, the muscles in Kit's shoulders began to burn and the shovel's wooden handle rubbed against her hand, making an angry red welt against the soft curve at the base of her thumb.

They had dug down so that Kit was almost knee deep in

the hole. Kit tossed her shovel aside, climbed out, stretched her back and arms and walked around the edge of the hole surveying their work from all sides. Her shoes and overalls were gritty with dirt but she didn't care. They were going to find water. At least she hoped they were. Caleb was still working. He had a steady rhythm, like a machine. His sleeves were rolled up and she could see how the muscles in his arms tightened and flexed under the skin. His movements altered only when he hit another root that had to be chopped or a large rock. He'd work around the edges of each rock to lever it loose, pick it up with both hands and throw it to the side.

It was getting late in the afternoon. The sun was lower now. It angled between the tree trunks in hazy bars of light. She could smell the dust in the air.

"How long before we hit water?"

Caleb straightened up and wiped his forehead with the back of his hand. "Hard to say. Could be ten feet. Or twenty. Maybe more."

Suddenly Kit felt exhausted at the prospect. The hole wasn't even two feet deep yet. It was going to take them days, maybe weeks, to dig that far. And the deeper they went the harder it would get. It was one thing to toss the dirt to one side, but it would be much more difficult when they had to bring it up by bucket. Kit plopped down on the ground.

"Have you ever done this before?" she asked.

"Nope."

Kit felt a niggling doubt. What if they dug and dug and there wasn't any water? All that work for nothing. Caleb had gone back to digging. Kit watched his back bending and straightening. Could she trust this strange boy? A boy who told fortunes and divined water. A boy she'd met only that morning. Maybe she was being foolish getting involved in such a crazy project with him. But she couldn't forget the dark bruise on his temple.

"Look," she said, determined to set things straight. "There's something I have to tell you…I haven't been completely honest. My father doesn't know you're here…"

~

Later that night Kit laid down her pen and picked up the paper to read what she had written.

July 26, 1924

Dear Mum,

I've been thinking about you every day and praying that you will be better soon. Please write again and tell me how you are doing. Has the doctor said yet how long you have to stay in the hospital? Or when you can have visitors?

Yesterday we went to the hospital charity picnic at the fairgrounds. There were swarms of people and it was so hot they must have sold a million gallons of ice cream. There were carnival rides and shows and a dance in the evening. I wish you could have been there. They raised a lot of money for the hospital and I'm hoping some of it will end up helping you.

Do you remember I told you about the well running dry? Well, we have a boy staying in the pickers' shack now and we're digging a new well. He's not just a regular boy, he's a runaway. He's had a terrible life and he's trying to make a new start. I told him he could stay in the pickers' shack. But there's one problem. Dad doesn't know. I was meaning to tell him, I really was. But for some reason Dad doesn't seem to want anyone else around. So I had to tell Caleb (that's the boy's name) that he can't let Dad know he's here. Caleb's a nice boy, Mum, and at first he said he wouldn't stay if Dad didn't want him to. But I begged him to stay and help me dig the well. I can't do it by myself. It's too much work for one person and Caleb is a very hard worker. This is my plan. When the well's all dug, we'll surprise Dad and he'll be so happy, he'll let Caleb stay as long as he wants. Don't you think that's a good idea? That way, Caleb gets a place to stay and we get a new well.

Kit was tempted to write about how her dad would disappear for long periods of time in the night and sleep in all morning, that he was very tight-lipped about the fishing and she had yet to see a single fish. But she decided against it as she picked up the pen again. All she wanted was for her mother to focus on getting better.

Mum, do you believe that some people have the gift of second sight? For instance, if someone told your fortune, and could divine water and seemed to know what you're thinking—what would you think about such a person? Could there be something to it? Or would you think it was all a sham?

I am glad you have met Lily and Ada in the hospital and that you can pass the time with them. They sound like nice friends. I miss you very much and I can't wait until we can be together again.

Lots of love,

Kitty

P.S. Yes, I have plenty of socks.

8   *Keeping Secrets*

Kit didn't like keeping a secret from her father, but what choice did she have? Kit and Caleb had talked it over and finally agreed. He would remain living secretly in the pickers' shack until they got the well dug.

Digging the well was the hardest work Kit had ever done. They usually worked early in the mornings while her father was still sleeping. Fortunately the site was far back amongst the trees, an isolated spot where no one else ever went. They took shifts, one at the bottom of the hole doing the digging and the other up top, pulling up the dirt-filled buckets with a rope and dumping them onto the ever increasing pile. She had found a couple of pairs of work gloves and a ladder in the lean-to behind the barn. As they dug, the ladder sank deeper and deeper into the hole.

Then one morning, about a week after they'd started the well, Kit was getting ready to go out when she noticed her father's shirt hanging on the back of the kitchen chair. One sleeve was stained reddish brown and the fabric was torn. She bent closer and her heart seized in her chest. It was blood. She tiptoed to his bedroom, eased open the door and was relieved to see the shape of his body under the covers. She crept closer. His chest was moving ever so slightly with every breath. Very quietly she left the room and eased the door shut behind her.

When she arrived at the pickers' shack Caleb was already up and dressed in the old work clothes Kit had found for him. He eyed Kit thoughtfully and said, "What does your dad do, anyway?"

"Do?"

"Yeah. How does he make a living?"

Kit didn't know what to say. "Well, there's the farm…," she started and then trailed off. They both glanced at the sad rows of strawberry plants.

"What does he do at night?" Caleb jerked his head towards the barn and continued, "He was out tinkering around the barn late last night and then I saw him pull a big, heavy wagon down to the wharf two or three times. Then he went out in the boat. It was well after midnight."

"Well, he told me he was doing a little night fishing," she said slowly.

"Night fishing?" Caleb's eyebrows were raised. "Why fish at night and not during the day?"

Kit shrugged her shoulders. An uneasy feeling stirred in the pit of her stomach. She had wondered the same thing herself. If fact, if she was honest about it, she had a lot of questions about the whole business. But Kit's father had made it clear he did not want to discuss the subject.

"I don't know. He doesn't tell me everything," she said, sounding more irritable than she intended. Then she pushed her thoughts aside. "Come on, Caleb," she said. "We better get digging before the day's half gone."

Caleb took the first turn down in the hole. The stones

were larger and more plentiful down deeper, and the dirt was heavy and clay-like. Kit strained to pull the bucket up to the top with a rope. She grappled with the bucket, heaving it to the side, dumping it and then lowering it down again. Their progress was slow.

Kit kept one eye towards the house, watching for the first sign that her father was up. Some mornings she'd see him pass by a window, or go out to the outhouse. Sometimes he'd sit on the veranda and smoke a cigarette. Then Kit would quickly nip farther back into the bushes, slip out of her filthy overalls, jump into her clean clothes and return to the house. Caleb would circle through the woods back to the pickers' shack. Usually they had several hours to work but this morning was different. They had been working only about twenty minutes when the back door opened and Kit's father emerged.

"Shhh. There he is," Kit hissed.

Immediately, Caleb's shovelling ceased. The ladder shook as he climbed to the top. They both crouched down low as they watched Kit's father cross the veranda and wobble down the stairs. One arm was clutched to his side. It appeared to be wrapped in a sling that tied up behind his neck.

"Kit," he called. "Where are you, Kit?"

"You'd better go." Caleb's voice was an urgent whisper in her ear.

"But I'm not even changed."

Kit's father had turned completely around as he looked for her. Now he stood facing the forest where they hid. Kit was not sure if he could see them. "Kit," he called again.

"Just go. Now. Before he comes looking for you," Caleb urged.

Kit jumped to her feet and hurried through the trees. As she got closer she noticed he was cradling his injured arm and there was a look of strain on his face. He had tied a thick makeshift bandage around the arm. And it was stained with blood—a blot about the size of an apple marking the halfway point between the shoulder and the elbow.

"Kit, there you are. I'm going to have to drive into town and have Dr. Swanson look at this arm. But I might need your help. I don't know how well I can drive."

"What happened?" Kit reached forward to touch the arm but he pulled away.

"Nothing. It's just a graze, that's all," he said quickly.

"But how did it happen?"

"I'll explain later. I just want to get to the doctor now." He opened the car door and eased himself into the driver's seat, muttering, "Darn if it didn't have to be my right arm, too. Of all the rotten luck."

Kit stole a furtive glance towards the trees where the new well was. She could see no sign of Caleb. Then she got in on the other side of the car. She was sitting next to her father's injured arm. The blood stain was fresh, the hand almost greyish in colour. The fingers didn't move. He took a deep breath and let it out again. She knew he wasn't looking forward to the process of starting the car and the drive into Sidney.

"Let me start it," Kit said. "I know what to do. I've watched you before."

"No." There was a determined set to his mouth. "I can do it." He switched on the ignition and adjusted the choke and the levers. Then he took another deep breath.

"I could crank the engine for you," Kit suggested.

"No, you stay here. It takes a lot of muscle to turn that

crank. Besides, it's too dangerous. It could backfire and break your arm."

Kit opened her mouth and then closed it again. She could see there was no point in arguing.

Her father heaved himself out of the car. With his one good arm, he turned the crank on the front of the car with all his might. The engine started. He slid gingerly back into the car and adjusted the idle on the engine. "All right, Kit. You can help me with this part. We've got to turn this wheel all the way around," he said. He pushed down on a foot pedal. "We're backing up first."

Kit grabbed the wheel and turned it hard. The car backed through the grass and came to a stop. Then he depressed another foot pedal and they pulled the wheel hard in the opposite direction as they circled forward until the car faced away from the house. Her father winced each time they went over a bump. Then they were edging out through the trees to the main road. The red flag on the mailbox was down. No mail again today, Kit thought. But at the moment, that was the least of her concerns.

Once they were out on the main road the ride became straighter and more even. "This is better," Kit's father said. "It should be pretty smooth sailing until we get into town. I might need your help again then."

Kit settled back into the seat. Her overalls were thick with dirt and her shoes wore a crust of mud, but her dad was too preoccupied with his arm to notice. The car whizzed between the farmlands, through the long evergreen tunnel and into the open again. Before long they were approaching the outskirts of town and the car slowed down.

"Help me with the wheel again," Kit's father said. "We'll turn onto the main street."

Together they manoeuvred the car around the corner and then angled into a parking space in front of the doctor's office. Kit's father turned off the engine and slumped back with a sigh. His face looked pale. Kit jumped out and ran around to the other side to open the door for him. She tried to help him as he struggled to get out of the car but he waved her away. His arm bumped against the car door and his face blanched whiter still.

There were several people in the doctor's waiting room reading magazines, but as soon as Dr. Swanson's nurse saw Kit's father, she whisked him into the office and closed the door. Kit was left behind. She sat down and waited. The nurse bustled out of the office and returned with a tray of metal instruments, a brown bottle of disinfectant and a thick roll of gauze. She closed the door behind her again. Kit listened carefully and could hear the low rumble of the doctor's voice and the higher sound of the nurse's. Then a muffled yelp—her father, certainly. Then a long time passed when no sound at all came from the other side of the door. The clock ticked on the wall. Kit secretly studied the faces of the other people in the waiting room. There was a woman in a hat with a snuffly-nosed boy curled up beside her. She noticed the way the woman in the hat eyed her dirty overalls and shoes. Two empty chairs, and then a man in thick suspenders and a plaid shirt. The skin on the back of his hands was covered in scaly, red patches.

Eventually the doctor's office door opened again and Kit's father emerged. He wore a fresh white sling and a brave grin. "I'll live," he announced, but immediately he sank down in the chair beside Kit.

The doctor had followed him out of the office. "You'll have to soak it every day in hot water with a little disinfectant." He held up the brown bottle. "Then put on clean dressings. Come back and see me at the end of the week."

"All right, doc," Kit's father said.

"And no more cat-and-mouse games." The doctor winked. "At least for a while."

Kit's father chuckled.

"Here's a little souvenir." The doctor handed him something wrapped in cotton. Kit's father closed his fingers around it and slipped it into his pocket.

When they left the doctor's office Kit's father squeezed her shoulder. "What do you say we go over to Stacey's for chocolate ice cream?"

A grin spread across Kit's face. "Chocolate ice cream in the morning?"

"Why not? I could use something sweet now. And a little breather before the drive back."

They were soon sitting on the bench in front of the shoeshine parlour licking their cones.

"Dad? What did the doctor mean when he said 'no more cat-and-mouse games'?"

Kit's father snorted. "Just trying to make me feel better."

"But what did he mean by it?"

"He was making a joke. Nothing to worry about."

Suddenly Kit was tired of being put off. "Well, I am worried. I want to know what's going on. I want to know what happened to you last night."

Kit's father stopped licking his cone and studied her. "You wouldn't understand. Maybe when you're older."

"But I'm not a little kid anymore." She could feel her heart beating out an angry rhythm. In the next instant her hand darted into her father's pocket and pulled out the cotton-wrapped bundle. Her father was not quick enough to stop her. She shifted away from him on the seat, unfurled the square of cotton and stared at what lay before her. A bullet! A square lead slug, almost as big as the end of her little finger.

Kit turned her shocked eyes from the bullet to her father. "Dad?"

His face took on a sheepish expression but he didn't make any effort to explain.

"A bullet, Dad. That's what happened last night? You were shot?" pressed Kit.

"It was just an accident," he said in an offhand manner with a shrug of his shoulders. He went back to his ice cream cone as if being shot in the arm was as commonplace as stubbing a toe.

"You were shot in the arm. You could have been killed! What kind of accident is that?" Kit's voice rose in protest.

"Shhh. Not so loud. Someone might hear you." As he spoke, two women passing by gave them a curious stare.

"How did you get shot in the arm?" Kit repeated in only a slightly quieter tone.

Kit's father took his time replying. "I heard a noise outside last night and I went out to check. There was something poking around the barn. A prowler, I thought, or maybe just a deer or a bear. I couldn't tell, it was too dark."

Kit's heart turned cold. Maybe it had been Caleb her father had heard.

His story continued. "I followed it through the trees trying to get a good look. It went over the road to old McCauley's place. It got quite close to the house. Planning to snoop around his place too, I figured. Then it went up the front stairs. It was so dark it was no more than a shadow. I called out to scare it away and that's when it turned around. I saw who it was then. It was old McCauley himself. He swung a rifle up to his shoulder and fired a shot. Bang, just like that. He shot me right in the arm."

"Did he see you?"

"No. I don't think so. He probably just thought he was scaring off an intruder, crazy old coot. He went into the house and there I was, my arm hurting like the blazes. I went home, washed it off, bandaged it up and went to bed. That's all there is to it. Accidents happen. Come on, finish off your ice cream and let's get home."

Back in the car Kit's father pulled out his keys and switched on the ignition. Then he glanced at Kit. "Look at you, Kit. How'd you get so dirty?"

Kit swallowed hard. "I slipped. Picking blackberries." It was all she could think to say.

"Well, a fine pair we make coming into town this way. What would your mother say?" he winked. Then he cranked the engine, settled himself behind the wheel again and looked over his shoulder. "Take the wheel, Kit. We're backing up."

When they got to the house Kit's father said he was going to lie down for a while. Kit waited a decent interval and then she went into the woods to see what progress Caleb had made while she'd been gone. He was nowhere in sight but the well looked perhaps another foot deeper. She took the path to the pickers' shack. A lone dragonfly hovered near the door for a moment and then darted off as she approached. She looked inside. The bed was smooth and Caleb's good shoes were lined up neatly underneath.

"Caleb?" Her voice seemed to ripple the silence like a

stone dropped in water. There was no reply.

She looked through the orchard and the upper field. Finally she found him down at the water, standing on the dock looking the boat over. He glanced up, waved and beckoned for her to come down.

"Just seeing what kind of boat a person would use for night fishing," Caleb said.

Kit didn't comment. Instead she said, "Caleb, did you see anyone else on the property last night?"

"Nope. The only person I saw was your dad. It was just like I told you. He was taking stuff down to the boat and then he headed out sometime after midnight."

Kit turned away, feeling confused. She pretended to rub some of the dirt off her pants. Could both Caleb and her father be telling the truth about last night? she wondered. Was it possible that her father had gone night fishing and also stalked McCauley and been shot in the arm?

"What happened to his arm, anyway? Why was it all bandaged?" Caleb asked.

Kit did her best to explain. "And this is the bullet," she concluded, digging into her pocket, unfurling the scrap of fabric again and holding it in the palm of her hand.

Caleb whistled when he saw it. Then they both stood in silence, considering the strange events that had led up to the shooting. "Maybe there's more to the story than he's telling you," he said.

Kit pretended to ignore him, wrapping the bullet up and stuffing it firmly back in her pocket. That was an idea she didn't want to think about.

Caleb shrugged mildly when she didn't reply, and turned his attention to the long, narrow boat bobbing gently in the water. "Doesn't look much like a fishing boat to me," he said. "I've seen lots of commercial fishing boats and pleasure fishing boats but none of them look like this boat. This boat is built for speed."

Kit shot him a sharp look. She had wondered the same thing. "Well, maybe he got a good deal on it," she said, slowly.

"Maybe," Caleb agreed. "But where's all his gear?"

Kit thought for a moment. "Well, you said you saw him going back and forth from the barn last night. He probably stores it up there," Kit said. Of course, that had to be what he did. "Come on, Caleb. Let's go back up," she said, anxious that her father might come out of the house at any moment and discover Caleb. Besides, she was tired of answering all the questions about the boat.

Kit started up the ramp. Its slope was gentle, the tide being up. Behind her, Caleb called out, "Wait, Kit." Kit turned.

"Look." He was pointing at the door of the cabin.

Kit sighed and thumped back down the ramp. The door was closed and locked with a heavy padlock. It was so short that a grown man would have to stoop to step through it. There was a round window in the door, trimmed with a tarnished ring of brass. And then Kit saw what Caleb was pointing to—a smear of brownish red, a distinct mark about halfway between the window and the padlock. Blood. It had to be. It looked as if someone had taken a rag and made a half-hearted attempt to wipe it off.

"And here." Caleb stooped down. At the edge of the wharf, right at the point where you could step across, was another drop of blood.

Kit stared over his shoulder. Her knees felt weak as an image of her father's bandaged arm flashed through her mind. Surely her father would not have come down to the boat after he'd been shot by Mr. McCauley. Hadn't he said he had just gone straight back to the house? Kit closed her eyes and felt a wave of dizziness. Something wasn't right. The pieces of the puzzle were not fitting together. Was her father lying?

"It might be fish blood," she said. "It doesn't have to be human blood, does it?"

"No. But don't you think that if this is fish blood you'd see fish scales somewhere too?" Caleb said.

Kit's eyes flew across the grey deck of the boat. He was right. There was not a single fish scale to be seen. No smell of fish either. There was nothing at all to indicate that this was a fishing boat. "Well, maybe…" She swallowed hard. Maybe what? She struggled to think. "Maybe he washed the deck down before he went to bed," she said. The explanation sounded flimsy as a strand of wet seaweed.

Caleb looked at her and then his expression softened. "Maybe," he said.

But neither of them believed it.

"Kit!"

The sudden voice made Kit and Caleb both reel around. And there, standing at the top of the bank, glaring straight down at them, was Kit's father.

9 Caught

Kit's father's face was as dark as a thundercloud. He grasped the railing with his good arm and stomped down the ramp.

"What are you doing down here, Kit—and who's this?"

She looked down at her feet. "We're not doing anything," she mumbled. "This is Caleb."

He turned to Caleb. "What's your interest in my boat?" he barked.

Caleb did not respond.

"Come on, boy. Speak up."

Kit's mouth felt dry as parchment but she knew she had to say something. "We're just looking, Dad. That's all. We didn't touch anything."

"Quiet, now. Let the boy speak."

"Well, sir…it's just as Kit said. We were just looking. We didn't mean any harm. Honest."

Her father studied Caleb long and hard. Then he turned his eyes heavenwards and let out a long breath as his shoulders relaxed. He turned back to Caleb. "You're not from around here, are you?"

Caleb shook his head.

"He was part of the travelling carnival at the charity picnic, Dad," Kit jumped in. "He was in the magic show act."

Kit's father narrowed his eyes. "The Great Martini?"

"Orsini. The Great Orsini. That's his father. Caleb was the one who did the water trick. But he ran away. His father beat him and so he ran away. I found him one morning in the old pickers' shack…and I said he could stay."

Kit's father took in a sharp breath. "How long has he been staying here?"

"About a week."

Kit's father stared at her. It felt as if his eyes were sharp pins pricking her skin. "Caleb, go back to the pickers' shack. I want to speak to Kit in private."

As Caleb climbed the ramp, Kit waited, miserably, for her father to speak. She studied the swirling water below as the seconds passed. The tension was almost unbearable.

Finally he spoke. His voice was low and measured. "Kit, I'm very disappointed in you. Why didn't you ask me if he could stay?"

"I know, Dad. I'm sorry," pleaded Kit. "I was afraid you would say no—that he couldn't stay. And then where would he go? Not back to his father. He'd only be beaten again."

"But don't you see? He needs to sort this out with his father. We're not his family."

Kit blinked back a sting of tears. "He's tried to talk to his father before. They can't sort it out. That's why he left. He wants to try to make a life for himself now."

"A life?" Her father tossed his head and made a snorting sound. "What kind of life does he have, sneaking around other people's places? That's no accomplishment. He should

113

get a job or learn a trade if he wants to make a life for himself. Do something useful."

"Well, he is doing something useful," Kit blurted out.

"What?"

"Digging a well."

"What do you mean, he's digging a well?"

"Just that. He's digging a well. He's doing it so we can have water again, water to wash with, water to drink and water for the farm. Sure, I let him stay in the pickers' shack and I take him food, but he's working hard for it. He's working as hard as any man and he has nothing to be ashamed of. He's earning his keep honestly."

Kit's father's eyes flicked over her overalls. "Have you been digging the well too? Is that why you're covered in dirt?"

Kit nodded. "We've been working really hard so please don't be mad. Let me show you what we've done." She led him up the ramp, past the house and into the forest.

Kit's father stared down the hole in amazement. "You've done all this?"

"Yup. Caleb and me. Just the two of us."

"But how do you know you're going to hit water?"

"He witched it. I saw him do it. He has the gift. Remember the water trick? It's practically the same thing."

Kit's father shook his head as he walked around the hole looking at it from different angles. "Well…," he said. "Well, well, well."

"It's a well, all right." Kit bit her bottom lip, unsure if her father was in the mood for a joke. But he glanced across the yawning black hole at her, the corners of his eyes crinkled, and he laughed. "That it is. It's a well." He nudged the blade of the shovel with the toe of his shoe. "And that's where my shovel's got to. I was wondering what happened to it the other day."

"It's going to be a good well. Better than the old one. So…can Caleb stay?"

Kit's father did not answer immediately.

"We really need a good well," Kit continued. "You can't dig with one arm in a sling. And I can't dig it by myself. Caleb's good and strong. He'll work hard and all he wants in return is a place to sleep and a little food."

She could see her father considering the situation. "He's a good worker, you say? And strong?"

"Yes. Strong as any man."

Kit's father made up his mind. "All right. He can stay a little longer."

Kit clapped her hands together. "You won't be sorry, Dad."

"Tell him to come up to the house for supper. I might as well get to know him a little."

Kit ran all the way to the pickers' shack and her feet felt so light it was as if she were flying over the grass. She banged on the door. "Caleb! Caleb, he says you can stay."

The door swung open and Caleb emerged, a wide grin across his face. He gave her a joyous hug and she stretched up on tiptoe so her chin would fit over his shoulder. Behind him on the table she could see his few possessions were stacked neatly. The bed had been stripped and the sheets and blankets were folded at the end of the mattress. Kit pulled away. "Were you packing?"

"I thought I might as well. I sure didn't expect your father would change his mind and let me stay."

"But where would you have gone?"

He shrugged.

"Well, you don't have to go after all. And he says you should come up to the house for supper. Come up in a couple of hours. I'm going to make you and Dad the best supper you've ever had," she said, determined to make their first meal together a special occasion. "Hope you like apple pie."

~

Kit brushed some flour off her nose and surveyed the kitchen. The table was covered with dirty bowls, forks caked with dough and stacks of unwashed dishes. A thick dusting of flour covered everything: the dirty dishes, the tabletop and even the floor. What had ever possessed her to promise apple pie? She'd never made a pie in her life.

The first thing she'd done was to find a musty old cookbook on the shelf. Then she'd got the wood stove going, adjusting the vents until the smoke went up the chimney. Next came the pastry. She didn't have a measuring cup but she'd estimated the best she could, scooping it from the tin flour drawer. It had crossed her mind that the flour had, very likely, been sitting untouched in the drawer for years. She hoped there were no bugs in it. In any case, the sifter could not be found. She'd cut in a lump of lard next, and then added some water.

She regarded the mixture. It looked dry so she added more water and dumped the gooey mess onto a floured board with a splat. She tried to knead it but it stuck to her fingers like paste. More flour, she decided. She added two generous scoops of flour and worked it into the dough until it was stiff. *Chill the dough for at least an hour before rolling it out*, she read. But she didn't have an hour to spare. She'd have to skip that part. It was supposed to be rolled until it was almost paper thin. But her pastry was thick as toast and twice as dry. No matter. It was only pastry. Everyone knew the filling was the important part of a pie.

She blew off the flour dust covering the recipe book to read the next step. Two cups of peeled, cored and sliced apples were called for. Kit ran out to the little orchard. It was too early in the season and the apples were small and hard and only just beginning to colour. She shimmied up the tree trunk, picked one and took a bite. Her mouth twisted with sourness. She was going to need a lot of sugar—at least twice what the recipe called for. She filled the bottom of her pail with apples and took them inside. Not only were they sour, they were hard to peel. By the time the first one was peeled and the core cut out, there were only tiny slivers of apple left. It was hardly worth it. That's when she decided not to peel them and just take out the core. The apples were then mixed together with plenty of sugar and cinnamon. The top crust was laid on, a slit was cut in the centre and the edges were pinched together. Kit opened the oven door and checked the temperature with her hand. Good and hot, she thought. Probably just right for baking. She slid the pie into the oven.

The fire in the wood stove crackled and popped. It was a hot afternoon and the stove made the kitchen even hotter. Sweat beaded on Kit's forehead as she propped open the back door and brushed her hands together. Now to the main course. The potatoes and carrots were boiled and the pork chops were cooked in the frying pan. She glanced anxiously at the kitchen clock. Almost five. Time for the pie to come out of the oven. Kit put on the oven mitts and opened the oven door. A lovely warm, spicy aroma wafted out and met her nose. She carefully slid the pie out and carried it to the back porch to cool. The crust had turned golden in the centre but the edges were black. The burnt parts could be broken off, she decided, and then it would be fine.

Next, she rushed to find a tablecloth. They'd eat in the dining room tonight, not at the little table in the kitchen where she and her father usually ate. But the only table-cloth was badly in need of a good ironing. No time for that. She covered the worst wrinkles with the plates and hoped no one would notice. Now, all that was needed was the centrepiece. A handful of purple fireweed from the yard would do. There was no vase to be had so she settled on a tall drinking glass. Just as she placed it in the centre of the table she heard a knock at the door.

"Hello?" Caleb's voice called through the screen door at the front.

Pushing her fingers quickly through her hair, and brushing the worst of the flour off her overalls, she ran to the door. "Supper's just ready," she said, swinging the door wide. He had slicked his hair back and he was wearing his jacket. The bruise on his temple had finally disappeared, and Kit thought to herself that he looked quite handsome.

"Kit?" a voice yelled down the hall from her father's room. "Someone's at the door."

"I know, Dad. It's Caleb. I'm just letting him in," Kit bellowed back and then, immediately, bit her lip. This was no way to start the evening. She lowered her voice and said, in her most ladylike manner, "I mean, Caleb, please do come in."

She had just shown Caleb to his seat in the dining room when her father appeared in the doorway. His eyes widened when he saw the table set with a cloth and flowers.

"Kit, you've gone to a lot of trouble," he said appreciatively as he sat down.

He seemed equally impressed when she brought the main course to the table. She'd cut his meat up into small pieces for him, knowing it would be difficult for him to use a knife with his injured arm. Then she sat down and took a bite. It all tasted delicious, and she looked from Caleb to her father, hoping this would be a good start to their friendship.

Her father asked Caleb if he was comfortable staying in the pickers' shack and if there was anything he needed. Caleb assured him it suited him very well. Soon they had settled into an easy conversation. Kit relaxed back into her chair. Everything seemed to be going well.

Then it was time for the pie. Kit whisked the dirty dishes away, set the pie down on the table and stepped back to admire it. Everything looked perfect—the tablecloth, the flowers and, most of all, the pie. Kit felt very proud of herself.

"You made a pie, Kit?" her father said, raising his eyebrows.

Kit grinned. She was just about to cut the first slice when there was a knock at the door.

"Yoo-hoo…," a fruity voice trilled. Before anyone had a chance to go to the door, Vivian sashayed into the room. Her eyes landed on Caleb. "Who do we have here?" she asked, looking him up and down.

Caleb stood up. "Caleb, ma'am."

She put her hand on his arm and said, "I'm Vivian. Be a dear, Caleb, and get me a chair. I want to sit right here between the two men."

Once seated, Vivian turned her attention to Kit's father.

"Jack, look at you, poor thing. What happened to your arm?"

"It was a bullet. That old McCauley shot me right in the arm. Can you believe it?"

"McCauley from across the road? I just drove right past the place not five minutes ago. He could have been out there waiting to take a shot at me too."

"Now, now, Vivian. The old codger's not going to shoot a pretty thing like you. You know I wouldn't let anything happen to you."

Her face looked as if it were about to crumble. "It just gives me the heebie-jeebies, that's all."

Kit's father put his good arm around her shoulders.

Kit squirmed in her seat as she watched. She cleared her throat. "What about the rest of us? Don't you think he might take a shot at the rest of us?"

"You might have a point there, Kit," Kit's father said. "He might get it into his head to take his rifle and come over here again. I think it would be best if you stayed indoors at night. No wandering around after dark, you hear?"

His reply was not exactly what Kit had hoped to hear, but she set her shoulders and forced herself to smile. She was determined the dinner was going to turn out well. "Vivian," she said brightly, "I made some apple pie. Would you like the first piece?"

"You made a pie? How clever of you. But just a small piece. I've got to watch my figure."

Kit cut into the pie. The knife slid in cleanly but balked at the bottom crust. She sawed away until she had freed up a chunk. As she was transferring it to the plate it fell sideways and broke apart. Kit pushed the pieces together again and passed the plate to Vivian.

Vivian took a tiny bite. "Such a tricky thing to get pastry right, isn't it, dear?" With that she laid down her fork and turned her attention to Caleb. "You know, I have a feeling we've met before. You look so familiar."

"He's from the carnival at the charity picnic," Kit's father said. "He's the magician's assistant. Remember when you went up on stage?"

"Oh, of course. I remember now. Caleb, tell me all about life in the carnival. I'm dying to know if it's as glamorous as it seems."

Caleb began telling tales as Kit glowered across the table. The three of them seemed to be getting along famously. She picked up the knife and tackled the dessert again. The next pieces were much easier than the first—perfect triangles. But when Kit passed Caleb and her father their plates they barely glanced at them. The men scooped up forkfuls of pie as they talked, not even noticing what they were eating. Caleb finished telling a story and they were laughing as if it were the funniest thing in the world.

It isn't that funny, thought Kit darkly. And why was Caleb making his life in the carnival sound so lighthearted? That wasn't what he'd told her.

She took a bite of her pie. Not bad, she thought. Granted, the crust was a little tough, and an apple skin stuck in her teeth, but for her first effort she had to admit it was not bad at all.

After dinner Kit's father smiled across the table. "Kit, that was a delicious meal. How about if Vivian and Caleb and I do the dishes tonight. You've worked hard enough today."

Kit felt a warm glow at her father's words, but then Vivian cut in. "Don't be silly, Jack. You'd be no help at all with one arm in a sling. You know I'm useless in the kitchen, and Caleb is our guest. We can't put him to work. Let's go into the living room and get out of Kat's hair. I'm sure she'll have it all done in a jiffy."

Kit glanced at her father, expecting he'd insist they all help—or at the very least point out Kit's correct name. But he was already following the others out of the room.

Kit looked over the dirty dishes with a sigh. She had a long and tedious task ahead of her. There was no water left in the stove reservoir so she'd have to pour water from a bottle into a big pot and heat it on the stove. The very thought of it made her feel weary.

Vivian's high-pitched voice floated down the hall. "Come on, Jack, put a record on the gramophone. Something we can dance to." Then came the sound of the gramophone being wound up and the first scratchy sounds from the record as the needle was set down. It was an upbeat, lively song, "I'm Just Wild About Harry."

Kit turned on the radio, thinking she'd drown out the sounds from the living room. The radio crackled as it warmed up. The reception was poor. She fiddled with the tuning dial and then, impatiently, turned it off again. Then she picked up a dishtowel, twisted it into a tight knot and threw it into the dishpan. She knew exactly what Vivian wanted. It was plain as day. Vivian had her sights set on Kit's father—even though he was already married. Vivian was counting on Kit's mother getting sicker and dying in the hospital. Then, as soon as she could, Vivian would marry Kit's father and move in. Kit could just picture it. Vivian would boss Kit around like her own personal servant. She'd have to do all the cooking and cleaning while Vivian sat and preened all day with her feet up. Kit gritted her teeth.

Well, she'd show her.

There were two full bottles left on the back porch. Kit heaved the first one up and carried it into the pantry. Then came the next one. She shoved them into a dark corner and covered them with a piece of tarpaulin. Then she straightened her overall straps, pushed back the hair from her forehead and marched into the living room.

The song had just finished. Kit's father was taking the needle off the record. The dancers were all flushed, grinning and puffing as though they'd run a mile.

"I couldn't clean up, after all. We're out of water." Kit made her face look innocent as she told the lie. "We'll have to get some more tomorrow."

"Don't worry. The kitchen can wait. Have a seat, Kit," her father said.

"Good idea. Let's all sit down," Vivian said, and she took both men by the hands and led them to the couch. She plunked herself down between them, looking as content as a cat with a bowl of milk.

Kit sank down into the only remaining seat in the room, a plush armchair facing the couch. She smiled sweetly at Vivian. "It looks like you have a bit of lipstick on your teeth," Kit said, indicating her front teeth with her index finger. "Maybe you should check in the mirror."

Vivian's smile vanished instantly as she retreated to the bathroom. Kit took the opportunity to move to the vacated position on the couch. When Vivian returned, she said frostily, "You'll have to get your eyes checked—maybe you need glasses. There was no lipstick at all on my teeth."

Kit felt a poke in her ribs from Caleb's end of the couch and she struggled not to laugh.

Vivian ignored Kit and perched on the arm of the couch,

next to Caleb. "Can you do any magic tricks for us now? I just love magic."

Caleb shrugged and gave an uncomfortable laugh. "I don't know…"

But Vivian persisted. "Oh, please. Just something small?"

Caleb relented with a nod of his head. He stood up and Vivian slipped into his place. From where they sat, looking upwards at him, he seemed suddenly taller. They all fell quiet. He put both his hands to his temples and closed his eyes. Then he turned in a complete circle in the middle of the room. He opened his eyes and looked straight at Kit. "I want you to wait until I leave the room," he said. "Then raise one arm in the air and hold it there until you have counted, slowly, to one hundred. Lower your arm again and tell me to come back into the room."

Kit nodded. When Caleb had left the room she raised her left arm straight in the air. She counted to one hundred and then lowered it. "All right, Caleb. You can come back in."

Caleb re-entered the room. He took both Kit's hands in his, and bent closely. At first Kit thought he was going to kiss them. But he didn't. He looked at them back and front and then raised her left arm. "This is the arm you held in the air." He did not say it as a question, but as a fact.

"How did you…?" Kit started to ask, but stopped herself, thinking that she shouldn't be taken in so easily. He'd had a fifty-fifty chance of getting it right, after all.

"Me next," Vivian said then. "Do me next."

Caleb let Kit's hand drop. He turned to Vivian, inclining his head slightly. "As you wish."

They all waited until he had left the room. His footsteps

retreated to the far end of the hall and then stopped. He would have no chance of seeing into the room from where he stood.

Vivian raised her right arm for the prescribed amount of time, lowered it and called Caleb back in. Kit watched closely as Caleb took Vivian's hands in his own. Vivian looked into his face, her eyes wide, her lower lip trembling. He stroked her hands, turned them up and down. "The right arm," he announced, stepping back with a flourish.

They all clapped, Vivian loudest of all. Her face was flushed with excitement. "Now do Jack," she said.

Kit's father shook his head, grinning. "I only have one arm I can raise, the other one's in the sling. It wouldn't be much of a choice, would it?"

"All right. Well, do me again, Caleb," Vivian said.

Once again, Caleb left the room. This time Vivian did not raise either arm. She giggled and winked at Kit's father. When Caleb returned to the room no one spoke. He examined both her hands. Then he let them drop. "Neither," he pronounced with certainty.

"Well done," Kit's father said. And they all clapped again.

Kit had watched carefully each time but she could not determine how he'd done it. It must be some kind of trick, she knew, some kind of parlour game. It couldn't really be magic. Caleb made a theatrical bow and sat in the armchair. Kit tried to catch his eye. She wanted some indication of what he was thinking, a hint—a secret wink, perhaps—that it was only trickery. But he did not look in her direction.

Kit's father stood up. "Well, that was fun. How about a game of whist next? I know I've got a deck of cards somewhere." He rummaged through the contents of the shelf near the door until he found the cards, while Kit pushed the newspapers on the coffee table aside to make space. The game was lively and fast-paced. Everyone laughed at the difficulty Kit's father had in holding his cards. For a while Kit even forgot how angry she'd been with Vivian. Eventually evening settled in. Kit found she had to put her nose right up to the cards to see them.

"Jack, this place is darker than a crypt," Vivian said. "I don't know when you're going to get electricity out here. Everyone in town has it."

Kit's father got up and lit some lamps. "One of these days…What do you say we have one more game before we call it a night?"

But Kit shook her head. "I'm all in." She could feel her eyelids beginning to droop. "Night, everyone."

"Good night, Kit."

Kit climbed the stairs to her room. It was sweltering, as if all the heat from the house had concentrated in one little room. She propped the window open and a cooler night breeze eased its way tentatively into the room. She slipped out of her overalls and into her nightgown in one quick motion. Then she peeled the blankets back, settled under a single sheet and laid her head down on the pillow.

~

Some time later Kit was roused from her dreams. Voices floated in through the open window. Kit turned over and opened her eyes.

"It's a nice night to be outside. And look at all the stars. See…there's the Big Dipper."

"Oh, Caleb," came Vivian's reply. "I think you're a little bit of a romantic, aren't you? Admit it. You are."

Kit jumped from her bed and stuck her head out the window. The light from the house illuminated the pair standing by Vivian's car.

"Oh dear, have I embarrassed you?" Vivian was saying. "Don't mind me. I practically melt whenever I'm around a handsome man."

Just then the screen door banged and Kit's father came down the stairs to join them.

"Jack, Caleb was just showing me the Big Dipper."

They all looked up and Kit pulled her head back inside so as not to be seen.

"I'd take you home, Vivian, if it wasn't for this bum arm of mine," Kit heard her father say. "Mind you drive safely, now."

"All right, sugar pie. Night, night." The car door opened and closed and then the engine started. Kit listened as the car moved down the driveway. A minute later it was quiet again.

Kit was just about to go back to bed when she heard her father say, "Caleb, I've got a business proposition for you. Come with me. I've got something to show you."

Kit poked her head out the window again. Caleb and her father were walking towards the barn. What kind of business proposition could her father possibly have? Kit wondered sleepily as she crawled back into bed.

~

"I've been thinking about the well," Kit's father said the next morning. "You're going to need a way to shore up the sides so they don't fall in."

This had not occurred to Kit. "You mean the whole thing could collapse?"

"That's exactly what I mean."

Kit thought about it giving way. All that work, wasted. But worse, what if she was down at the bottom when it happened? She thought of the crushing weight of the dirt and mud and the horror of not being able to move or breathe, of being buried alive.

"I think you're at a point now where it's getting dangerous," he said. "There's a pile of two-by-eights out back that you could use to shore up the sides, at least for the time being. And then we'll have to figure out something more permanent..." He swirled the coffee in his cup as he considered what would have to be done. "Bricks and mortar. And then, after that, there's the platform to be built over the top. Blast this arm of mine. I wish I could be more help. It's a good thing we've got Caleb. He's a good hard worker. He can do the work of two men."

Kit ran her finger back and forth along the tabletop before she spoke. "Dad? Remember last night when Caleb could guess which arm had been raised? How do you think he did that?"

Her father laughed as he set his cup down. "That's an old parlour game. A trick. Do you want to know how it works?"

She nodded.

"When the arm has been raised for a minute or two, the blood flow to the hand slows down. It looks pale compared to the other hand. That's how he does it. He's a clever boy, I'll give him that. But there's no magic involved, if that's what you're thinking."

Kit turned this over in her mind. She had suspected as much but a renewed wariness began to stir inside her. If it had been only a trick last night, was it possible that everything else—the fortune telling, the witching of water—was a trick as well? Was it all a ruse so he could have a place to stay?

Just then Caleb poked his head in the back door.

"Speak of the devil," Kit's father said, by way of a greeting. "Finally dragged yourself out of bed, did you? Well, come in and have some coffee."

"Coffee? Thought we were out of water," Caleb said.

"Oh..." Kit felt her face redden. She thought quickly. "I found a couple of extra bottles after all. They'll do us for another day."

Caleb pulled up a chair and they discussed the plan for shoring up the well. After breakfast they went out to the lean-to behind the barn. There was a dusty pile of lumber stacked against the back wall.

"This will do the job nicely," Kit's father said. "How about you two get that wheelbarrow, load it up and take it over to the well? I'll see what other tools we have in the barn." But he waited until they had started to push the loaded wheelbarrow over the bumpy ground before he pulled out his keys.

When Kit and Caleb started unloading lumber at the well site, Kit said, "Do you know what my father keeps in the barn?"

Caleb paused. "Do you?"

"I'm asking you."

She waited. Still, Caleb did not answer.

"Caleb?"

"I know. I heard you." He straightened up and faced her. "If you're so interested in the barn why don't you ask him yourself?"

"I already did. He won't tell me. Come on, Caleb. You

know, don't you? What's the big secret?"

Caleb looked as if he was about to say something, but then his eyes shifted down the path. Kit's father was approaching through the trees.

They spent the rest of the morning constructing a wooden framework completely lining the inside of the well with struts across the middle to provide support. They finished by rigging up a sturdy windlass over the top so that the buckets could be drawn up cleanly instead of knocking against the sides of the well and spilling the contents.

There was not another word spoken about the barn.

10 Talking to Strangers

August 1, 1924

Dear Kitty,

I was so happy to get your letter. I feel you are growing up and I am missing it all. Every morning the nurse comes around with the mail and I wonder if there will be anything from you.

In the last letter you said you had taken in a strange boy without your father's knowledge. Kit, this does not sound wise to me. You should tell your father immediately. Your father, after all, has your best interests at heart and has much more experience judging a person's character than you do. What do you know about this boy after all? He may appear to be a gentle person, and hard-working as you say, but you cannot always trust appearances.

As far as digging the well, I hope you are going about it in a safe manner. This is another matter your father needs to know about. What if something happened when you were digging down in the bottom? Please take care, Kitty. I worry about you.

Forgive me. I have just reread what I have written so far and I know it seems I am fretting over everything. To be honest I am feeling a little low today. We have just had a very sad event here, at the hospital, and I am still getting over the shock of it. Do you remember Lily, the older lady who was so good at playing hearts? I am sorry to say that she passed away in the night. The nurses said she went very peacefully and that is of some comfort. Ada and I had been quite concerned about her for the past few days. She was hardly eating at all and had been too weak to come to the sun porch. I suppose we should not have been surprised. She was so very frail. There will be a service for her tomorrow in the hospital chapel.

I don't want you to think that everything here is grim. It is not in the least. The nurses are very kind and our Ada keeps us laughing. She is full of stories and wedding plans—a real chatterbox. In fact, she is getting healthier by the day. She has a good colour and she's regained a great deal of energy. She can walk up and down the corridor several times now—and with considerable vigour—without getting short of breath. She tells me that she came in to the hospital the first of February, and that makes it six months to the day she has been here. Half a year in the hospital is half a year too long, she says. I know that seems like a long time but some people have been here much longer than that. The doctor may discharge her soon and she tells me she has her suitcase already packed. I shall miss her when she goes.

You asked about the gift of second sight in your letter, Kitty, and whether I believed in such a thing. All I can tell you—all that I know for sure—is that there are some things we do not have the knowledge to explain yet. I do think that mankind, at the moment, probably only has a very basic understanding of how the world works. There is much left to be discovered.

Kitty, if anything should happen to me, please don't dwell on sadness. Try to remember the happy times we had together. Do try to mind your father and work hard when the school year *starts again. You are a smart girl and you can do anything you want with your life. I have faith in you.*

I must close my letter now. It is late and I am tired. Do you remember how, at the end of the day, we would take turns reading to each other until we were both sleepy? How I wish I could do that now.

All my love,
Mum
P.S. Are you sure you have enough socks?

Kit sighed as she folded the letter carefully, put it back in the envelope and placed it with the other letters she kept under the photograph of her mother. She wasn't going to think about what would happen if her mother died. Her mother was not going to die. She couldn't. With one last look at the picture, she went downstairs.

Kit's father was up and stirring in the kitchen. "Vivian's coming this morning to pick up the water bottles and get them filled," he announced. "Wasn't that nice of her to offer? She knows it's hard for me to drive with my arm all bandaged."

Kit felt her face freeze at Vivian's name.

"Not only that," he went on to say, "she wants to take you shopping in Victoria."

"Do I have to?" Kit said immediately. The thought of going shopping with Vivian was about as appealing as swallowing a slug.

"Come on, Kit. Give her a chance. She's just trying to be friendly. Besides, she could use a hand with the bottles."

"Aren't you coming?"

" 'Fraid not. With the two of you and all the bottles there won't be room for another person. Besides, Caleb and

133

I have to take the boat up to the marina to have some work done."

Kit pressed her lips together. Obviously it had all been decided without her.

Her father looked at his watch. "She'll be here in a few minutes. I'd better get ready. Maybe if you're looking for something to do you could put all the bottles out in the driveway."

Kit sighed heavily as she picked up a couple of empty bottles on the back porch. Just then Caleb came up the path. "Morning, Kit." He took one look at her expression and his smile vanished. "What's wrong?"

"I have to go to Victoria with Vivian."

"That doesn't sound so bad."

Kit glared at him. "Maybe not for you. I bet you'd just love to go to Victoria with her. You're stuck on her." The words were out of her mouth before she could stop herself.

Caleb shifted uncomfortably from one leg to the other. "Sounds like someone's a little jealous."

"No. I am not."

"Come on, Kit. Admit it."

"I just don't like her, that's all."

Caleb shrugged his shoulders. "Fine. Let's not fight, okay? Do you want me to help you with those bottles?"

Kit nodded. They were both silent for the next few minutes as they carried the empty bottles from the back porch, around the house and to the driveway. When they were done, they sat on the front stairs.

"What kind of business proposition did my dad make you?"

It seemed to Kit that Caleb's body stiffened. But in the next moment it had relaxed again as he laughed and said,

"What makes you think he's done that?"

"I heard him say it the other night." Kit waited for him to answer the question. "Well…?"

"Well, nothing. He just wants me to help around the place until his arm gets better."

"That's all?"

"Sure, that's all. What else could there be?" He pushed a lock of hair back off his forehead and then said, "Listen, Kit. Promise you won't go outside at night, all right? You don't want to run across old Mr. McCauley, do you? They say he's crazier than a rabid dog. He sleeps during the day and wanders around at night."

Kit tapped her foot impatiently. The sun was still young, but already it was burning hot on the back of her neck. Her foot stopped tapping and she turned to Caleb. "You know that trick you did the other night when we raised our arms? How did you do it?" She was testing him. She wanted to see if he would tell the truth.

"Magic," he said, and grinned his lopsided smile.

"I'm being serious, Caleb. How did you do it?"

"Don't tell me you don't believe in magic."

He was deliberately being obstinate. Well, she could be just as stubborn. "Of course I don't," she said irritably, and moved to the step below so she didn't have to look at him.

Vivian's car approached down the long, winding driveway. It nosed out through the trees and came to a stop beside the bottles.

"Morning." Vivian waved gaily and turned off the engine. "Isn't it a beautiful day?" She opened the door, stepped out and adjusted her skirt.

"Morning, Miss Vivian. I'll get these for you." Caleb was down the stairs in a fraction of a second. He opened the back door and began loading in the bottles.

"Look at you," she said with an admiring glance. "So industrious. My! It makes the rest of us look like perfect sloths."

Kit, still sitting on the stairs, made a face—one, she thought, vaguely resembling a sloth's. Vivian looked in her direction disapprovingly. "You're not wearing *that* to town, are you?"

Kit looked down at her overalls, her best pair and freshly washed. "What's wrong with them?"

But before Vivian could reply, Kit's father came out of the house. "There she is. Looking as lovely as ever." He edged past Kit on the stairs and gave Vivian a kiss on the cheek. "Is that a new dress?"

Vivian turned around so she could be admired from every angle. "I just got it last week. Isn't it the cat's meow?"

Kit eyed the black and yellow outfit complete with a cloche hat in matching trim. Despite its fine silk georgette fabric Kit couldn't help thinking about hornets. The outfit was perfect all right—for someone who packed a nasty sting. And she couldn't imagine how anyone could possibly fill bottles wearing a skirt so snug.

"You're as pretty as a film star," Kit's father said.

"Really? Do you really think so, Jack?" Vivian was flushed with the praise.

"Of course, Vivian. You're as pretty as any film star I've ever seen."

Vivian's eyes were bright. "Do you think I could have a career in show business? Do you think I'd have a chance?"

"I think you'd be a natural," he said smoothly, giving her another kiss.

Kit turned away, still making her sloth face. She covered

her ears and squeezed her eyes shut. She wanted to roll under the stairs and curl into a ball until Vivian had gone. But her father tapped her on the shoulder. "Kit? Come on. It's time to go. Vivian's waiting."

Kit stood up reluctantly. She took one step down the stairs and then stopped. "Just a minute," she called out. And she ran back into the house, grabbed the remains of the pie, covered it with a tea towel and jumped back into the car.

Vivian turned the car around and headed down the driveway. "What have you got there?"

"The rest of the pie. Dad said we were supposed to drop it off for Mum at the hospital." She shot a furtive sideways look in Vivian's direction.

Vivian's eyes narrowed. "He did? He didn't say anything about that to me."

"Oh, yeah. He made me promise we'd stop in to see her. Guess he forgot to tell you."

Vivian clicked her tongue in annoyance. "Well, maybe after shopping. I'll give you five minutes, that's all. And don't expect me to come in."

Kit wrapped her arms around the pie plate and turned to look out the window. She could see her reflection in the glass smiling back.

~

They stopped at a gas station in Victoria. Vivian took some lipstick from her purse and preened in the rear-view mirror as she applied it. "I've got some shopping to do. I won't be long. You be a good girl, Kat, and do the bottles while I'm gone."

Kit, Kit wanted to say. *My name is Kit.* And weren't they supposed to be going shopping together? But she bit her tongue. What was the use? She didn't want to go shopping with Vivian anyway. Besides, she'd put up with just about anything if it meant she could go to the hospital and see her mother.

"Then we'll go to the hospital, right?"

Vivian's laugh was almost a snort. "For goodness' sake, Kat. It's not like I have all the time in the world." She smacked her lips together to even out the lipstick. "Maybe another day."

"But you promised…"

"I did no such thing." And with that she dropped the lipstick back into her purse, snapped it shut and marched off.

Kit grumpily hauled the bottles out of the car and filled them with the hose at the back of the gas station. Why hadn't she seen this coming? Of course Vivian had no intention of fiddling around with water bottles. She hadn't so much as laid a hand on them. Neither had she any intention of taking Kit shopping, let alone going to the hospital. Mean old Vivian. Kit returned the heavy bottles to the car, gave the spokes of the wheel a kick and sat down in a slump on the running board of the car. She was so mad she felt like walking all the way home. The street was noisy with cars and city people hurrying along the sidewalk. No one looked in her direction. She fumed and fumed—and then she had an idea. She looked both ways to make sure no one was paying attention, then picked up the water hose, opened the tap and deliberately trained the flow of water onto the brown fabric of the driver's seat. She waited a good five seconds. Then she turned off the hose and pressed her hand down onto the seat. It was soaked through and soggy.

Half an hour later, Vivian reappeared carrying several

bags and a hat box. "Look what I found in Spencer's," Vivian said, all out of breath from her excursion. She pulled out a pair of high-heeled shoes and a flashy hat with the brim turned up at the front.

"Nice," Kit managed to say through clenched teeth.

"Oh…," Vivian said as an afterthought. "I got something for you." Vivian produced a slim paper bag.

Inside, something green. Kit pulled it out, holding it up so it unfolded to its full length.

"It's a scarf," Vivian said. "Like the one at the charity picnic. I thought you might want one, after all."

Kit blinked her eyes. She had not expected Vivian to be so thoughtful. Could Vivian have a kind side to her, after all? Kit ran her fingers across the soft fabric. It was lovely, perhaps not exactly the same shimmering green as the other one, but lovely just the same. "Thank you, Vivian," Kit said, offering her a cautious smile. "Thank you very much."

"I thought you'd like it," Vivian said, looking genuinely pleased. "You can wear it like this…" She wrapped it around Kit's head, pushing the hair back out of her eyes, and tied it in a bow at the back. "There. It makes you look more like a girl."

Kit decided to ignore the last comment.

Vivian tilted her head to one side, gave her an appraising look and said, "You really should make more of an effort, you know, Kat. You're never going to catch a boyfriend looking like Little Miss Sourpuss all the time."

Kit felt annoyed all over again. She pulled off the scarf and shoved it into the pocket of her overalls. "I'm not looking for a boyfriend," she muttered. But Vivian did not appear to hear. She flung open the car door and tossed all her parcels in the back with the bottles. Kit caught a glimpse of the sopping wet car seat just as Vivian was about to sit down.

But then Vivian stopped. "Oh, I forgot. There's just one more thing—it won't take me a second. You don't mind staying with the car, do you? You can keep an eye on my parcels. Make sure no one steals them."

Vivian teetered off and Kit sank down dejectedly onto the running board once again, covering her face with her hands. She wanted nothing more at that moment than to be with her mother.

Just then a brand new, shiny convertible car pulled into the gas station. A dapper young man sat in the driver's seat and a bigger man sat in the passenger seat smoking a cigar. They both got out as the gas station attendant came running over.

"Fill 'er up," the big man said in a deep, confident voice. He peeled an American bill off a thick roll. "And keep the change." He moved away from the gas pumps to finish smoking his cigar and the other man followed. They were standing closer to Kit now. Not only could she smell the warm, spicy aroma of the cigar, she could plainly hear what they were saying.

"Randall, what do you say we head over to the hospital and see how Fletcher's doing?" the big man said. He wore a pinstriped suit, a starched shirt and a tie fastened with a diamond stick pin.

"Of course, Mr. Olmstead. He won't be expecting a visit from you. It'll be bound to lift his spirits." The smaller man spoke with a trace of an English accent. He held a pair of chamois driving gloves in one hand.

"Sounds like he had a real close call with those hijackers. He's lucky to be alive." The big man blew a puff of cigar smoke into the air.

Kit picked up the pie and took a few steps towards them. She wasn't sure what she was going to say. All she knew was that they were going to the hospital and that was exactly where she wanted to be.

"Excuse me, sirs…"

Both men looked at her.

"Um…um…I wondered…um…"

"What's he saying?" the big man said to the other man.

The other one shrugged. "Speak up, boy."

Kit stared back at the two men. They thought she looked like a boy too. It shouldn't have bothered her, but it did. Quite unexpectedly, a hot, angry tear coursed down her cheek. Kit felt disgusted with herself as she wiped it away with the back of her hand. The last thing she wanted to do was start crying.

But then she noticed the two men's reaction. They were looking very concerned and the big man was actually lowering himself down to one knee to study her face closely. Maybe she could make this crying business work in her favour, after all.

The big man took the hat off his balding head and let out a low whistle. "By jiminy, you're a girl! And a right pretty one at that. Here, take this…" He offered her his handkerchief. "And please accept our apologies. We're truly very sorry."

Kit dabbed at her eyes with the crisp linen handkerchief and then snuffled her nose moistly. She looked at them through her watery eyes. "It's not your fault," she said. "I'm just having a bad day, that's all."

"What's wrong?"

"It's just that I'm trying to get to the hospital to see my mother but my ride hasn't come." It wasn't an outright lie, just stretching the truth a little.

"Well, we'll give you a ride. That's where we're going right now."

"You will?" Kit's face brightened.

"Sure we will." The big man stood up again with a wide grin and slapped the other man on his back. "Won't we, Randall?"

"Whatever you say, Mr. Olmstead. You're the boss."

The big man chuckled. "What's your name, little lady?"

"Kit."

"All right then, Kit. You can call me Roy. And Mr. Randall here is my driver. Now, you hop in the back and we'll have you up to the hospital lickety-split."

Kit had second thoughts as they pulled out onto the road. She was leaving Vivian's car with all her parcels unattended. She had deliberately and thoroughly soaked the car seat. She had not left a note to say where she was going. And, perhaps the worst thing of all, she was going off with two strange men. She wasn't even supposed to speak to strangers, let alone go off in a car with them. What would her mother think?

The big man turned around in his seat and grinned at her. "Too breezy for you, Kit?"

The wind was whipping her hair into her eyes. "Oh, no, sir. I'm fine."

"Call me Roy, remember?"

"Roy...maybe I should have told someone where I was going."

"Don't you go worrying yourself now," he assured her. "You'll be with your mum in no time. You can trust us. Honest. We're a couple of fine, upstanding men, aren't we, Randall?"

Randall nodded and said, "Mr. Olmstead is even a policeman."

"Ex-policeman," Roy added and let out a loud guffaw.

Surely a policeman, even an ex-policeman, could be trusted. Kit settled back in her seat. Her hair was being blown first one way and then the next. She thought she would tie it back out of her eyes with the green scarf. But when she fished it out of her pocket, the wind snatched it out of her fingers and carried it away. Her last glimpse of it was as it rose up, darting and curling, towards the clouds.

True to the men's word, it was only a short time before they arrived at the hospital. The first thing they did was check at the front desk. "Do you know where we can find a Mr. Charlie Fletcher?"

The young woman checked her roster, flipping through the pages. "Mr. Fletcher? Let me see. Here we are. Mr. Fletcher was discharged home this morning."

Roy rocked back on his heels. "Well, good for him. I guess he wasn't as badly off as we thought." Then he turned to Mr. Randall with a wink. "We're a tough breed, aren't we?" Next he turned to Kit. "Now, what about your mother? Do you know where to find her?"

"She's in the Tuberculosis Pavilion," Kit said, and noticed a quick look exchanged between Roy and Mr. Randall.

Roy gave Kit's shoulder a pat. "Come on, then. Let's go find your mum. I'm sure it will do her a world of good to see you."

The Tuberculosis Pavilion was behind the main building. It was long, low to the ground, and fronted with a sun porch that ran the entire length. Instead of stairs up to the door there was a ramp. Kit clutched the pie as she stepped up the incline, wondering for the first time if her mother was in a wheelchair. Her throat felt dry. She paused before knocking and looked back over her shoulder. At the foot of the ramp, Roy and Mr. Randall gave her encouraging waves. Then she turned back to the door and rapped sharply.

A nurse in a cap and starched white apron opened the door. "Can I help you?"

"I'm here to see my mother, Mrs. Jean Avery."

The nurse spoke softly. "I'm sorry, dear. Mrs. Avery cannot have any visitors."

Kit felt a pain as sharp as a sword slice through her. "But…but…I've come a long way to see her…and it's been such a long time."

"I'm afraid it's impossible. Doctor's orders." She shook her head. "Besides, even if she were allowed visitors, only adults can come in. No children. I'm very sorry." She began to pull the door shut.

"Wait!" It was Roy. He was up the ramp in a flash and stood towering over Kit and the nurse. "This young lady would like to see her mother. And I'm sure her mother would like to see her. Surely, it would be the best thing for both of them."

"I'm sorry, sir. It's against the rules." The nurse was firm.

Roy pulled out his pocketbook, peeled off a bill and offered it to her, with a winning smile. "Well, maybe we could bend the rules a little. Call it a charitable donation… to the hospital."

The nurse refused to accept the money. "That's not the way we do things around here." She paused, studying him, and then said, "I've seen your picture somewhere…You've been in the papers, haven't you? I recognize you. You're Roy Olmstead, the King of the—"

144

"That's right. I'm Roy Olmstead." He cut her off quickly. "And I can see by your name tag you're Miss Denton. Well, Miss Denton, now that we're properly acquainted...I suggest you let my young friend in to see her mother." His voice had taken on a hard edge.

Miss Denton wavered slightly as she repeated, "No, sir. I'm afraid I can't. It's against the rules."

"The rules." He spat the words out, his face becoming dark with anger. "Do you think I care about the rules?"

The nurse shook her head. "No...sir."

Kit felt her heart skip in alarm at Roy's sudden change in temperament. She knew he was only trying to help her, but she felt frightened all the same.

It looked as if the nurse was just about to step aside and let them in when a man in a white lab coat appeared behind her in the doorway. "What's going on here?"

"Doctor, it's Mr. Olmstead...Mr. Roy Olmstead..." The nurse tilted her head in their direction, her eyes wide with meaning. "He's brought a visitor for Mrs. Avery. I've already told him she's not allowed any visitors."

"Mrs. Avery is too ill to have visitors at the moment. I'm afraid I'm going to have to ask you to leave."

"We're not going until the girl sees her mother."

"I'm sorry, but if you don't stop this disturbance and leave immediately, I'm going to have to call the police."

Just then Mr. Randall joined the group. "Mr. Olmstead." He spoke quietly and evenly. "Maybe we should go...You don't want any more trouble, do you? Especially two days before your wedding. You've got to get back home to Seattle tonight."

Roy took a deep breath, tipped his hat to the nurse and said, "Good afternoon to you."

They walked back to the car in silence, but the air still prickled electric and Kit's heart beat furiously against her ribs. She looked down at the checked pattern of the tea towel covering the pie. She hadn't even thought to leave it.

Roy opened the car door and stood back. "How about we take you home, Kit?" he said, his voice gentle now.

Kit hesitated. "I live way out on the Saanich Peninsula. It's a long way to drive."

"Don't you worry about it. In fact, if we're going out that way, I might as well go right up to Canoe Cove and check out some of my boats. We can do that, can't we, Randall?"

Mr. Randall tipped a finger to his cap and started the engine.

Kit crawled in and Roy closed the door behind her. Then he put his face down close to hers. He spoke quietly. "I'm sorry you couldn't see your mum. I really am."

Kit swallowed hard and nodded. "Me, too."

"I hope she gets better soon."

She looked back at him. The face that only a few moments ago had blazed with anger now seemed like the kindest face she had ever seen. She allowed her lips to form a wary smile. "Me, too," she said again.

Roy straightened up, winked and said in a louder voice, so Mr. Randall could hear, "I'd say a stop at the ice cream parlour is in order, wouldn't you? Nothing like ice cream to cheer us up."

～

A short while later, the three of them sat on the running board eating the rest of the pie with big dollops of ice cream. Mr. Olmstead had persuaded the woman at the counter to lend them some plates and spoons.

"This is the best pie I've ever tasted," Mr. Olmstead said between bites. "And you made it yourself?"

"Yup." Kit grinned. "Mr. Olmstead, I mean Roy, did you say you were getting married soon?"

"You bet I am. Day after tomorrow. Across the border, down in Seattle."

Kit ran her tongue all around the spoon to get the last of the ice cream. "What are you doing here in Canada, then?"

Roy laughed. "I guess you could say it's a little business trip. I'm going back tonight." He popped another spoonful into his mouth. "What kind of work is your dad in?"

"He has a farm but we didn't have a good crop this year. He's gotten into another line of work lately."

"Oh, yeah? Doing what?"

"Night fishing."

Roy stopped chewing. "Night fishing?"

"Uh huh."

Both Roy and Mr. Randall were looking at her intently now. "Let me guess," Roy said. "He works late at night, sleeps until noon and you've never seen a fish?"

Kit stared back at him. "How did…"

A knowing smile played on his face. "Call it a sixth sense. What's your dad's name?"

"Jack. Jack Avery."

Roy looked at Mr. Randall, one eyebrow raised. Mr. Randall shook his head ever so slightly.

"Does he have his own boat?"

"Yup. He keeps it right in our bay. He had a wharf built and everything. It's called the *Nighthawk*."

"The *Nighthawk*. That's a good name for a boat." He finished his ice cream and stood up. "Well, what do you say, Kit…time to take you home?"

147

~

Mr. Randall and Mr. Olmstead dropped Kit off at the end of the driveway. "You take care, you hear?"

"I will. Thanks for the ride…and I hope everything goes well on your wedding day."

Mr. Olmstead tipped his hat and waved as the car pulled back onto the road again.

Kit walked down the shady drive. Birdsong filled the treetops and she whistled back. Then she heard another sound, a vehicle approaching from the direction of the house. An unfamiliar dusty black truck rounded the curve ahead and hurtled towards her. Kit had hardly enough time to jump out of the way. She tried to get a look at the driver but all she could see was a hat pulled low and a cigarette dangling from the corner of the mouth. The truck sped by without slowing down at all.

11 *A Shadow in the Night*

Kit found Caleb and her father at the barn. They snapped the padlock shut as she walked towards them.

"Hey—what happened to you?" Caleb said. "Vivian came by a while ago. She said she didn't know where you'd got to."

"I...uh..." She had to think of something quickly.

"You had us worried half to death," her father said, giving the padlock a yank to make sure it was locked.

"I'm sorry. I...uh...just thought I'd look around the town a little while I was waiting for Vivian. But when I got back, she'd already gone." It was almost the truth.

"Well, for goodness' sake, Kit. I thought we were going to have to send out a search party. How did you get home?"

Her tongue faltered for a moment. She knew her father wouldn't want to hear how she had been driven around by two strange men. The rest of the lie unrolled so smoothly and convincingly she almost believed it herself. "The train. I remembered where the station was from the last time I took it. I had just enough pocket money to buy a ticket. And I knew I had to get off at the Saanichton stop. I walked the rest of the way."

Her father laughed. "That's my Kit. But don't do it again. All right? You gave us all a real scare. You should've seen the state Vivian was in. She wouldn't even get out of the car."

Suddenly Kit remembered the thorough dousing she had given the car seat at the gas station. "Did she say anything else?" she asked tentatively.

"No. She just wanted to get home. She could barely wait for us to finish unloading the car."

Kit knew she should feel ashamed of her behaviour, but a smile threatened the corners of her mouth. She turned away, trying to suppress it. "What are you two doing out here at the barn?" she asked, hoping to change the topic.

"Oh, nothing," Caleb said vaguely. Something about his manner had changed. Kit tried to catch his eye, but he wouldn't look at her.

"Who was that man in the truck?" she asked.

"What man?"

"The one driving the truck that almost ran me down in the driveway," she said, feeling a stirring of unease as she pushed the question.

"Just someone looking for directions," Kit's father said lightly, and he put his arm around her shoulders and steered her away from the barn.

~

That night Kit was roused from her dreams by a noise outside. It had sounded like a low voice. She sat up and listened. All she could hear was the wash of the waves. A minute passed and then the voice came again, followed by a second voice: two people talking outside. Kit slipped out from under the covers and crept to the window. There was only a sliver of moon like a great eye that was almost asleep. A dusting of stars glimmered above. Then she saw a movement in the dark near the barn. Kit strained her eyes. She could just make out two figures, Caleb's and her father's.

~

The next morning dawned fresh and dewy. Kit woke very early. She stepped into her overalls and running shoes and tiptoed to her father's room. Asleep. Quietly, she let herself out of the house and crossed the yard to the pickers' shack. Caleb was asleep too.

She ran to the barn and gave the padlock a sharp tug. It would not open. She dragged a wooden packing case from the lean-to at the back of the barn, placed it under the window and climbed up. Inside, just like the last time she had looked through this window, she could see hundreds of boxes stacked high along the walls. She turned her head this way and that, trying to see better. It looked as if they were wrapped in thick burlap.

Kit jumped down and ran back to the house. Very quietly she poked her head into her father's room. His clothes were folded over the back of a chair. She tiptoed across the creaky floor, keeping a watchful eye on the bed, then slipped a hand into his jacket pocket. Just a package of Lucky Strikes and some loose change. She checked his trouser pocket next. There they were—his keys. She drew them out and recrossed the bedroom floor. Back at the barn, she fumbled with one key after another, trying to fit each into the padlock. Finally a thin, gold-coloured key slid in. She turned it in the lock until it clicked. She grabbed the base and yanked. The hasp came free.

Kit pulled open the heavy door. It sagged on its hinges

so much she had to push it up so it would clear the ground. Sunlight poured in. There were stacks and stacks of cases almost as high as she could reach. Her toe caught the corner of a box as she stepped inside. There was a clinking sound from inside but the box did not budge. Whatever it held had to be heavy. The box was wrapped in a coarse gunny sack material. She looked around furtively and then her eyes fell upon a knife on the window ledge. In a moment she had slipped the knife under the flaps of the burlap, sliced through the material and pushed it aside. Underneath she found a corrugated cardboard box stamped with a picture of a raccoon. *Coon Mountain Bourbon Whisky*, it read. She ripped open the box. It was full of bottles. Six rows of four. Twenty-four bottles. She pulled one bottle out. It was small and flat. There was no label. She held it up, letting the sunlight shine through the amber liquid.

She grabbed the next case, sliced through the rough burlap and opened the box. Twenty-four more bottles. Kit sat back on her heels and looked around her. She was surrounded by towers of boxes and each one held twenty-four bottles of whisky.

She knew her father enjoyed a drink once in a while but she was pretty sure the same bottle of whisky had sat on the pantry shelf the whole time she'd been staying at the house. No, all this whisky in the barn was more than her father would drink in a lifetime.

So what was it doing here? And why was he so secretive about it?

Kit closed the flaps on the boxes as she thought. Whatever her father was up to, Caleb was in on it too. She'd seen the two of them at the barn more than a couple of times in the last few days.

Kit half dragged, half lifted the door back into place and snapped the padlock shut. Then she silently returned the keys to her father's trousers.

She paced, restlessly, back and forth in the kitchen. Thoughts were spinning around in her head like a dog chasing its tail. The more she thought, the more uneasy she became. Settle down, she told herself. Don't jump to conclusions. But still her thoughts whirled. She wished her father and Caleb would wake up. She had to talk to them and find out what was really going on. Maybe it wasn't as bad as she feared.

She checked the clock. Ten-thirty. She could wait no longer. She took a pan and purposely dropped it on the floor. Then she picked it up and dropped it again for good measure. Sounds of stirring came from her father's room.

As soon as he walked into the kitchen she confronted him. "What are you storing in the barn?"

He was taken aback by the question. "Nothing."

It was an outright lie. She pressed on. "You've got something stored in there. I can see it through the windows."

His mouth tightened. "I told you. Nothing. Stop asking so many questions, Kit. And stop poking around the barn. It's got nothing to do with you."

She could see he was angry now. But she was angry as well. She didn't like being treated like a kid. She knew very well something was going on and she had a sick feeling in the pit of her stomach that it was something dangerous. "Just tell me. I have a right to know."

"Kit." His voice carried a warning. "That's enough. I don't want to hear any more about it."

But she persisted. "What do you do at night when you go out?"

His face darkened. He took a couple of breaths before he answered. "I'm a night fisherman. I've already told you."

He was lying. She knew it. The lies were flying out of his mouth like a swarm of bees.

He turned and walked back to his room. "Well, where's all the fish, then?" she called after him.

He stopped and turned around. "What I do at night is my concern. Stay out of it." He went into his room and slammed the door.

Kit stomped out of the house. Her own father was a liar and who knew what else? Certainly he could not be trusted. It was as if he were someone else, a stranger, not her own father.

She marched down to the pickers' shack and stood in the doorway with her arms crossed. Caleb was still asleep with his back towards her. "Caleb. Caleb, wake up."

He groaned and buried his head further under the covers.

"Caleb! I need to talk to you."

"I'm sleeping." His voice was muffled by the blanket.

"Caleb, it's about the barn."

Slowly he roused himself and turned his tousled head towards her. "What's going on?" he asked, his voice thick.

"You tell me," Kit said. "You tell me what's going on. What are you and my father up to at the barn?"

"Kit…" He sat up and rubbed his eyes. Then he focused on her and said, "You gotta stop worrying about the barn."

"Something's going on. Why won't you tell me?"

But instead of answering, he lay back down again and pointedly pulled the covers over his head.

"You're not going to tell me, are you?"

"No."

She turned away from the door, seething with anger and frustration. She kicked a weedy tuft of grass, hard, with the toe of her shoe. She kicked it again and again. Puffs of dust rose up with each kick. Then the tough ball of roots finally broke free. She stooped to pick it up and threw it as far as she could into the trees.

~

The next evening Kit dried the last supper dish and hung up the dishtowel. She was just about to switch off the radio when she heard "Mr. Roy Olmstead." She bent closer to catch every word.

"…Seattle's notorious police officer turned rum-runner was married today."

There could not be two ex-policemen with the same name getting married today. She turned up the volume.

"It is widely believed that Mr. Olmstead, sometimes known as the King of the Northwest Bootleggers, heads the largest liquor-smuggling operation in the region. His criminal activities involve extensive networks on both sides of the Canada–U.S. border. Police say his rum-running empire employs more people than any other business in the area, and includes fleets of boats, warehouses, lawyers and messengers. Over the past few years he has undermined American Prohibition by smuggling tens of thousands of cases of illegal alcohol, mostly Canadian whisky, into the United States. He has been quoted as saying, 'One shot of my whisky has been known to stop a man's watch, snap his suspenders and crack his glass eye all at the same time.' Although authorities are well aware of his activities, to this date, he has successfully avoided prison. He and his new bride, Elsie, plan to continue living in the Seattle area."

Kit found herself shaking as she turned off the radio. Mr. Olmstead was the biggest criminal in the area. A gangster! And she'd ridden in his car! She recalled his manner with the nurse, his temper—and then remembered the ice cream afterward, and his kindness. How could she be sure what to think of this man?

A wave of unease washed over her. How could she be certain of anyone anymore? She put both her hands on the table to steady herself. She closed her eyes, took in a deep breath and let it out again.

~

A few days later Kit sat down to write a letter to her mother.

August 10, 1924

Dear Mum,

I tried to see you at the hospital but they said you could not have any visitors—and that children were not allowed at all. Can't you ask them to make an exception? Surely a visit would only do you good. It seems very unfair to me that I am not allowed to see you. Promise you will let me know the very minute they let you have visitors. Dad and I will come right away.

I hope you are getting stronger. You are feeling better, aren't you? You didn't say in your last letter. How long will it take to get better? You said that your friend Ada had been in the hospital six months. They are not expecting you to be in the hospital that long, are they? Six months would be an eternity. I thought you might be there a month at the most. No one ever said it could be half a year—or more!

I was very sorry to hear about your other friend, Lily.

She sounded like a fine person. I am glad, though, that you had some time with her and you were good company for each other. Did you go to her service in the chapel?

Tell me, Mum (and please be honest), do many people die from tuberculosis? I am worried about you every day now.

You say you are worried about me as well. But you mustn't be. I am healthy and fit and there is absolutely nothing to worry about.

The well is getting quite deep—maybe fifteen feet. We have it shored up now and there is no risk of danger. Digging it is the hardest work I've ever done. Dad knows about Caleb now. He says it's all right for him to stay. In fact they are getting along like the best of friends. Caleb can do a lot around the place to help out. It's a good thing he came along when he did, because Dad had a little accident and hurt his arm the other day.

Kit bit her lip as she wrote this. What would her mother say if she knew the whole truth—that he'd been shot? Or that the barn was full of whisky? Part of her wanted to tell her, but another part did not. She took a new piece of paper and considered what she would write next.

The doctor says it will take a few more weeks to heal completely but he's doing just fine. He tells me it doesn't hurt as much anymore, but he still needs help to drive and he can't write yet. I am sure he would write you himself if he could.

I have been watering your roses every day with the dishwater and they look pretty as can be. There are some glorious, huge blossoms on the pink one and the climbing

157

rose has gone all the way up the side of the house. You would be very impressed to see how they are thriving.

When you are well enough to leave the hospital maybe it would be a good idea to come here to get strong. I think Dad would like that.

Kit read what she had just written. She wasn't at all sure her father would agree to the arrangement, let alone like it, but she'd written it now. She set her pen to the paper again.

Please hurry and get better.
All my love,
Kitty
P.S. I have enough socks. Truly. You mustn't worry.

~

That night she lay down, fully dressed, on top of her bed, her thoughts turning in her head. One of these nights she knew something would happen. The window was propped open. She heard the wind stirring the dark trees, and farther away the wash of the waves. She lay awake for hours, listening and waiting, until her eyelids grew heavy and she eventually fell asleep.

She did the same thing the next night, but still nothing happened.

Then, on the third night, she heard the creak of the screen door opening and a soft, dampened thud as it closed again. A moment later, footsteps down the veranda stairs.

Kit leapt to the window. She was just in time to catch a glimpse of her father's shadowy figure disappearing into the darkness like a phantom. He was headed to the barn.

Kit grabbed her sweater and rushed down the stairs. She fumbled at the door as she pushed her feet into her shoes. Then she slipped out of the house, careful that the door closed soundlessly behind her.

She ran nimbly down the slope to the orchard. The air had cooled and the grass was damp beneath her shoes. She huddled in the shadows under a tree. There was a flicker of movement and the faint sound of footsteps whispering through the grass. Kit froze. Could it be old Mr. McCauley with his rifle wandering around the property? She pushed herself against the tree trunk. No. It was Caleb. If he had come any closer she could have reached out her hand and touched him. But he did not see her and he passed by.

Kit waited another few minutes, her heart pounding in her chest. Then she quietly moved forward to one of the trees closer to the barn. She could hear them talking in low voices. The glare of a flashlight illuminated the padlock on the barn door. Her father's face hovered above the light as he bent to turn the key.

The two disappeared into the barn and their light flashed now and again through the window. Then Caleb emerged with a case wrapped in burlap. He loaded it onto the big wooden wagon and disappeared back into the barn. He returned with case after case until the wagon was stacked high. Then he picked up the heavy handle and leaned his body forward, straining every muscle to start the wheels turning. He pulled it across the grass towards the water. Minutes passed—ten? fifteen? Then he returned. The wagon was empty. Twice more he loaded it up, grabbed the handle and hauled with all his might until the wheels started to turn. The last time, Kit's father pulled the barn door shut, locked it and walked along with him.

Kit waited a minute and then crept through the trees. Even though it was late at night, the moon was nearly full and she wanted to stay out of the open as much as possible. At the bank near the top of the wharf she could see the dark outline of the loaded wagon. There was Caleb, now picking up a case of liquor and carrying it down the ramp. Her father was nowhere to be seen. Probably already down at the boat, she reasoned. Kit waited until Caleb descended the ramp. Then she darted across the field and threw herself down flat on her stomach amongst the tall grass. From there she could see down to the boat bobbing restlessly in the water. Caleb stepped from the wharf to the boat, set the box down and jumped back onto the wharf again.

Now Kit could see why her father had enlisted Caleb's help. There was no way her father could pull the wagon or move the boxes with one arm in a sling. Caleb carried the cases one by one down the ramp and loaded them into the boat. Then he pulled the empty wagon back up the sloping grass towards the barn.

As soon as Caleb was out of sight, Kit heard the boat's engine start up with a rumble. This was her chance. She pulled herself through the tall grass, keeping as low as a snake. At the top of the ramp she paused for a heartbeat. Her father was leaning over the engine behind the cabin. She stood halfway up. If he looked up now he'd see her for sure. She scampered down the ramp. She could hear the thump, thump, thump of her feet as she ran. The engine was thumping away as well, and Kit hoped that, to her father's ears, it was drowning out every other sound. She stopped when she reached the boat, then inched towards the stern. Her father was struggling to place the lid back on the engine cover with his one good arm. Hurry, she kept thinking. Caleb would be coming down the ramp any minute. But finally Kit's father got the engine cover back into position and ducked into the boat's cabin.

Kit slipped onto the boat, stealthily as a cat, a shadow in the night. Boxes were stacked waist-high with barely a foot between them to squeeze through. She scrambled to the very back of the boat and crouched behind one of the stacks. She kept her head tucked as low as she could, all around her the dusty smell of burlap.

It was only a matter of a few moments and she heard her father say, "All right, then. We're all loaded up. We've got a full tank of gas. It looks like we're all set. Cast her off."

Caleb jumped into the boat. Kit could see his shoes only a foot or two away. She held her breath until the shoes moved out of view, forward, towards the cabin.

Slowly Kit let out her breath. She'd done it. She'd managed to get aboard without being noticed. She was a stowaway.

12 *Stowaway*

The engine strained at a high pitch as the boat shot forward through the water. The salt air blew harsh and biting. Kit crouched behind the burlapped boxes of whisky.

Travel on water. Caleb had used those words when he had told her fortune weeks ago. And it was almost as if she could hear his voice whispering into her ear now. *Travel on water.* She hugged her knees and shivered in her light sweater and overalls. Everything Caleb had predicted had come true. One by one, starting with the tricks, lies and deception of the Moon card, her fortune was unfolding just as he said it would.

Kit raised her eyes towards the heavens. There was the real moon now: luminous, grown plumper in the last few nights, almost a full moon. It hung just out of reach, and its reflection danced, tantalizingly, across the water. The boat rushed eastward, along the path of moonlight. They were chasing the moon.

The sky was a massive canopy of stars. Other than the moon and the stars there was no light, not even in the cabin. There was blackness in every direction, but still the boat raced onward.

Something flashed brightly up above—a shooting star—blazing white across the sky. Kit caught her breath and it was gone. Could it be a star for good luck? It was almost the middle of August, and the Perseid meteor shower would be at its peak. There might be hundreds of shooting stars tonight, but a thin, gauzy layer of cloud was gathering across the night sky.

The wind was stronger now and the waves were growing larger. The boat pitched up and down as it forced its way through the swells. Kit could feel the sickening lurch of her stomach with each rise and fall. Sometimes the boat took a sudden roll sideways when a larger wave broadsided the hull, and Kit would be knocked against the side of the boat or one of the piles of boxes. The boxes themselves shifted against one another, threatening to fall, the bottles clinking inside. Kit kept reaching up to steady one box in particular. It was close enough to land on top of her if it tipped in her direction.

They were out in the open now, out of the protection of the islands. The full force of the wind and sea bore down upon the little boat. Sometimes a wash of icy salt spray swept across the deck and Kit felt the sting against her face. They battled forward against the choppy water. Kit thought she was going to be seasick and she struggled to swallow down the bitter taste that rose in her throat. On and on the engine throbbed. It seemed an endless journey.

But then, gradually, the waves began to diminish. The boat did not lurch as much and the ride became smoother. Kit could make out the dark outline of trees passing to the side. They were no longer in open water. The engine cut speed, its whine and thump softening to an even drone. The boat edged along the shoreline, a furtive creeping. Caleb came out of the cabin and stood at the side of the boat.

Kit's father called out from the cabin. "All right. This is Whidbey Island, just south of Point Partridge. We've got to keep our eyes open. There. Did you see that?"

"What?"

"A light on the shore. That's our signal." He came out with a flashlight and flashed back.

The boat pulled in closer to shore and then the engine cut out completely. Caleb scrambled up to the bow and tossed the anchor into the water.

After the engine stopped, the quietness of the night descended upon the boat like a thick blanket. At first it seemed to Kit that there was no sound at all, but as she listened she became aware of the whispering lap of the water against the hull. And, farther away, the sound of waves against the beach.

Then, in the distance, she heard the regular rhythmic splash of oars. Kit peered through the darkness. The long shape of a rowboat materialized out of the darkness like a vision. The oars dipped down, stirring the water into a phosphorescent froth, and then rose up again.

"*Nighthawk*?" a man's low voice called out from the rowboat.

"Yup," Kit's father replied. He fished in his pocket and produced a crumpled ball of paper. "You got the other half of this dollar bill?" The two boats were now side by side. Kit's father knelt over the edge, stretching his arm out to receive another small piece of paper. He smoothed out the two halves on the deck, shoving his face up close so he could see.

"They're a match," he announced. "We're in business.

Throw us a line and we'll tie you up."

A rope came whistling through the air. Caleb grabbed it and wrapped it around a post. Then he hoisted a case of liquor and passed it over the side. A set of hands reached up from below to receive it, and the case was lowered out of sight.

One by one the cases were passed from the larger boat down to the smaller. As they were removed, Kit began to worry. It would be only a matter of time before she was discovered. But then the man in the rowboat said, "That'll do for this load. Cast me off. I'll take it ashore and be right back."

The sound of the man unloading his rowboat at the shore travelled clearly over the water. Kit heard the scrape of the boxes on the rocks almost as clearly as if she were there herself.

"Is this whisky any good?" Caleb asked Kit's father quietly as they waited.

"You bet it is. I get it from a guy called Moonshine Lou. He's got a big still in the back of his property. Everything's copper…big copper kettle, coiled copper tubing…all the best equipment. I've seen it. He makes high-quality whisky and he tests every batch. Takes a spoonful and lights it. If it burns a bright blue, it's good. He doesn't let many people back there, mind you. Keeps two guard dogs who'd tear your throat out in a second."

"But it's not against the law to buy alcohol in Canada. So why moonshine? Why go to the trouble of making it himself?"

"I'll tell you why. No government taxes. More profit for us. That's why. Lou and I have a good little business going this way."

"Do most rum-runners buy from the big distilleries?"

"That's right. They buy in Canada and sell in the States, and they turn a handsome profit, no two ways about it. They can sell it for three, four, even ten times the price in Canada, depending on the buyer. It's big business. You've heard of Silver Springs and Victoria-Phoenix Brewing, the distilleries in town? If you go down to Wharf Street in Victoria, you'll see their warehouses with iron bars on the windows. They're full of government-bonded liquor all waiting to be loaded up onto ships. Up until that point everything's fair and square, all according to the law. But take one guess where those ships are headed?"

"The United States?"

"You bet. Ever hear of Roy Olmstead?"

Kit caught her breath when she heard the name.

"He's the big cheese all up and down the coast. He's dealing in thousands of cases of liquor every month. But to take it out of Canada he's got to pay a government tax on it called a duty. He pays the duty and it's all above board—at least on the Canadian side. Of course, they don't say it's headed for the States, but everyone knows it is."

"So," Caleb said slowly, "the way we do it, dealing in moonshine instead of government-bonded liquor, we turn an even bigger profit. We take it across the line, and no one's the wiser...least of all the government. There's no duty, no taxes—and that leaves more money for us."

"Exactly."

The wind was stronger now. The boat bobbed in the swelling waves. Kit eyed the sky overhead. Some of the stars were now covered by heavy, brooding clouds.

Kit's father began pacing the deck nervously. "Keep an eye out for the Coast Guard," he said. "Just look at that moon—bright as a new silver dollar. The worst kind of moon for rum-running…the more light, the more chance of getting caught. And it's a U.S. jail for us if we're caught. I wouldn't be out here tonight if the money wasn't so good. Come on. Come on. What's taking that rowboat so long? The man moves slow as molasses." He hugged his arms together and shivered. "Let's go in the cabin out of the wind. We can wait just as easily there."

Kit poked her head out from behind the edge of the boxes to see them return to the cabin and close the door. Only a few moments passed and then her ears pricked up. There was the steady, low, rumbling beat of a boat's engine in the distance. And it was getting closer. Kit waited for Caleb and her father to spring into action. But the minutes ticked by and nothing happened. The sound of the boat was getting louder. Surely they had to hear it now. But being closed off in the cabin, they obviously did not.

Kit shifted anxiously in her hiding place. She knew they wouldn't see the approaching boat until it rounded the headlands of the bay. And then it would be too late to make a getaway. They'd be trapped in the bay with no escape. Maybe she should warn them, she thought. But that would mean revealing herself.

Come on, Kit, she told herself. Don't be foolish. You can't hide forever. They're going to find you soon enough.

Kit struggled to her feet. The muscles in her legs had cramped and a tingle of prickly pins and needles shot down one side. It was difficult to keep her balance as the deck rolled side to side with the waves, and with one leg asleep. When she took her first step toward the cabin, the leg half collapsed. She lurched sideways, leaning heavily on one of the boxes for support. The box began to shift under her weight. It angled precariously off the box below. Kit tried to right herself and at the same time steady the box. But the box slipped from her hands. It crashed to the deck with the deafening sound of shattering glass. And Kit slipped down onto one hip, banging the side of her head as she fell.

The cabin door burst open. "What the heck was that?" Kit heard her father shout, and she knew she was about to be discovered.

But then Caleb yelled, "Look! It's a boat with a huge light."

"A spotlight like that can only mean one thing…the Coast Guard!" Kit's father leapt to the engine. "Help me get this cover off." The top of the heavy wooden cover hinged back. Kit's father grabbed a long metal pole and they cranked the engine over hard. In the next instant the engine roared to life.

"I'll cut the anchor. There's no time to haul it up," Caleb yelled above the noise. He was already scurrying up to the bow.

The boat jerked forward with sudden power, the bow thrusting through the waves. Kit was doused with a cold splattering spray of salt water. Her hip and her head ached. And the deck beneath her was awash with a mix of salt water and whisky from the broken bottles.

But Kit barely noticed. She pulled herself up to see over the stern. The spotlight was bearing down on them. It was so bright it was difficult to see much of anything. She twisted around. Caleb was scrambling back towards the cabin, hanging on the best he could.

A loud voice boomed across the water. "This is the U.S. cutter *Arcata*. Stop and surrender for inspection." It was so loud it had to have been amplified through a megaphone.

"Stop and surrender!" Louder still.

But the *Nighthawk* did not stop. It kept pushing forward through the waves. And then a sharp retort. Something whistled by like a flash of lightning.

"They're shooting!" It was Caleb's voice from where he clung to the side of the cabin.

"They're not trying to hit us. It's just a warning shot," Kit's father yelled back. "Hurry. Get into the cabin."

But a split second later there was another shot. The window in the cabin door shattered.

Kit ducked her head, and even though it was freezing cold, a sweat broke out on her forehead. The engine strained to a screaming pitch and the boat surged forward. No running lights and madly careering into pitch black.

Two more shots.

Kit squeezed her eyes tightly closed and prayed.

13 *Pirates*

The boat rounded a point of land at a furious speed. Kit half opened one eye. They had pulled away from the Coast Guard. Even though they were a much smaller vessel, they had the advantage of speed.

They rushed headlong into a waterway between two islands. The boat's roaring engine eased to a low-pitched throb as it inched into a small, rocky cove, out of sight. Then the engine was cut even further until it purred like a kitten. There was a strong, tangy smell of salt and seaweed and rotting wood in the cove, as if the water and the air here lay stagnant.

"Keep your fingers crossed," Kit heard her father say, his voice low. "If we're lucky they didn't see us turn in here."

Several minutes passed. They waited. The sound of the other boat's engine was getting louder. Then the searchlight swept across the opening between the two islands. It flicked across the water like a skipping stone, first one way and then the other, through the trees on either side of the cove.

"Be ready, Caleb. If they come any closer we're going to have to dump the cases overboard...get rid of the evidence.

Then they won't be able to charge us." Kit's father's whisper was tense.

Kit held her breath. Another minute passed and then the Coast Guard moved farther away. Gradually the sound of the boat became quieter. Then they could no longer see the spotlight. Kit felt herself relax again.

"I think we did it. We outran the Coast Guard!" Kit's father was jubilant. "We were lucky this time. I've heard the *Arcata* has a semi-automatic one-pound cannon mounted on her deck. Good thing for us they just fired a rifle at us and not the cannon. We wouldn't be sitting here if they had, I can tell you that."

"I didn't know this boat could go so fast," Caleb said.

"She's a fast one, all right. She might be the best little rum-runner on the coast. She's not the biggest. Not by any means. But the *Nighthawk* might just be the fastest of them all. She's built for speed—low and narrow with the biggest Liberty engine she can take. Do you know what a Liberty engine is? An airplane engine. I'm not kidding you. We've got a converted airplane engine specially rigged up for this boat."

"It's no wonder we're fast, then," Caleb said, sounding impressed. "That's why we get so much work."

"And not only that—we take the load right across the border. Some of the others don't do that. They stay on the Canadian side of the border where it's safe. That way if they get caught they're not breaking any laws, you see. It means they can use slower boats. They meet up with an American speedboat in Canadian waters—places like Discovery Island or Saturna Island. D'Arcy Island is one of the favourites. You ever heard of D'Arcy Island?"

"Don't think so."

171

"That's where the leper colony used to be, up until just a few months ago."

"Lepers? People with leprosy? Isn't that the disease where parts of the body rot away? Fingers…noses…toes…drop off?"

"That's right. D'Arcy Island is where the lepers used to be sent. There weren't many of them, mostly Chinese. They'd live there, all to themselves, away from everyone else, so that no one else would get it. And even though the colony's closed down now, people still think of the island as diseased. Not only that, it's got dangerous reefs around it. Most people would go a mile to avoid D'Arcy Island. It's like it has a hex on it. No one wants to go near the place and that's why the rum-runners like it. They can come and go and do their business and there's no one around to see what they're up to."

"Makes sense. So they meet American boats on the Canadian side of the border…?"

"Exactly. They pass over their cargo and pocket the money. That's all they've got to do. An easy business. The American speedboat takes all the risk. That's the difference between us. We take the risk. We take it right across the border. Costs them a little more, but they're willing to pay for it."

"It takes a brave man to do this job," Caleb said.

"Either that, or a foolish one." They both laughed.

Kit kept herself very still as they were talking, a few yards away—allowing herself only a rare peek around the edge of a box.

After a moment Caleb said, "You're not thinking about going back now to finish unloading, are you?"

"No. They know about that location now. They'll be

watching it. We'll have to wait and arrange a different location another night. What I'm thinking about is going home to a nice, warm bed." He paused and then continued. "You look like you could do with a good rest. You keep rubbing your forehead. You got a headache?"

"No. It's just…maybe we should wait here awhile longer. Make sure the coast is clear."

"They're gone now. It's as good a time as any. I think we could make a run for it." Kit's father sounded impatient.

"I don't know, Jack…I've got a pretty strong feeling…"

Kit's father sighed. "All right, then. We'll stay awhile longer. Just keep an eye on the shore. We don't have an anchor and we might drift in too close." He lit up a cigarette and inhaled deeply.

Caleb was examining the cabin door. "The window's shattered completely. And look at this…" He bent closer. "The bullet is lodged right here in the wood."

Kit's father whistled. "Well, what do you know?"

Then Caleb straightened up. "Jack? You never told me what happened to your arm. Was that a Coast Guard bullet too?"

"Afraid so. That was another close call. It was north of Anacortes—a rocky stretch of coastline with a cove that was just the right size to meet in. I had an arrangement that always worked out…that is, until that night. That night everything seemed to be off. My delivery was ten boxes short and the meeting hadn't been confirmed. The last I'd heard it was supposed to be a midnight rendezvous. I set out anyway. There wasn't much of a moon that night—barely enough light to see the back of my hand. About halfway across, I hit a log. It was submerged about a foot under the water—a deadhead, we call them, the worst kind of log. They're hard to see even in the daytime. So…WHAM…just on the port side of the bow. I was lucky it didn't rip a hole right through the hull. Then it hit again at the stern. I knew right away it had bent my propeller. It still turned, but not with the same force. It slowed me down. I was late getting to the meeting spot. No one was there. A half hour went by. Then an hour. I was cold to the bone. The tide was at its lowest and I had to sit farther out from the shore than I like. I had just decided to head back home when who do you think came around the end of the point?"

"The Coast Guard?"

He took a puff of his cigarette. "That's right, the U.S. Coast Guard. I fired up the engine full tilt but I couldn't get any momentum with that darn bent propeller. They were right on top of me before I could pull away. They were yelling at me to stop and then they started firing. When I was hit I thought I'd pass out from the pain, it was that bad. But I wouldn't stop. I knew I was close to the border and I'd be safe as soon as I crossed over into Canada. I tied my jacket around my arm nice and tight and kept on going. I don't think I've ever been so glad to get home as I was that night."

"So that's why we had to get the boat pulled up out of the water in Sidney the other day…that's why the propeller had to be replaced?"

"That's right. I guess you can call it one of the hazards of the business." Kit's father finished his cigarette and flicked the butt into the water. "What do you say, Caleb? Do you think we should be heading home?"

Caleb pressed his hand to his forehead. "Can't we stay here until the morning?"

But Kit's father had already made up his mind. "The

wind's really picking up. Looks to me like a storm's brewing. We better make a run for it." Kit's father handed Caleb a heavy oilskin coat. "Here. Put this on. We'll be home before you know it." He took another coat down from the hook, shrugged into one sleeve and draped the other over the shoulder of his injured arm. Kit hugged herself tightly and wished she had an oilskin coat too.

Caleb was still hesitating. "I don't know, Jack. I have a funny feeling about this…Why don't we put up here for the night?"

Kit's father laughed. "I've been in this business for a lot longer than you have. Don't you trust me?"

"It's not that. It's just…I really think we should stay here. It's safer. We can go back in the morning."

It may have been the sway of the boat, or it may have been the way Caleb spoke, but Kit felt a twinge of uneasiness stir in her stomach, as if something ominous was about to happen.

But her father seemed unconcerned. "It's just nerves, Caleb. You'll get used to it when you've been doing this awhile longer. Now, let's get ready to go. I've got a tarpaulin in here somewhere…" He began rummaging through the cabin. "We can cover the load with it and lash it down. It'll stop the boxes from getting wet."

Kit stiffened. If they did that, they'd be sure to find her.

Then her father came out of the cabin and checked the sky again. "No. Let's take a chance. I think we'll be all right without the tarp. If we start now we'll probably be home before the worst of the rain starts."

The engine thrummed a little louder and the boat nosed forward out of the cove and between the two islands. Kit watched Caleb and her father check cautiously in every

175

direction. Then they were out in open water. The wind buffeted the water into choppy waves and tossed the boat side to side like a piece of driftwood. Kit felt the rise and fall of each wave and her stomach did a corresponding flip-flop. The bitter taste rose in her mouth again and she swallowed it down with difficulty. They had to be in the middle of the strait now, completely away from the protection of any of the islands. The smell of the salt and the whisky made her feel worse. Then, overhead, a flash of lightning arched across the sky, and a few seconds later came the low rumble of thunder. Heavy raindrops began to pelt the boat. The wind lashed furiously, and Kit huddled miserably in her cold, wet clothes.

The boat pressed on and on until, finally, the waves began to subside. The rain stopped as suddenly as it had begun. They slowed to a quieter pace and Kit saw the dark shape of an island slip by. They must be on the Canadian side of the border, she reasoned, now that they were not running so fast. They were safely out of the range of the U.S. Coast Guard. No risk of bullets or jail now. These thoughts, and the easing of the wind, the rain and the waves, made Kit's stomach feel steadier.

The cabin door swung open and Caleb surveyed the boxes in the back. "Looks like we didn't lose anything in the crossing. Boy, that was rough," he yelled into the cabin.

Kit heard her father laugh. "You can say that again. But we're through the worst of it now. The storm has passed and we're safe in Canadian waters."

"Guess we should have covered the load with that tarp, after all."

"Guess so."

The boat puttered along for a few minutes and then

Caleb said, "What's that?"

"Where?"

"Over on our starboard side."

"I don't see anything," Kit's father said.

"I thought I saw a light. Maybe it was a lighthouse."

"There aren't any lighthouses over there."

"A house on the shore?"

"Maybe…better keep our eyes open. The last thing we need tonight is to run into pirates."

"Pirates?" A note of worry had crept into Caleb's voice. "What do you mean, pirates?"

"Pirates, hijackers, whatever you want to call them. Mind you, it's more of a problem on the American side. Not so much happens on this side of the line. But even so, we can't be sitting too easy."

"You're pulling my leg, aren't you?"

"Nope. Wish I were. Ever hear of the Eggers boys? They're the worst of the bunch. The Eggerses have been hanging around these parts for a few years now. One night they hijacked a couple of rum-runners up at D'Arcy Island and towed them clear across the strait. Then they ripped apart the engine, stole their load and left them there, adrift."

"Really?"

"Really. Just this spring, they hijacked another rum-runner over at Bedwell Harbour. Shot a guy in the shoulder and ankle to do it. Then they took the cargo and abandoned that boat too. They're ruthless, those pirates. They'd bump someone off as soon as look at them. That's why most of us carry a shotgun these days…just in case."

"Do you?"

"I've got one stowed away. Never had to use it, though.

I've been too fast for them, I guess. And so far I've been lucky."

After another minute Kit's father said, "Listen. Do you hear that?"

Caleb stood completely still, listening. "I'm not sure. Cut the motor so we can hear better."

The engine cut out but a steady, rumbling background sound continued. Another boat's engine. Just then a dark ship loomed up beside them, seeming to emerge out of the night like some kind of ghostly apparition. It was completely black. It had no running lights. No light at all.

Caleb saw the boat first. "Fire her up again. Hurry!" he yelled.

But before the engine could start two men leapt from the ghost ship to the deck of the *Nighthawk*. The first man shouldered roughly past Caleb, knocking him to the deck, and then yanked Kit's father from the cabin and tossed him down beside Caleb. "Don't bother getting up if you know what's good for you," he growled, standing with his massive tree-trunk arms akimbo.

"It's not a big haul," the other man said, shining a flashlight across the stacks of boxes. "Thirty, maybe forty cases—that's about all." He had the fidgety manner of a rat, with a rat's darting eyes, a long nose and a weak chin.

"Better than nothing," grunted the first man. The light flashed in his direction, clearly revealing a thick neck and short, close-cropped reddish hair.

The rat-faced man tossed him a coil of rope. "Help me tie these two up and then we can load up the goods."

First they tied Caleb's hands behind his back. Then Kit's father's. He yelped in pain as they forced his sore arm backwards. They left the two lying face down on the deck. Kit knew that as soon as they started loading boxes they'd find her too.

"Go back to our boat and I'll pass the cases over." The rat-faced man's voice was oily.

Over the next few minutes they worked in silence; the only sounds were the grunts they made as they hoisted the cases. Then the rat-faced man shouted out, "Hey! What do you think you're doing?"

The red-haired man had ripped open a case and taken out a bottle. "Checking the goods. Making sure it's top quality." He cracked it open and took a long swig.

"Put that down. You'll be no good to me if you get flat out drunk again."

"I'll do what I want." He took another swig. "Stop telling me what to do."

"You're supposed to wait until we've finished a job, Red. That's the rule."

"Yeah? Well, I never agreed to that. Besides...you just broke another rule. We're not supposed to use our names... even nicknames."

The rat-faced man swivelled around and glared nastily at Caleb and Kit's father. "Reckon you're right, Red," he snarled. "Not only that...they've seen our faces. We can't have these miserable two knowing who we are, can we? Guess after we've finished loading up we're going to have to do something about that." He laughed and the one called Red sloshed down some more whisky from the bottle.

Kit felt her stomach twist. What did they mean by that? Were they planning to kill Caleb and her father? The two pirates were busy swinging the cases from one boat to the other. She shifted herself up onto her hands and knees and crawled along the far side of the boat towards the cabin.

Thank goodness it was dark—but that still did not make her invisible. Her heart was beating so hard it felt as though it filled her entire chest. Her limbs were stiff, not only from the cold but also from not moving for so long. Just as she reached the cabin door, something sharp stung the side of her hand—a sliver of glass from the shattered cabin window. She brushed it away, barely taking notice, as she glanced over her shoulder. There was Caleb, in the light of the flashlight. He was lying on the deck, his head twisted to one side, looking right into her eyes. He had seen her. She put a finger to her lips, slipped into the cabin and ducked out of sight in the corner.

It was slightly warmer in the cabin. The door swung on its hinges in time to the waves. Every time it opened she could see the rat-faced man heaving up the cases.

Where would her father stow the shotgun? It wasn't in plain view, not behind the door, not stashed under the steering wheel. She quietly lifted the seat of the bench and looked into the storage bin below. It was hard to see in the dark. She held up the lid with one hand and felt inside with the other. Her stiff, cold fingers searched frantically. There was a map, a flashlight and a rope. If she found the shotgun, she'd have to use it. And she didn't know how.

But there was no shotgun. Her father had stored it somewhere else. Just as she was closing the lid, it slipped from her fingers and slammed down with a loud bang.

Suddenly the activity outside stopped. "What was that?" one of the pirates said.

Kit sank down into the corner. She could hear the ragged sound of her own breathing.

"It came from the cabin," the other one said. Already his speech had slowed and had a slur to it.

The rat-faced man was at the cabin door. His fingers curled around the edge of the door and he pulled it towards him.

But then, without any warning, there was another loud crash and a wrenching sound of splintering wood. The entire boat shuddered and lurched violently sideways. The pirate at the cabin door was almost thrown off his feet with the jolt. He shouted a curse, looked over the side and cursed again. "Looks like we hit the reef. There's a hole ripped in the hull you could drive a truck through." He straightened up. "We better finish this job up and get out of here before we ground our boat too."

The two men hastily resumed passing the cases from one boat to the other. Then one case slipped from the red pirate's hands and smashed to the deck.

"Idiot. Watch what you're doing," the rat-faced pirate shouted at him. The next case also slipped but it fell with a splash into the water. "You're drunk already!" the rat-faced pirate yelled. "You're no help."

"I'm not…" The red pirate put out a hand to steady himself. Slowly his legs folded and he sat down on the deck, with his back against a stack of cases. "…drunk."

"For the love of…," the rat-faced pirate muttered angrily. "For a big guy, you get drunk faster than any man I know."

"I might have had a few nips…earlier in the evening," he said sheepishly.

"Phhhhffft…." A disgusted snort from the rat-faced pirate. He swivelled around and eyed Caleb and Kit's father. "Let me see. We got us here a man with a bum arm and a kid. You." He kicked Caleb's leg with his boot. "You're young, but you look strong enough. You'll have to do." He produced a switchblade from his pocket, snapping it

181

open so it glittered menacingly in the moonlight. He sliced through the rope at Caleb's wrists with one quick motion. "Get over to the other boat and make yourself useful," he ordered, giving Caleb another kick.

Caleb scrambled to his position. The remaining cases were loaded up in a few minutes and then the rat-faced pirate leapt to his own boat. "Come on, Red. Get up and start the engine."

"What about the boy?" the red pirate said as he got sluggishly to his feet.

"He's coming with us. We're going to need him to unload...seeing as I can't depend on you," he said, sourly. Then he added, "We'll deal with him later."

"What about the other one?" the red pirate said, indicating Kit's father, still lying face down with his hands tied behind his back. "He'll talk."

"He's not talking to anyone. He's going down on a sinking ship."

The pirates' engine rumbled loudly as their boat pulled away. Kit watched helplessly. She wanted to yell out, to tell them to let Caleb go. But it was too late. Caleb and the pirates' boat had already disappeared into the darkness.

The *Nighthawk* listed awkwardly and the bottom of the boat scraped along the rocky reef with every wave. There was no doubt they were grounded and maybe even taking on water. A rush of anger boiled up inside Kit. Not only had the pirates kidnapped Caleb and stolen all the boxes, but they'd let the boat drift onto the rocks, and then, to top it off, they'd left Kit's father tied up and helpless. How could they be so heartless?

She jumped to her feet and stepped through the cabin door. When her father saw her his eyes grew as big as sand dollars.

"Kit!" he said in disbelief. "Is that you, Kit?"

She bent to unfasten the knots as she nodded.

"What in heaven's name are you doing here?"

Kit loosened the final knot. "I followed you. I had to see what you do at night."

Her father winced as he brought his sore arm forward. "Well, of all the crazy things. Don't you see how risky this is? Anything could happen. It's dangerous."

Kit eyed him steadily. "So, why do you do it then? Don't you think I worry about you?"

"Worry about me?" He made a snorting sound, almost a laugh. "I've never been in a scrape yet that I couldn't find my way out of."

At that moment Kit wasn't sure whether to be more angry with the pirates or her own father. But there was no time for argument. In the next instant the boat groaned and lurched farther sideways, knocking them both off their feet. The deck now sloped down at a precarious angle. They pulled themselves upright and then leaned over the side of the boat to examine the damage. The water swirled, white and hissing, around the barnacled rocks and up against the hull of the boat. A jagged gash ripped through the wood, as if a giant had kicked it in. Her father pulled up the floorboards and looked into the bilge. Water slopped back and forth. "We could try to patch it but I'm not sure it will hold." He lowered himself down into the cramped space and crawled towards the hole. Just then the boat listed again and another rush of water flooded in. He came out gasping. "That's not going to work. It's too big. We don't stand a chance."

"How far are we from land?" Kit tried to gauge the

distance, but in the darkness it was difficult to see.

There was a fearful creaking and then the boat lurched even farther on its side. They both slipped down against the bulwark. The waves were lapping right into the hold, water washing over their legs, so shockingly cold it was painful. The boat held for a moment and then it lurched again.

"Dad!" Kit was pummelled by a wave but she managed to grab hold of a stay.

"Hold on, Kit." His voice was a distance away.

Kit twisted around as far as she could without letting go. Where was he?

"Dad?" she called out, but all she could hear was the rush of the waves. "Dad!" The wind snapped up her call and swept it away. She slipped farther into the water. It was up to her waist now.

Then she saw him. His head bobbed in the water about a stone's throw from the boat. He was trying to swim. But he had only one good arm. He coughed and sputtered and gasped for air. And then he sank down below the surface.

14 *Shipwrecked*

Kit let go of the boat. She slipped under the water, and when she bobbed up again, she was gasping with the shock of the cold. She could no longer see her father.

Then her feet touched bottom. The rough barnacles of the rocky reef scraped against the soles of her shoes. She stumbled on the uneven rocks, leaning against the hull for support. The wood was ripped and splintered. Kit looked anxiously across the water. Still no sign of her father.

She scuttled, crablike, along the length of the boat. But the reef dropped away beneath her feet. Her body plunged down again and the water swirled over her head. She came up sputtering, numb with cold and frantically treading water. She looked all around but could not see far in the early-morning darkness. Maybe he had made it to dry land already.

Kit pushed hard against the boat with her legs and swam towards the land. The waves were carrying her along, helping her progress, but it was still farther away than she had thought. Finally her feet hit the gravel and she dragged herself out of the water.

"Dad! Dad!" she called repeatedly.

But there was no answer.

She stumbled across the gravelly beach, desperate with fear. Her sweater flopped soggily as she ran, cold as a fish. The ground was wet and slippery with seaweed. Her feet splashed through shallow tidal pools and then sank down into soft, grasping mud. Each step became mired in the ooze, pulling her back, slowing her down. She thought her shoes were going to be sucked right off her feet. But then the beach became firm again, a rough patch of oysters crunching under her feet. She hopped across them towards another gravelled stretch. Running faster now, calling as she went. Five minutes had already passed, and then she finally saw him. He was still out in the water, barely visible in the gloom. And he was not moving.

Kit raced straight back into the water. Her arms flailed and her legs kicked furiously. Then her hand brushed against him. She struggled to grab hold of him. He was heavy and limp, the weight of him almost pulling her down. Somehow she managed to get both arms around him and pull him up so his mouth and nose were above water. He began to gag and cough. He took in a huge breath of air and then his arms and legs began to struggle. His writhing was pulling them both under the water.

"Dad! Dad. Stop fighting. It's me," Kit yelled through a mouthful of water.

He turned, wild-eyed.

"I'll hold you up," she yelled. She held on tightly until his efforts calmed and they could float more easily. "That's better. Now we're going to have to try to get to shore."

"But the boat…"

"Don't worry about the boat," she shouted above the

wind and the waves.

She kicked her feet, clutching his shirt tightly. He now seemed limp with exhaustion.

Finally she felt the ground beneath her feet. She dragged her father up on the beach and slumped down beside him, panting hard with her effort. She saw that he was breathing regularly but his eyes were closed.

"Dad? Are you going to be all right?"

His eyes flickered open. He groaned and looked around in a daze. "I think so. Thanks, Kit. I couldn't have made it without you," he managed to say and then closed his eyes again.

Kit scanned the beach and the water. The sky was beginning to lighten as dawn approached. But the wind blew harder and with a sharper bite. Steel-grey waves churned restlessly, breaking into crests of white. A seagull swooped down low over the water with a lonesome cry. Kit could not think when she had been so cold. She was soaked to the bone and she couldn't stop shivering. The *Nighthawk*, in the distance, shifted on the rocky reef and sank a little lower. Now the bow of the boat was all that was visible above the waterline.

The tide was coming in. Already it was licking and slurping at her father's feet. They'd have to move to higher ground. The bank behind her looked to be heavily treed, and a good shelter from the wind. She managed to urge him up, letting him lean against her as they stumbled across the rocks, through reed grass, up amongst the salal on the bank and into a flat, mossy area, protected by the trees. He slumped down and closed his eyes.

"Rest here." Kit tried to keep her voice calm. She didn't want to make it sound as if she was worried.

He opened his eyes briefly. "Kit? Kit?"

"I'm right here, Daddy."

"Tell Caleb to watch the boat. Make sure it doesn't run aground."

This caught Kit by surprise. Didn't he remember the pirates had taken Caleb? That the boat had already run aground and capsized? He had to be delirious. Of all the things that had happened so far, nothing frightened her as much as this.

"Hush, now. I'll get you home, Dad. Don't you worry," she made herself say evenly. "Let's get you covered now, so you'll be warmer." She gathered armfuls of dry arbutus leaves from the bank and laid them like a crazy patchwork quilt over her father. The sky in the east had taken on a rosy glow and the air was finally beginning to lose some of its chill. Kit's sweater hung long at the sleeves and hips, stretched with the weight of the water. She unbuttoned it, peeled it off and squeezed out streams of water. Then she laid it out flat on a rock to dry.

When she straightened up and looked out towards the reef, she saw the bow of the boat just slipping under the water. A bubble broke the surface as the boat sank out of sight. Kit swallowed hard. She looked back at her father, hoping he hadn't seen the *Nighthawk* go down. But his head was buried under the leaves.

How were they going to get home? It was all up to her now. The coastline was thick with fir and arbutus and maple. There was no sign that anyone lived here, and no obvious route out. If she lit a fire it might attract the attention of a passing boat…not to mention getting them both warmed up. Maybe she could even cook some clams and oysters for breakfast. There were plenty of branches scattered around the bank, perfect for a fire. But how would she light it? Rub two sticks together? That would take forever. Her father's matches! But then she realized they'd be soaked through. Useless. With a sigh of frustration she let the idea of a fire go.

There were no two ways about it. She was going to have to leave her father and try to find help. She set off towards the point. The rocks took on larger, more angular shapes as she walked. Some shifted unexpectedly under her feet. She hopscotched over the smaller ones and picked her way between the larger ones, splashing her way through the barnacled and seaweed-choked tidal pools. It didn't matter; she was entirely wet as it was. Some of the rock formations were as tall as she was. Towards the point, the rocks began to stretch out flatter. It was easier going and she was able to move faster.

At the tip of the point the wind blew her hair wildly and buffeted her body. There was no protection from the elements here. A few scraggly, wind-sculpted trees clung to the rocks. Even the rocky bluff had been worn into sweeping curves by years of wind and waves. The sea was a swirl of whitecaps. Over and over, with the rhythm of breathing, the waves roared in and crashed, roared in and crashed. With each wave, a spectacular white spray burst over the rocks.

Kit's ears were filled with the sounds of wind and waves. She stood back from the water, high on a rock, and shielded her eyes against the first rays of sunlight glancing off the water. On the other side of the point, trees crowded the shoreline; no sign of anybody living there, either. Far across the water, hulking shapes of other islands lurked like sleeping giants. Then, far in the distance, no more than a dot, a boat appeared. Kit watched the dot become bigger. Now she could make out the large net wheel at the back, the distinctive mark of a fishing trawler. It was travelling much too quickly to be fishing, though. As it drew nearer, Kit waved her arms back and forth. She tried to shout, but the wind snatched her voice from her mouth and swallowed it up. She jumped. She waved. The boat cut through the waves at full throttle. She saw the fisherman come out of the cabin. He bent to pick up a coil of rope. He was close enough for Kit to make out the heavy green straps of his hip waders where they crossed his shoulders.

Kit yelled. She ran close to the sea, waving frantically. The man looked up. He saw her. But he just gave a friendly wave back. It was a wave that simply said, "Hello. Good morning." Then he went back into the cabin. Kit's disappointment felt heavy and sickly, like a bad case of stomach flu. She slumped down onto a washed-up log as she watched the fishing boat getting smaller and smaller as it moved away.

Then something else caught her attention. There was something in the trees farther along the shore. The point of a roof? She squinted her eyes. Yes, it was a building. There was the roofline sticking up through the trees. And farther along, another building, and another. They were so hard to make out, it didn't surprise her she had not noticed them at first.

Kit raced down the beach, stumbling over the rocks, righting herself and continuing on. A stitch formed in her side and she had to slow to a walk. She was breathing heavily. The first building she came to was a house. She knocked on the front door and waited. No one answered. It was still very early in the morning. Perhaps no one was awake yet.

She rapped more insistently on the door. There was only silence. Kit peered in the window. A broken chair lay on its back, but otherwise all she could see was an empty room. Then she tried the doorknob. The door creaked open.

"Hello?" Her voice echoed against the bare walls. "Is anybody home?"

There was no answer. She stepped inside. Dust covered the floor. A ripped woollen blanket lay discarded in the corner of the room. She tiptoed down the hall to the other rooms. The floorboards creaked beneath her feet. It was darker towards the back of the house. The air smelled musty. She checked each doorway but all she found were empty rooms. The cupboard doors in the kitchen were open and there was nothing on the shelves. A solitary spider scurried soundlessly across the floor and pushed itself into a crack in the corner. One of the panes at the kitchen window was broken. Shards of glass lay scattered on the floor. A tree outside had worked a branch in through the jagged opening, a sly intruder.

It was obvious that whoever had once lived here had moved away, but Kit still felt as if she was trespassing—as if someone might come back at any moment and find her there where she had no right to be. The silence was oppressive. She retraced her steps, closed the front door firmly behind her and took a big breath of fresh air.

Perhaps there was someone at one of the other buildings. The woodshed nearby housed a rickety pile of split wood. A rusty axe was wedged into a stump, its handle raised up like a cat's tail. The next two buildings were set at a distance farther away. Each had a covered porch across the front, facing the sea. All was quiet.

The stairs of the next building slanted down crookedly.

Some of the planks were missing. She stepped up carefully. At the top, balanced on the porch railing, she found a bent spoon and a dented tin plate. The door was already open. Kit held her arms tightly around her as she entered. For some reason she did not want to touch anything. Inside, she found a series of small, dark rooms, every one of them empty. All around, she felt an air of abandonment, sadness and loneliness.

There was only one building left. As she approached she heard a noise from inside—a furtive, scratching sound. She hugged herself tighter and made herself go up to the door.

"Hello?" she said.

The noise stopped. A second later, it began again.

Kit stepped inside. "Hello." Louder this time.

Once again it stopped. Kit steeled herself and walked towards a shadowy room at the end of the hall. Inside were two wooden barrels and a bulging gunny sack labelled as rice. No sign of anyone there. She let out her breath, realizing, only then, she'd been holding it for quite some time. She wasn't sure if she was more disappointed or relieved to find no one there.

She was about to turn and leave. Then, suddenly, something lurched out from the far side of a barrel. A face—a face with huge, dark eyes. Kit screamed and jumped back. Her heart thudded against her ribs. The face ducked out of sight behind the barrel again. Kit pushed her back against the wall as she stared at the spot where it had been. A moment later it reappeared. A face covered in black and white fur. A raccoon. That's all it was. Kit laughed aloud at herself for being so scared. The animal was probably more scared than she was. The raccoon watched warily as she backed away.

Outside, Kit surveyed the site. She had explored all the

buildings. There was no one here. But, even so, there was an eerie feeling about the place that was almost palpable. A flurry of shivers crawled up and down her skin. Something sad had happened here. She could sense it.

Then she noticed a narrow path covered in a carpet of rust-coloured conifer needles. It led away from the settlement through the trees. Kit followed it along. To one side the bright blue of the ocean glinted through the trees. A short distance later, the path turned inland, and then opened into a small, grassy glade. All around, towering trees circled like sentinels. The ground in the clearing rose and fell in a series of dips and mounds. It was very quiet here. No sound. No wind in the trees. No birds singing. Not even the waves on shore could be heard. Kit stood absolutely still, staring at one of the mounds. It reminded her of something. It was about six feet long and not very wide, the earth rounded over the top. And then she recognized the shape. It was a grave. She was standing in a graveyard.

Kit took a step backwards, her thoughts scattering in every direction. What kind of strange settlement could this be? No one lived here anymore. There was a graveyard in the trees. There was sadness everywhere.

A possibility occurred to Kit, and, suddenly, she knew without a doubt that it had to be true. This was D'Arcy Island. This was where the leper colony had been until just a few months ago. The people who had lived here had been shunned from society, thrown out and forgotten. Outcasts.

Kit hated the idea. It made her think of her mother in the sanatorium. She did not want to be here anymore. She turned and fled, running until she could run no longer. When she stopped, gasping for breath, the buildings were far behind her and once again obscured by the trees.

She continued on, walking now, around the point and back to check on her father. The leaves still covered him completely. She brushed them away and found him curled up in a ball underneath. He was not moving. She leaned in closer to check his breathing. Yes, she was relieved to see, his chest was rising and falling evenly and rhythmically. And his skin felt slightly warmer now. She covered him back up again, careful not to wake him.

What now? She would have to wait until another boat came by, she decided as she walked back to the point. That was all she could do.

Perhaps half an hour passed. A boat passed, off in the distance. Too far away. Kit ran back and checked her father—still sleeping—and then returned to the point. At least another hour passed and then another boat appeared, like a mirage. It drew closer, the white hull and handsome wood trim of the motor yacht becoming more distinct. Once again, Kit leapt to her feet and began jumping and waving. She yelled until she was hoarse. "Heeeelp. Heeeelp."

This time the boat slowed down. A man came to the side of the boat. He was looking in her direction through a pair of binoculars. Kit was waving so hard her arms began to ache. "Help. Our boat's gone down," she yelled as loud as she could. "We're stranded."

The man shouted back but the wind and the crashing waves made it impossible to hear the words.

"Help us, pleeeee...ease!" she hollered.

The boat moved around the end of the point into the more protected water of the bay. The man dropped an anchor off the bow and then lowered a small dinghy off the stern. Kit ran to the edge of the water.

The little dinghy bobbed in the water as the man rowed

to shore. Something about him looked familiar. Kit waded in up to her knees. Then she recognized him and her mouth gaped open. "Mr. Randall!"

"Good morning, Kit." He greeted her as casually as if they had just met on the street, as if coming to her rescue was nothing out of the ordinary. He rolled up his pant legs, took off his shoes and socks, and stepped into the water. His shirt was bright white and crisply ironed. "As you see, I have been lured to this godforsaken island by the siren's call."

Kit was not entirely sure what Mr. Randall meant by the siren's call—something to do with Greek mythology. But Kit hardly gave this a thought. She was more concerned about other things. "Our boat's gone down," she rushed to tell him. "And my father almost drowned. I thought we were never going to be rescued. And something terrible's happened to Caleb."

"Hold on. One thing at a time. Start from the beginning and tell me the whole story."

Kit hesitated. How could she tell the story without letting on that her father was a rum-runner? It was her father's business, her father's secret. And he would want her to keep it a secret. She was sure of it. "How did you know I was here?" she said instead.

"Mr. Olmstead asked me to keep an eye on you and your father."

"Mr. Olmstead? Mr. Olmstead asked you to watch us? But why?"

"He took quite a shine to you, young lady."

Kit turned this over in her mind. There had to be more to it than that. "And...," she prompted.

"Well, let's just say he likes to know what the competition's up to." He paused and then added, "Besides, he knows business on the water can be dangerous—especially at night."

"But how did you know we were in trouble?"

"I took a run by your bay this morning and I saw the *Nighthawk* wasn't there. I know that when your dad takes the boat out at night he has it back well before sunrise. And I knew it wasn't getting gassed up because I'd just come from the gas barge up at Canoe Cove." Mr. Randall sat down on a log and put his socks and beautifully tooled leather shoes back on.

Kit chewed her bottom lip as she watched him. Then she said, "You know all about what my dad does, then? His comings and goings? Everything?"

Mr. Randall looked up from rolling down his pants and gave her a wink. "Down to the last bottle."

Kit felt her eyebrows rise. "You do?" Her father's shady business dealings had not been such a secret after all. But then she remembered their conversation over ice cream in Victoria—the way they had questioned her about the night fishing. It was no wonder they had figured it out.

Mr. Randall nodded. "So tell me what happened last night. I might be able to help."

"All right, then…" And she told the whole story, from becoming a stowaway, to Caleb's capture, to the *Nighthawk* sinking.

Mr. Randall listened carefully, nodding thoughtfully. "So one of the pirates was called Red. Mmm…tell me. Was the rat-faced pirate a small man, narrow across the shoulders? Hair dark and slicked back?"

"Yes."

"Joe Lupini," he said quietly. Then he asked, "And did

they say where they were going to take the load?"

Kit shook her head. "They could have gone anywhere—one of the islands, a bay along the coastline. I have no idea. And we don't have much time. They said that when they finished the job, they were going to kill Caleb. He might even be dead right now!"

Mr. Randall put both hands on her shoulders and looked her straight in the eye. "First things first. Let's get your father. Then we'll figure out how to find Caleb. Okay?"

"Okay. I'll take you to my dad." As they made their way along the beach, Kit asked, "This is D'Arcy Island, isn't it? Where the leper colony used to be?"

"That it is. Although the only people you'll run across here these days are rum-runners." His stride was jaunty and his manner was as cheerful as if they were going for ice cream.

Kit led the way up the bank and through the salal. "Like us, you might say." She glanced back at him, to catch his expression. So far, Mr. Randall had allowed only a few hints to drop. He had not actually come straight out and said he was a rum-runner.

Mr. Randall grinned. "You might say that."

Arbutus leaves still covered Kit's father entirely, and from somewhere below came the obvious sound of snoring. Kit shook his shoulder until a groan came from under the leaves. Then he sat up, groggily, leaves showering off in all directions. One lone leaf remained stuck in his hair. He looked from Kit to Mr. Randall. "Who are you?" he asked.

Mr. Randall offered his hand. "Franklin Randall. I was passing in my boat and your lovely daughter flagged me down."

Kit's father looked somewhat bewildered as he shook

Mr. Randall's hand weakly with his injured arm. "I'm Jack Avery. Pleased to meet you."

~

An hour later, Kit and her father were wrapped in blankets and sipping tea in the cabin of Mr. Randall's boat. They were speeding home. Kit was relieved to see her father no longer seemed confused, though his colour remained pale and he still shivered. He had been in the water longer than she had, after all. Kit knew he had to be feeling miserable about everything that had happened the night before. She caught his eye and he attempted a smile but it faded as soon as it had appeared.

They pulled up to the dock, home again to Home Again Bay. No other sight could have been more welcome to her eyes. The slope of the bank up from the water, the tops of the apple trees, the morning sun glinting off her little bedroom window under the eaves—it was like seeing old friends.

It felt as if ages had passed. Had it been only last night that she'd hid in the grass waiting for a chance to board the boat? And everything that had happened since—the sneaking on board, the U.S. Coast Guard, the pirates and the shipwreck—who would have thought so much could happen in a single night?

As Mr. Randall was tying the boat up, Vivian appeared at the top of the wharf. She stared at the unfamiliar boat for a moment, but when she recognized Kit's father she flounced down the ramp.

"Jack? What's going on?"

Kit's father patted her shoulder. "Everything's all right, Vivian. We just had a little accident, that's all."

"Where's your boat?" she demanded.

"Well, that's the thing, Vivian. We lost the boat," he said through chattering teeth. "The important thing is that Kit and I made it back safe and sound. But Caleb—"

"You lost the boat?" Vivian interrupted, her voice sharp. "What do you mean, you lost the boat?"

Kit's father started to explain, but Vivian crossed her arms and turned away huffily. "I knew it was a silly idea to get involved with you. I just knew it."

"Now, now, Vivian. Don't say that. Aren't you glad to see us?"

But Vivian would not reply. Instead, she turned her attention to Mr. Randall. "Well, hello," she said, checking her curls with a coquettish gesture. "I'm Vivian—who are you?"

"Franklin Randall." He took her hand in his. "A pleasure to meet you."

Vivian blushed. When Mr. Randall started to remove his hand she held on tighter. "The pleasure is mine," she replied.

15 *The White Orchid*

"Take his temperature every hour. Keep him wrapped in warm blankets. And fetch the doctor if he doesn't improve," Mr. Randall said.

Vivian looked doubtfully at the bed where Kit was covering her father with another blanket. "What about Kat?" she said. "She could watch him as easily as me. Nursing is second nature to her. She looked after her mother before she went into the hospital."

Kit put a finger to her lips. "He's sleeping now," she whispered and indicated they all step out of the room. "I can't stay with him," she explained once they were in the hallway. "Mr. Randall and I are going to find Caleb."

Vivian smiled sweetly at Mr. Randall. "I have a better idea. I'll help Mr. Randall find Caleb and Kat can stay here with her father."

Kit felt her anger rising quickly. She turned to face Vivian and squared her shoulders. "Kit. My name is Kit. K...I...T. Kit."

The simpering look faded from Vivian's face. "All right, *Kit*. No need to get snippy." Her voice was icy. "Now, as I was saying, I'll go with Mr. Randall. You stay here." She took Mr. Randall by the arm. "It's all settled."

Kit glared at Vivian. She had seen Vivian checking Mr. Randall's hand to make sure he did not wear a wedding band. She had seen how easily Vivian had shifted from one man, whose fortunes were down, to another, more promising prospect. It was obvious Vivian was only interested in suiting herself.

Mr. Randall disengaged himself from Vivian's clutch and said, "It's better if Kit comes with me. She knows what the pirates look like, she's seen their boat and she heard everything they said."

Vivian was clearly disappointed. She pressed her lips together. "Well, I don't see why I have to be left behind. Jack's a grown man. He can look after himself."

"He was in the water a long time," Mr. Randall explained patiently. "He has hypothermia. He needs someone to keep an eye on him."

～

They left Vivian standing on the wharf. Her arms were crossed tightly around her. The breeze played with her skirt, chasing it around her legs. Her hair blew across her face. She did not look happy.

The boat rounded the point and Kit scanned the wide strait ahead of them. "How do we know where to start looking for Caleb?" she asked.

Mr. Randall adjusted the steering wheel and checked the compass as he thought. Then he replied, "They could unload anywhere along the coast. Chances are they've got a truck hidden somewhere. I've heard of those two pirates. They've got connections in Seattle and I figure that's where they'll end up…at one of the blind pigs downtown. They'll want to deliver their load and turn a pretty penny as soon as possible."

"Blind pig?"

"Blind pig. Some people call them speakeasies. They're both names for secret clubs that sell alcohol."

"So that's where we're headed? Seattle?"

Mr. Randall nodded. "Seattle it is."

Kit knew Seattle was a big port city in the United States down in the Puget Sound. It was a city she'd never been to, but she'd heard it was bigger than Victoria. Mr. Randall said it would take almost four hours by boat. He knew the route well, he assured her. Doing business for Mr. Olmstead, he often travelled between Victoria and Seattle.

Kit nodded sleepily as Mr. Randall talked. Her eyes felt heavy. She'd been awake all night. She lay down on the bunk, pulled a blanket up over her shoulders and fell soundly asleep.

～

Caleb was floating just out of reach. Kit's arms stretched towards him through the air…or was it water? His eyes were closed, the lashes forming dark crescents against his skin. He held a white flower to his chest. Kit was not sure he was breathing. She called to him. His eyes flickered open and he turned towards her, his face dreamy, a half smile on his lips. He extended an arm to her. Their fingers touched briefly. The flower passed from his hand to hers. And then he closed his eyes again.

Kit looked down at what she held. It was no longer a flower but an orange, peeled and pulled open, the segments forming a star. Its citrus aroma, overwhelming and powerful, filled the air…

Kit woke up. The scent of oranges faded away with the dream. She was not sure how long she had slept but she had the sense that hours had passed. She sat up in the bunk and looked around. The boat was swaying gently. Through the porthole she could see a huge, sprawling city. The waterfront was a mass of docks and boats. Large buildings marched up the hillside as far as she could see. Seattle was bigger than she had imagined. How would they ever find one boy in such a big city?

Mr. Randall turned around at the wheel. "Ah, you're awake. We've just arrived." He cut the speed as they came closer to the shore. Then the boat nosed slowly into a boat-house. "Take this line and jump to the wharf," he said. "Hold her steady."

Kit tied the boat fast and Mr. Randall turned off the engine. He checked his watch. "We made good time. I bet you're hungry, aren't you?"

Her stomach felt empty and hollow. She realized she hadn't eaten since dinner the day before and now it was mid-afternoon. "I'm starving. But we have to start looking for Caleb right away. It sounded like the pirates were planning to kill him when they were finished with the job."

"Come with me." Mr. Randall led her up the ramp, across a busy road and then up three long flights of stairs. They were both out of breath when they reached the top.

"Pike Street Market," Mr. Randall announced.

They stood at the end of a long building. Stalls lined each side and crowds of people thronged like bees in a hive. It was a hubbub of noise and, everywhere the eye looked, colour. Here, fish vendors slapped bright red snappers onto a counter, wrapped them in brown paper and tossed them to customers. There, perfect pyramids of purple plums and brilliant green snap peas tumbled into baskets. A man zigzagged through the crowd, pushing a cartload of deep red beets. "Coming through," he called. "Coming through." Great armloads of flowers were stuffed into buckets. One stand sold newspapers from all over the world, some with headlines in letters from a strange alphabet. People with bulging shopping bags squeezed past each other. All around, smells of spices and honey, olive oil, coffee and dust filled the air. A woman wearing an elaborately feathered hat pressed past them, leaving behind a lingering scent of perfume. Someone was shouting above the din, "Hot bread. Fresh from the oven."

Mr. Randall took her by the arm. "This way. There's the man I want to talk to." They wove through the shoppers to the bakery stall. Long loaves of golden bread were laid out in a beautiful, tempting row. There were dinner rolls and breakfast crescents and gingersnap cookies. Kit's mouth began to water.

"A baguette," Mr. Randall said, and the man with the apron behind the counter picked out the longest, thinnest loaf of bread Kit had ever seen. Mr. Randall broke it in half and gave Kit a piece. "Try it. It's good."

The crust was firm and chewy, the inside wonderfully soft. Kit thought she had never tasted anything more delicious. She devoured it hungrily. Mr. Randall was still talking to the baker. At first she didn't pay much attention but then her ears pricked up at the words "blind pig."

"Notice any unexpected deliveries today?" Mr. Randall was asking.

The baker wiped his hands on a towel and shook his head. Then he pointed across the street. "Go up that way a couple of blocks and ask Harry the butcher. It's on the corner. He might have seen something at the one near him, The White Orchid."

"Thanks." Mr. Randall handed him several bills. "Keep the change."

Kit and Mr. Randall crossed the road and walked up the steep sidewalk. The butcher's shop sported a fluttering of long, coloured streamers at the open doorway. Inside, the ceiling was high, twice the height of a regular ceiling, and ornamented in geometric designs of pressed tin. A shining brass register sat prominently on the counter. Great loops of pink sausages and chicken breasts rolled in spices and tied neatly with string were displayed behind glass. The shop was empty but from somewhere in the back they could hear whistling. Mr. Randall rang the bell. The butcher appeared through a swinging door.

"What can I do for you?" His eyes were round and brown, his head bald except for a little fringe of hair.

"The name's Randall. I work with Roy Olmstead…" He paused, waiting until the butcher gave the slightest nod of the head to indicate he understood. Mr. Randall continued. "I'm looking for information about a certain club in this area."

The butcher eyed him. "You mean…?"

"That's right." Mr. Randall's voice dropped to a near whisper. "The White Orchid."

"What kind of information are you looking for?"

"I'm wondering if you noticed any unusual deliveries today."

The butcher's eyes flicked from Mr. Randall to Kit and back again before he answered.

"Why don't you just go over there and ask them yourself?" He nodded his head towards the back of the shop.

"It's just out back, down the alley."

"Sometimes the people who run these clubs don't like to talk much. Especially about where they buy their liquor. And especially if it's from someone undercutting Roy Olmstead." Mr. Randall jingled the coins in his pocket. "Information pays well these days. I can make it worth your while."

The butcher considered this briefly and then he spoke. "About half an hour ago. A truck I'd never seen before pulled up. Two men and a boy."

"The boy…" Kit nudged Mr. Randall. "Ask him about the boy."

The butcher looked down at her. "A little older than you, I'd say. Fifteen, maybe sixteen. Dark hair."

Kit's heart flip-flopped. "Caleb. It has to be. And the men? What did they look like?"

"One's small and wiry. Oily looking. He did all the talking. The other one's a redhead. Seemed real sleepy—just sat in the truck the whole time."

"It's them. I'm sure it is."

The butcher studied Kit. "They friends of yours?"

"Just the boy. Caleb's my friend. The other two took him against his will. I'm trying to rescue him."

Mr. Randall put some bills on the counter. The butcher looked at the money and then pushed it back. "I don't want your money. I just want what's right. If the truth be told, I didn't much like the way they treated that boy." He opened the door to the back room. "Come with me. They might still be there."

Kit and Mr. Randall followed the butcher into the back room. The air was as cold as a winter's day. Huge blocks of ice were stacked in straw against the walls. The floor was covered in sawdust, and dripping, red animal carcasses hung from hooks in the ceiling. The butcher had already crossed the grisly room and opened the next door that led to the alley. Kit hurried to catch up with him.

The alley was narrow and dingy. Garbage bins overflowed with refuse. An acrid, rotten smell hung in the air. The backs of the buildings, hidden away here, were roughly finished and ramshackle, so unlike their polished fronts presented on the street side.

"There…" The butcher was pointing to a dark green truck idling halfway down the alley. "That's the truck." But as he spoke, the truck began to pull away.

Kit could make out the shape of the three heads through the windshield. "Caleb!" she called as it turned the corner at the end of the alley. She could see his profile. Caleb's head turned slightly. Had he seen her? And then the truck was gone.

Kit stamped her foot in frustration. They'd come so close and they'd missed their chance. The pirates had finished the job and now they were going off to kill Caleb. Tears stung Kit's eyes, but she blinked them back stubbornly. She wasn't going to let herself cry—not in front of Mr. Randall and the butcher.

Then, over and above the squalid stink of the alley, came another smell, the smell of citrus, sweet and fresh. An elusive scent of oranges, just like in the dream. The scent tingled her senses.

"Do you smell that?" she asked the two men. "Do you smell oranges?"

Mr. Randall and the butcher both shook their heads. "Let's go back inside," the butcher suggested.

"Just a minute…" She took a step down the alley and

then another. She was walking toward The White Orchid. Faster now, and the smell of oranges was growing stronger. She reached the spot where the truck had been and her feet stopped.

The door was unmarked. The windows had been painted over black. The smell of oranges was overwhelming. She felt light-headed, almost dizzy.

Behind her, she heard Mr. Randall's voice. "Kit, come back. That's not a good idea." But she was only half aware of the warning. His voice seemed to come from a long way away.

Her arm stretched forward and her knuckles rapped the door.

The slit in the door, narrow like a mail slot, but set up just above her head, squeaked open.

"What do you want?" It was a man's gruff voice. It was very dark through the slit and Kit could not see the face. In the background she could hear music and laughter and the clinking of glasses.

"Is this The White Orchid?" she asked.

"What do you want to know for?" The voice sounded irritated.

"I'm looking for my friend, Caleb. I think he was just here making a delivery. Do you know where he went?"

"We haven't had any deliveries. Now scram, kid." And with a rattle and a clank, the slit closed again.

Kit turned back towards the butcher's shop. Mr. Randall and the butcher were waiting for her, both looking concerned. She started to walk back towards them. The smell of oranges was so strong it made her head spin. Where was it coming from? The alleyway was strewn with garbage but there were no oranges that she could see.

Then, from behind her, she heard her name being called. "Kit! Wait."

She spun around. No one was there. The alleyway was empty. The windows on either side were blank. Even though she could not see the person, she knew the voice. She would have known it anywhere. It was Caleb's.

"Caleb? Where are you?" she called out. She ran to the corner where she had last seen the truck. She looked both ways. The street was teeming with streetcars and honking motor cars. But he was not there. She ran back into the alley, calling his name as she went: "Caleb! Caleb!"

Mr. Randall caught her by the shoulders. "Kit. Calm down. Caleb's gone."

"But I just heard him calling me. Didn't you?"

"No, Kit. He's gone. He left in the truck."

Kit knew Mr. Randall was right. She had seen Caleb go with her own eyes. Was it possible she'd only imagined his voice? But it had seemed so real.

"Come back to the shop, Kit. We'll go inside and sit down. You need to calm your nerves."

Kit let herself be taken back to the shop. Just before she went back inside, she looked up and down the alley, just to make sure. But there was no sign of Caleb.

~

Kit sat in a chair in the butcher's shop. The two men were talking quietly across the room. "She's exhausted," she heard Mr. Randall say. "She was up all night. And she's been through a terrible ordeal."

"Poor sausage," the butcher said, as he locked the door at the front of the shop and put up the Closed sign. The clock above the door said five o'clock. "What are you going to do now?"

"Good question," Mr. Randall said. "I think it's about time I gave Mr. Olmstead a call. Do you mind if I use your telephone?"

"Go right ahead. It's behind the counter."

Mr. Randall placed the call. "Hello? Is Mr. Olmstead home? Tell him it's Randall from Victoria...Yes, I'll wait... Hello, Mr. Olmstead. You must have just got back from your honeymoon...Congratulations, sir...and give my best to your lovely wife...Something's come up. I thought you'd want to know...All right...All right...I understand." Mr. Randall hung up the phone.

"Why didn't you tell him?" Kit asked, surprised.

"There were clicking noises on the phone line. Mr. Olmstead thinks someone might have been eavesdropping on our conversation—listening in, trying to collect evidence against him. He's going to another phone."

A few minutes later Mr. Randall dialed another number. He spoke quietly and it was hard for Kit to catch more than a few words. "...Kit...the old leper colony on D'Arcy...taken by pirates...The White Orchid..." Kit strained her ears but she could not hear more than a mumble. Then Mr. Randall handed her the phone. "Mr. Olmstead wants to talk to you," he said.

"Kit?" It was Mr. Olmstead's booming voice. "Sounds like you've had a busy night. How're you holding up?"

"Fine...sir."

Mr. Olmstead laughed heartily. "Roy. You call me Roy, all right? We're old pals, after all. Now this friend of yours, Caleb...Don't you worry. I'll send out some of my men and tell them to turn this city upside down until they find him. By the end of the day there won't be a door in town they haven't checked. We'll find him. And that's a promise."

"Thank you, sir…I mean, Roy." Kit felt the weight of her worry lighten.

"Your mum all right?"

"I think so. I haven't heard anything from her lately."

"And your dad?"

"Shook up pretty bad, I'd say."

"Well, chin up, my girl. They're lucky about one thing… and that's having a daughter like you. You can tell them I said so."

"Roy, thank you for everything and…congratulations on getting married. I wish you all the happiness in the world."

"You too, Kit. You too."

~

Ten minutes later a big black car pulled up outside the butcher's shop and Mr. Randall ushered her into the back seat. "Mr. Olmstead sent us this car and two of his men to help. We're going to check out a few other blind pigs. Those pirates might try to unload their cases at a couple of places in town," he explained.

Kit sank back against the plush seat beside Mr. Randall as the car moved out into traffic. She looked out the window at all the cars, the stores, the people on the sidewalks. On the far side of the street was a building with a door so big a giant could have walked through without bending his head. She craned her neck but the building stretched up so high, she could not see the top of it. She felt small by comparison. In the front seat the two Olmstead men were both wearing dark suits and hats. Their hair was cut neatly at the nape of their necks, both exactly the same.

Then she caught a whiff of something and she sat up

straight. She took a deeper breath. She knew what it was. Oranges. Her scalp began to tingle and the fine blonde hairs on the backs of her arms bristled. She remembered the voice in the alley, Caleb's voice calling to her, "Kit! Wait." She could hear it now in her head. It sounded urgent. Almost pleading.

But she was not waiting. She was being driven off in a big black car by strange men in suits. She knew one thing for sure. She had to go back.

"Stop!" Kit cried out suddenly. "Stop the car."

16 *The Star Card*

The car jerked to a stop and a horn beeped behind them. Kit's hand was on the door handle. "I'm going back to the butcher's shop. Go ahead without me." She caught the look of surprise on Mr. Randall's face before she jumped out of the car and slammed the door. As it pulled away Mr. Randall stuck his head out the window. "Kit, stay at the butcher's shop. We'll come back and get you later," he yelled above the traffic noise. The car was already halfway down the block.

A truck honked as it swerved around her and Kit leapt to the safety of the sidewalk. Her heart was beating hard. She ran all the way back to the butcher's shop, but the door was locked, the lights were out, and the Closed sign still hung in the window. She pounded on the door. But the shop remained dark. Kit ran around to the alley planning to try the back door.

Just as she entered the alley, a green truck turned in from the far side. Quickly, Kit ducked down behind a row of overflowing garbage cans. The truck pulled up to The White Orchid and stopped. A man stepped out. Kit caught her breath. It was the rat-faced pirate. He looked shiftily up and down the alley, then tossed the butt of his cigarette down on the ground and rapped sharply on the door of The White Orchid. "Second load," he said. The club door swung open. Several men emerged. They pulled the tarp off the back of the truck. "The first row's oranges, in case I was stopped by the police. Stack them up over there. I'll sell them down at the market later," ordered rat-face. "The rest of the load you can take inside."

The men began unloading boxes from the back of the truck. Kit shifted behind the garbage cans, trying to see whether Caleb was there. She caught sight of one man with a cap pulled down low over his face, a slim build and a loose-limbed way of moving. She watched him heave up a box and take it into The White Orchid. A few moments later he was back again. The cap was still drawn low, still obscuring his features, his face cast in shadow. Was it Caleb? It had to be. But what if it wasn't? If only she could get a better view. She started to creep forward. Then she brushed against one of the garbage cans, and the lid slid sideways and rattled to the ground. The men in the alley froze. The offending lid clattered noisily as it rolled and finally came to a rest several feet away. Kit held her breath.

"Rats," one of the men said, and they all laughed as they went back to work. But the one with the cap remained looking in her direction.

"Get back to work," one of the others growled, giving him a shove.

Then, with a screech of tires, a police car pulled into the end of the alley. The lights were flashing. The doors burst open and policemen jumped out. "Stop right there! This is a raid."

People scattered in every direction like marbles thrown to the ground. Well-dressed men and women poured out of The White Orchid and ran up the alley towards Kit. The rat-faced pirate frantically cranked the engine on the green truck and leapt in. Then it was lurching forward, careering into the stack of orange boxes and knocking them sideways. People leapt out of the way. The vehicle raced down the alley, crushing the garbage lid lying directly in its path. A sharp report. Had it been the crumpling garbage lid…or a gunshot?

Kit did not know for sure. All she knew was she had to get away. But first she had to find Caleb. She leapt to her feet and ran down the alley towards The White Orchid. People were shouting and rushing, wide-eyed. Kit dodged amongst them, looking in every direction and seeing only a confusing kaleidoscope of panic, clatter, disorder. A woman being dragged by the arm. A policeman grabbing a man in a business suit. A long-legged man darting past with a trumpet tucked under his arm. Kit reached the end of the alley, all out of breath. But there was no sign of the young man in the cap. He had disappeared already.

A portly man pushed past her, knocking her against the rough brick wall. "Better get outta here, kid. Everyone's being rounded up and taken to jail," he yelled as he bolted around the corner.

But instead of following him out of the alley, Kit steadied herself and turned around. She would try to get back to the butcher's shop. It was the only place she knew where she could hide. She prayed that the back door was still unlocked. She didn't have time to think what she'd do if it wasn't. Her feet were pounding. She passed a crushed box of oranges, the scattered contents lying splattered, bright, splayed open. Overwhelmingly fragrant. She was at the butcher's shop. Her hand was on the doorknob.

"Kit! Wait."

The skin on the back of her neck prickled. It was the same call she'd thought she'd heard before. She whirled around. There he was, the young man with the cap. Caleb.

He was just down the alley from the butcher's shop. He was half sitting, half lying, almost hidden amongst a smash of boxes and crushed oranges. No wonder she had not seen him before.

"Get up." Kit grabbed his hand, pulled him to his feet and dragged him, limping, to the butcher's shop door. He leaned heavily against her as she tried the handle. It turned. She pushed her shoulder hard against the door and then, mercy upon mercy, it gave and Kit and Caleb tumbled inside. In the next instant Kit had snapped the bolt into place, locking it behind them.

They both sank down on the sawdust floor. Huge carcasses of beef and pork hung in the shadows all around them. The air was so chilly their breath came in white, feathery clouds. From the other side of the door they could hear shouts and the sound of gunfire. They waited, listening, and hoping no one had seen them come through the doorway.

"Kit? What are you doing here in Seattle?" Caleb whispered. "How did you know where to find me?"

"Long story," Kit whispered back. "Are you all right?"

"It's my ankle. I got knocked over by the truck." Caleb rubbed his foot. His face twisted as he attempted to stand. "It hurts like the dickens."

"Shhh." Kit put her finger to her lips. "Listen." There'd been a sound from the front of the shop. A man's voice. Then footsteps. They both huddled down next to a block of ice. The door swung open.

"Who's there?" The voice was deep and resonant. The butcher.

Kit let out her breath. "It's just me, Kit."

The butcher pulled the light switch on and the room was suddenly illuminated. "Kit? But I thought you'd gone off with the Olmstead boys."

Kit explained what had happened: that she'd returned to the alley and found Caleb and then they'd escaped the pirates and the police just in the nick of time. "And we're supposed to wait here at the shop until Mr. Randall comes back," she finished.

"That's fine. That's just fine." The butcher gave her a reassuring pat on the shoulder. "I was back here and just about to lock up when I heard someone pounding on the front door."

"That would have been me."

He nodded. "By the time I went up front, no one was there. I checked my cash register for day's end, and then I heard a commotion in the alley. I remembered I hadn't locked the back up."

Kit glanced at the door and the sturdy bolt that held it closed. What would have happened if it had been locked?

Suddenly there was a tremendous banging from the other side. The door shook on its hinges. "Open up. It's the Seattle police. We know you're in there."

"Hurry!" The butcher's voice was urgent as he hustled them towards the front of the shop. "Out the front door. Quick."

Kit grabbed Caleb's hand. "This way." She was dragging him down the sloping sidewalk back towards the Pike Street Market. Caleb limped along as fast as he could, but their progress was slow. "Here..." She took his arm and draped it over her shoulders. "Use me like a crutch."

They were able to move faster now as Caleb leaned against her, half walking, half hopping. When they crossed the intersection and looked down the side street, they saw the green truck stopped half a block away. It had been blocked by a police car. The rat-faced pirate was pushed up against the car and the police were frisking him. The other pirate was already sitting in the back of the police car.

Kit and Caleb hurried away, down the hill. The street sloped down at a greater pitch here. Ahead they could see the sign for the Pike Street Market. Over the rooftops, the bright blue of the ocean shone. Kit knew somewhere along the waterfront Mr. Randall's boat sat waiting in its boat-house. She just hoped she could remember the way.

"Where are we going?" Caleb asked.

"Mr. Randall's boat."

"Mr. Who?"

"Randall."

"Who's that?"

Kit had forgotten Caleb had never met Mr. Randall. She filled him in, sketchily, as they entered the market. The crowds had gone. People had done their shopping and gone home. The news vendor reached up and, with a great rattle and clank, pulled a corrugated tin blind down over his wares. A Chinese lady at the fruit and vegetable stand was throwing overripe produce into a refuse bin. The baker had already gone. His shelves were bare. The man at the fish stand took off his big rubber apron and stepped out of his gumboots. The light at the coffee shop turned off.

Kit and Caleb continued through the market stalls. They passed a man sweeping up, whistling a tune as he pushed the broom through the empty aisles. He put two fingers to his eyebrow, in a salute. "Good night," he said.

"Night," Kit and Caleb replied.

Caleb was starting to slow down. "It's not much farther," Kit assured him. "We'll come to the stairs soon. We just go down the stairs and then we'll be at the waterfront."

"I've got to stop for a minute." Caleb sat down and rubbed his ankle. He pulled the sock down. The skin was an angry red and starting to swell. Kit stood over him looking down. It reminded her of something—a wisp of a memory, a strange dream she'd had a long time ago. A boy in a harlequin suit, riding a unicycle. His feet were bare. And a snake rose up to strike the tender, white flesh of his foot.

A tingle ran down Kit's spine. She'd had the dream even before she'd met Caleb. And, just like in the dream, he had fallen into danger. And then his foot had been struck...

"Hey!" A distant shout.

Kit swung around. A policeman was standing next to the man with the broom. The man was pointing towards them.

"Hey, you two kids," the policeman yelled again, and his voice echoed from the walls. "Stay where you are."

Kit pulled Caleb up in a panic. "Hurry. We're just about at the stairs."

Caleb managed only a few limping steps before saying, "Go ahead without me, Kit. I'm only slowing you down."

"No. I've got you this far. I'm not going to leave you now." She was determined to get him to the boat.

The policeman was gaining ground. They were at a covered passage between two buildings. To the right, a long series of stairs stretched down the hill.

"This is it," Kit urged Caleb on. They made their way

awkwardly down the first flight, and then ducked into a doorway alcove, pressing themselves up to the corner and listening. A moment later they heard the sound of running feet. The sound stopped at the top of the stairs. Kit and Caleb both held their breath. She knew the policeman would be looking down the stairway for them. Then the sound continued on into the next building, gradually getting quieter as it moved away.

"We have to get down the stairs before he comes back." Kit led Caleb the rest of the way, down to the busy road at the bottom. They crossed over to the marina and down the ramp. Kit was relieved to recognize the tin roof of the boat-house and to find Mr. Randall's sleek boat moored inside.

They both sank down onto the cushioned benches, their breathing slowing down as the minutes passed. It was dark here, out of the glare of the evening sun. The only sound was the water lapping gently against the hull. They were safe, at least for the time being.

~

Hours later, a dozing Kit heard footsteps on the wharf. The boathouse door opened. A flashlight shone in her face. She pulled herself straight up. Her heart started to gallop in her chest. They'd been caught.

Then came a laugh. "Don't look so scared, Kit. It's just me, Mr. Randall." He angled the flashlight away and then Kit could make him out, as well as Caleb's eyes shining in the shadows like two huge coins. "I see you've retrieved the prodigal pirate," Mr. Randall said. "Good work. You outwit-ted the pirates, the police *and* the Olmstead boys. When the butcher told me you'd left the shop I thought I might find you here."

Kit grinned. "This is Caleb...and Caleb, this is Mr. Randall."

"Pleased to meet you." Mr. Randall shook Caleb's hand and then started up the engine. "Now, let's get you two home."

~

Kit's eyes slowly focused on the wall in her room. It was splashed with sunlight. The clock on the chest of drawers read a few minutes past two. Why had she slept until such an hour? Then she remembered. She had been to Seattle and rescued Caleb and she hadn't got home until late last night. Her father had answered the door, bleary-eyed and wrapped in a blanket.

"We've brought Caleb home...," she began to explain, but she was so exhausted she could not continue. "I'll tell you the rest in the morning." Then she'd stumbled upstairs and thrown herself onto the bed, not even bothering to put on her nightdress.

Now it was the middle of the afternoon. She pushed back the covers, stretched out her legs and wiggled her toes. Then she padded to the window, opened it wide and leaned out. A breeze played in the treetops, stirring the leaves and making them rustle. There was no sign of anyone about.

Downstairs, her father was resting on the couch. He sat up as she entered the room. "Feel better?" he asked.

"A hundred percent. How about you?"

"Finally warm again. Thought I was never going to thaw out," he grinned.

"Where's Vivian?"

"She left."

"But she was supposed to keep an eye on you."

"I guess she had other ideas." He patted the seat beside him. "Come and tell me what happened in Seattle."

After Kit had told him the whole story she went into the bathroom and checked her reflection in the mirror. Her face was brown from the sun—and a layer of dirt. Her bangs formed a long fringe over her eyes. And her overalls were rumpled and filthy. She hardly looked the same pale girl who'd arrived in a clean, starched dress at the beginning of the summer. She wondered if her mother would recognize her. She barely recognized herself.

Kit pushed the bangs off her forehead and then poured water from the pitcher into the wash basin. She scrubbed her face and gave herself a sponge bath. The water was brown as tea when she had finished. She pulled on her dressing gown and ran upstairs where she picked the blue-and-white-striped dress from her closet. Then she ran back downstairs again to heat a flatiron on the stove and give the dress a pressing. She had grown so much this summer it was difficult to do up the buttons. She tugged the skirt down to try to make it cover her knees.

Her stomach was rumbling. She cut several slices of bread, spread them with butter and strawberry jam, and ate quickly. Then she poured herself a tall glass of milk.

She knew Caleb would be hungry as well, so she went back into the kitchen and sliced more bread, poured another glass of milk, and set them on a tray. Outside, the afternoon air was hot and muggy. Heat waves shimmered off the ground. It was so hot the birds sat still in the trees, not even bothering to sing. The tall yellow grass rasped against her bare legs as she walked. A couple of drowsy grasshoppers leapt out of her path at the last minute, narrowly avoiding her footsteps.

The door of the pickers' shack was open and she found Caleb wrapping his foot with a bandage. "How's the ankle?"

"It's just a sprain, I figure. The bandage helps."

"Thought you'd be hungry." Kit set the tray down on the little table. She watched him finish the bandaging, then limp to the basin to wash his hands. When he'd sat down again and ate some of the food, she continued, "Caleb, why didn't you tell me about the rum-running?"

He stopped chewing. "Your dad made me promise not to say anything. I would have told you if it wasn't for that. Honest."

"Why did you get involved, anyway? You of all people. You'd think you'd know better, seeing what alcohol did to your dad. And the way he treated you because of it."

"I know." He couldn't meet her eyes, looking down at the plate instead. Finally he said, "You're right, Kit. That's what I wanted to get away from. I hated being around my dad when he was drinking. People talk about the evils of drink, and I can tell you, I've seen it first-hand." He swallowed hard. "And that's only part of it. Remember when I told you my mother died in a car accident?"

Kit sensed an uneasy tension in the question. She gave a slight nod, afraid of what he was going to say next.

"It was a drunk driver that killed her." He shook his head. "Who'd have thought such a thing could happen? Like being struck by lightning."

Kit felt her throat constrict into a tight knot. Even though she had been expecting something tragic, the words still came as a shock.

"It was a warm evening, almost dusk." His voice was quiet, barely audible. "We were up the Fraser Valley, near

Hope. We'd just finished setting up the tents in a field outside of town. My mother said she wanted to walk into town and look around. She said she wouldn't be long. She walked away..." He stopped, closed his eyes and continued. "She was on the side of the road, right at a point where the road curved. A car came along. The driver'd been drinking. He was going too fast. He didn't take the curve sharp enough. And he hit her."

Kit put out a hand to touch his shoulder but he shrugged it off. His brusqueness surprised Kit at first, but then she realized it was a front. He was only trying to be brave. "I'm sorry about your mother," she said very quietly.

He acknowledged her sympathy without comment, leaning forward, his elbows resting on his knees, pretending to show interest in a fat black beetle crossing the floorboards. A strange silence filled the pickers' shack. Although there was no sound, the air seemed to hold the ring of the words she had just spoken.

Kit made herself stumble on. "But what I don't understand is...after all that's happened to you...why did you ever...?"

He leaned back against the chair, a wry twist to his mouth. "Get involved in rum-running?" he said, finishing her sentence. "It's hard to explain." He took a deep breath of air and said, "Your dad asked me to help him when he hurt his arm. I thought I was doing the right thing since he was letting me stay here and eat his food and all. But it was more than that. The whole business—the night runs, the risk of getting caught, the secrecy—it was all so...so... what's the word? Exhilarating...like a carnival ride. And the money...I could make more money in one night than a whole year doing the magic show." He looked directly at her. "Kit, I'm sorry I didn't tell you." There was a long pause and then he said, "You shouldn't have snuck on board the boat. It was too risky."

"Too risky?" Kit drew herself up and planted her hands on her hips. All thoughts of approaching the subject delicately had now vanished. "Why was it too risky for me, but not for you or Dad?" she snapped. "Tell me that. And another thing…where would you be right now if it wasn't for me going all the way to Seattle to save you? You'd have been thrown in jail…or worse, you might even have been killed by those pirates. And Dad might have drowned. Drowned, Caleb. It was a good thing I did sneak on board!"

Caleb shook his head. "No, no. That's not what I meant. I am grateful for everything you did." His voice softened. "What I meant was that I wouldn't want anything bad to happen to you. Ever."

Kit felt her face redden. She looked down at the skirt of her dress, unsure of how to reply.

"I've never seen you wear a dress before, Kit. You look… pretty."

Part of her wanted to hear these words, but another part of her felt uncomfortable. "My overalls are in the laundry basket," she mumbled, as she tried to think of something else to change the subject. Her eyes shifted towards the patch of sunlight on the floor, near the window. The fortune cards were spread out there, like tiles on a strangely patterned floor.

He noticed her glance. "They got a bit damp when it rained the other night. The hole in the roof…I'm just drying them out." He scooped them up and tapped them into a neat deck. "A little warped, but they're still good." Then he looked up, caught her eye and grinned his crooked grin. "I never finished telling your fortune, did I?" He passed the cards to Kit. "Cut the deck anywhere you want."

Kit took the cards in her hand. No trace of dampness remained but the deck felt thicker than before, the cards no longer lying as smoothly together. There was a musty smell about them. Her fingers fumbled as she split the deck in the middle and laid the bottom half on top. Caleb turned over the top card. Kit felt her mouth fall open. It was the card with the long-haired woman looking into the pool of water. Kit felt a fluttering in her chest, like a bird. Her mind flew back to the first day Caleb had told her fortune, when she'd thought she'd seen—just for a moment—this same woman reaching up for a star.

"It's the last card in your fortune," Caleb said. "The one remaining to be read."

Kit tried to calm herself. "What does it mean?" she asked, her voice very quiet.

"The Star. It is a good card. It means hope. Hope and healing."

The muscles in her shoulders relaxed. One by one, she allowed her hopes to rise to the surface of her mind. First of all, she hoped her mother would get better. Hope and healing—that's what the card predicted. And what else did she hope for? That her father would give up rum-running. That the well would strike water and the farm would be revived. Maybe even that her mother and father would get back together again. There were so many things to hope for.

"What are your secret hopes, Kit? Tell me," Caleb said, teasingly.

She made a dismissive snort through her nose, like a horse. "No. And don't you go grinning, Caleb. They're nothing to do with you." She plucked the card up and looked at it closely, turning it first one way and then the next in the light. The image remained unchanged. "Before…when we looked at these cards…just for a moment…it looked like the woman was reaching up to the sky."

Caleb looked into Kit's eyes deeply, right to the very core of her, as if he was searching for something. "Right from the first day I met you I thought you had the gift," he said.

Kit felt the fearful flutter of wings in her chest again.

He was still looking at her closely. "When you can see a change in a card, it means you have the gift of second sight. Like me. You do. You know you do."

No, she wanted to say. *It's all foolishness.* But if that was the case, why had she dreamed of Caleb, before she ever saw him? Why had the witching rod shaken in her hands? Why, in the alleyway in Seattle, had she had a premonition of Caleb telling her to wait?

Caleb leaned in closer. "What about the oranges, Kit?"

Kit drew back sharply. She had not told him she'd dreamt of oranges. Or at least she didn't think she had. But how else would he know? Unless…

No. She would not consider the notion a moment longer. She pushed the troubling thoughts away and whisked up the remaining cards. "It's all a trick. The witching…some kind of trick. And telling fortunes…just a trick. You keep cards up your sleeves, don't you? Or you've marked the cards. That's how you do it."

"Come on, Kit. Stop playing around." Caleb tried to take the cards from her hands.

"No." Kit wrenched away from him, almost dropping the cards. "If you have nothing to hide, why don't you let me look at them?"

"Kit, it's not a trick. Honest."

"How do I know it all hasn't been a trick? Everything—the cards, the water trick with the glasses, the witching for the well. For all I know we've been breaking our backs digging that stupid well and we'll never find any water. There is no water there. That's what I think."

"Believe what you want, then." He said this very softly.

She could see she had hurt him but she wasn't sorry. She was not going to be taken for a fool any longer. She bent to examine the cards. One had a little nick out of the edge. Another had a bent corner. Was that purely coincidence? Or perhaps the trick was in the way he shuffled or dealt the cards. "Let me tell your fortune then," she said, determined to figure it out. She sat down at the table again and shuffled the cards well. Then she turned over the top card. A castle tower hit with a jagged bolt of lightning. A figure was falling from the crumbling tower. She pulled her hand back, not wanting to touch it, and a bitter taste rose in her mouth.

Caleb had fallen silent, his face pale.

She swallowed hard, forcing the bitterness down again. "Tell me what it means."

"Sudden change. Drama. Upheaval." He stared at the card as he spoke.

"Well, that's already happened, hasn't it? It's easy enough to know that." She tried to sound assured, but her voice came out barely a whisper.

Caleb shook his head. "No. It's yet to come. A prediction for the future. Something else is going to happen."

Kit started to turn the card over, but Caleb put his hand over hers and stopped her. He was looking directly at her. She could see her reflection in the dark of his eyes. "This will come true. Believe me," he said. "You have the gift."

That night Kit paced restlessly in her room. Then she took a pen and a piece of paper and sat down by the window.

August 14, 1924

Dear Mum,

I haven't heard from you in such a long time. Why haven't you written? I am starting to wonder if you are ever going to get better. Please write and let me know how you are.

Things have changed a little here at the farm.

Kit tapped her pen as she wondered how to word the events of the past few days.

Dad lost his boat in a storm. It hit a reef and went right down. He is safe though, that we can be grateful for. And Caleb is safe as well. But I don't think they'll be doing any more fishing—at least for a while. I'm not sure what is going to happen now.

Caleb says we should keep working on the well but, to be honest, I'm not sure we're ever going to hit water. We must be down twenty feet now and it's hard going. The rocks are enormous—some of them barely fit in the bucket. Sometimes I wish we never started on that well.

Don't mind me. I know I'm running on. I just wanted to drop you a short note to let you know that I am praying for you. My dearest wish is that you get better and we can all be together again.

Your loving daughter,
Kitty

One day Kit and Caleb were at the back of the house. They were working through a sack of corn from the market, pulling the tough, green husks from the tender yellow ears of corn.

Kit had just finished saying she never thought she'd see the day when they'd be buying corn instead of selling it, when they heard the sound of a car turn into their driveway and approach the house. The engine stopped and a door slammed.

"Were you expecting someone?" Caleb asked.

"No." Kit dropped a cob into the basket and walked around the corner of the house, Caleb right behind her.

Then they both jumped back out of sight. A car was sitting in the driveway. Painted on the side in glaring purple letters were the words *The Great Orsini. Magician.*

Kit heard Caleb's sharp intake of breath and felt the way he tensed beside her. In the next instant he had retreated down the path, through the trees to the pickers' shack. Kit ran to catch up with him. He was already stuffing cards and clothes and belongings into a sack.

"What are you doing?"

"I'm going." Caleb's voice was a strained whisper.

"Don't go. Just hide in the woods until he leaves."

"He'll know I've been staying here. He's smart." Caleb took a fleeting look around the room and limped towards the door. "I've got to get away now, before he finds me."

"But where will you go?" Suddenly everything was happening so quickly.

"As far away as I can. I'll get a job somewhere. Maybe Seattle. I'll be okay."

Kit ran to catch up with him at the door. "Caleb! Aren't

you coming back?"

He stopped and turned around. She felt her face flush red as she rushed on, "I'm afraid you won't come back. I'm afraid you're going for good…and I'll never see you again."

He smiled his lopsided smile, one corner turned up but not the other. He took her hand very gently and said, "Kit…thank you. Thank you for everything. I won't forget you…ever." He squeezed her hand tighter, leaned closer and whispered, "Remember the Star card. Have hope."

Then he let go of her hand and was gone.

17 *A Clean Start*

Caleb entered the woods behind the pickers' shack and vanished in a heartbeat. All his belongings were gone as well. There was nothing left to indicate that he had ever been there. Caleb's fortune was coming true—sudden change, drama, upheaval.

The high-pitched tones of a woman's voice could be heard from the driveway. Even without hearing the exact words, Kit knew, from the simpering rises and falls, who it was. Vivian.

Kit edged closer through the trees and ducked down behind a huckleberry bush.

"Aren't you going to open the door for me?" Vivian was pouting in the passenger seat.

"Of course, baby cakes." The Great Orsini whisked open the door with a flourish.

Vivian stepped down from the running board, straightened her skirt and flashed a brilliant smile. Side by side, they made a curious couple. Not only was he considerably older but he was short—several inches shorter than Vivian—and stocky like a bulldog. Still, Vivian looked at him adoringly and took his arm. "He's been staying in the pickers' shack, but he eats up at the house," she said.

"Where's the pickers' shack?" He had taken off his hat and was mopping his brow with a handkerchief.

"Through the trees. Down that path." Vivian pointed. "You go look. I don't want to ruin my new shoes."

The Great Orsini put his hat back on and set his mouth in a determined line. He moved silently down the path, as if he were stalking a deer. He approached the shack carefully, then flung the door wide and rushed inside.

Kit crouched low behind the bush, waiting. The minutes ticked by. Vivian fidgeted by the car, taking a stick of chewing gum from her purse and popping it in her mouth. Then she pulled out an emery board and began to file her nails. Finally, The Great Orsini reappeared in the doorway of the pickers' shack. He wore a satisfied sneer on his face as he slunk back up the path.

"Any luck?" Vivian asked.

"He wasn't there. But I found this." He held up something between his thumb and finger.

"What is it?"

"A hair. His hair. It was on the pillow. He's been there, all right."

"Of course he's been there, silly. I told you. Go ask at the house. Jack will tell you where he is." She was still chewing her gum as she talked.

"Why don't you go talk to him? He's your friend."

"He's not my friend anymore," she said emphatically. "We're through. He was a fool to lose that boat, and I told him so. 'No boat, no business,' I said. 'No business, no money.'"

The Great Orsini mounted the front steps and rapped

on the door. He waited impatiently but there was no answer. He rapped harder. Still no answer. Then he knocked so hard the windows shook. Finally Kit's father came to the door.

"I've come to get my son, Caleb. Where is he?"

"Caleb?" Kit's father repeated warily and his posture straightened slightly, almost imperceptibly.

"Yes, Caleb. Don't pretend you don't know who I'm talking about. He's been staying here. I know all about it."

Kit's father blocked the doorway, trying to stall. "What makes you think your son's been staying here?" Then his eyes strayed towards the car and he noticed Vivian. "Vivian... you came back?"

Vivian offered a weak smile. "Hello, Jack." She ran a hand back and forth along the car door, a nervous gesture.

"She's with me," The Great Orsini growled possessively. "Aren't you, baby cakes?"

Vivian swallowed. "That's right, Jack. I am."

Kit's father studied her. His eyes moved to The Great Orsini and back to Vivian again. "How did you get involved with this man?"

Vivian raised her chin. "I always wanted to get into show business. You know that. I heard he was asking questions around town, trying to locate his son. I went to talk to him, didn't I, sweetie?" She looked towards The Great Orsini and he responded with a smirk.

Vivian continued, "He remembered me right away from the charity picnic. He said he never forgets a pretty face. And he said he'd help me start my career in show business. He says I could go places. I could be a big star."

The Great Orsini crossed his arms assuredly and said, "So...are you going to tell me where my son is, or aren't you? It's no use denying it. Vivian told me everything."

"Vivian…?" Kit's father stared down the steps at her.

"I just…I just…" Her face coloured. "Well, what did you expect me to do? He's Caleb's father, after all. He has a right to know."

"The lady's right," The Great Orsini said. "Now, come on, buster. I've wasted enough time looking for that boy as it is. I gotta find him, and then catch up to the carnival so I can start making regular money again. Now, are you going to tell me where he is, or aren't you?" There was a menacing tone in his voice. Even though The Great Orsini was a short man, he was burly, heavyset and obviously not afraid to get into a fight.

Kit's father held his injured arm folded like a broken wing, making him appear weak by comparison. Kit could not sit still any longer. She leapt up. "He's gone," she shouted. "Caleb is gone."

Everyone turned to her in surprise. "Caleb left." She made her voice speak calmly as she walked towards them. "He said there was no point sticking around here anymore, with the boat gone and no work."

The Great Orsini descended the stairs. He studied her with narrowed eyes. "Where did he say he was going?"

She opened her mouth, not even knowing what was going to come out. "Vancouver," she said. "He was going to take the ferry to Vancouver and then head up to…to…" Her mind suddenly went blank.

"The Cariboo," finished her father, smoothly. "He got an offer to work on a ranch up in the Cariboo."

"That's right. He's going to work on a ranch up there," she gulped and shot her father a grateful glance.

The Great Orsini hooked his thumbs in his suspenders and rocked on his heels as he considered this information.

All the time he kept an appraising eye on Kit. Finally he spoke. "He doesn't know anything about ranches. And he hardly knows the first thing about riding a horse."

Kit's heart was thumping against her ribs, but she made herself calmly meet his eye. "He told me he's always liked horses and working outdoors. Besides…he's a fast learner."

His eyebrows crept together. "He does like horses. Ever since he was a young kid." Then he fixed her in a hard stare. "You wouldn't be telling a lie, would you?"

She shook her head. "No, sir," her answer sounding as honest as a saint.

"What's the name of the ranch?"

"He didn't say."

The Great Orsini's mouth tightened. "All right, then." He yanked open the car door. "Get in, Vivian. We're leaving."

Vivian sulked as she wiggled into her seat. "Don't tell me we're going up to the Cariboo. I don't want to go traipsing from one stupid old ranch to another, getting all hot and dusty. Smelly cattle buzzing with flies. Lord! Besides, what do you need Caleb for? You've got me to be your assistant now. That's what you said."

The Great Orsini put both hands on the steering wheel, and his jaw tightened. He took in a deep breath and let it out again. "Just stop talking for one second. Can you do that? Stop talking and let me think." Then he got out and cranked the engine. The car roared out of the driveway, sending gravel and dust spinning from under the wheels.

The sound of the retreating car faded away. Silence settled back over the farm. Kit's father came down the stairs and draped his good arm around Kit's shoulders. "We make quite a team, don't we?"

Kit looked up into his face. She saw a man who was

not perfect. He made mistakes, there was no doubt. But, then again, she had made mistakes as well. One thing she knew for sure, he was her father, and she would forgive him almost anything. She grinned up at him. "We sure do."

His eyes crinkled at the corners as he smiled back at her.

"Caleb really did leave, you know," she said.

Kit's father nodded. "I thought as much. It looks like it's just you and me."

Kit thought for a moment and then said, "Dad, what do you think is going to happen to us now?"

"What do you mean?"

"Well…" There were so many things. "You're getting out of rum-running now, right, Dad? What with your boat gone and it being such a risky, dangerous business and all? Please tell me you are…"

He didn't answer immediately, plucking a green shoot of grass and chewing on it. As Kit waited, a niggling suspicion began to form in her mind. She remembered seeing Mr. Randall and her father talking earnestly and quietly together the day of the rescue. Had Mr. Randall been offering him a job? Her stomach did a series of somersaults as she waited for his answer. Finally he looked sideways at her and grinned. "I'm not as foolish as I look."

Kit considered his answer. "What does that mean?"

A low chuckle sounded from the back of his throat. "It means I'm weighing my options."

"But you want to get out of the business, don't you?" Kit persisted. "You could end up in jail…or worse."

"You want to know something, Kit? Rum-running isn't against the law in Canada. In the United States it is, but not in Canada."

"Well, if you're caught in the United States you'd go to jail."

"But it's bigger than that, Kit. Think of it this way. What right does the American government have to say people can't drink alcohol? Shouldn't that be something people decide for themselves?" He looked at her with one eyebrow raised.

"But what if they drink too much? Look at Caleb's father—whenever he'd drink he'd beat Caleb. And his mother—she was killed by a drunk driver. Did you know that? Caleb would have had a better life if it wasn't for alcohol."

Kit's father took this in and swallowed hard. "I knew about his father…but he didn't tell me about his mother. I'm sorry to hear it." He shifted uncomfortably, and then he said, "It's not easy for some people. I'm the first to admit it. I don't have all the answers, Kit. I don't think anyone does. But I can tell you a law against alcohol doesn't stop drinking. It just adds another layer to the problems. Prohibition isn't the answer. I honestly believe that. No matter how you look at it, the law is wrong."

Kit considered her father's reasoning. Maybe the law was wrong. Maybe it was each person's right to decide for him or herself. Prohibition in the United States had not stopped people drinking, it had just forced it underground. And if a man or a woman wanted to have a drink, was that always a bad thing? Maybe not. Her own father was a good example. She had seen him enjoy a drink now and again, but never had she seen him drunk. He had not turned into a monster. He had not caused harm to himself…or anyone else. She lived in a province where there was no Prohibition and, even so, it functioned in a civilized way—at least as far

238

as she could tell. Her father's explanation did make some sense.

Still, Kit struggled. Even though she could understand his point of view a little better, she was still convinced about one thing. She wanted him to quit the business. "But there must be other ways of making a living," she said. "Rum-running is too risky. And it's not just you to consider in all of this. You have to think about how it affects me…and Mum."

Kit stopped. She was hoping he would say something but he didn't. Suddenly she felt all her other worries come bubbling up. "And what about Mum? Is she ever going to get better? We haven't heard from her in ages. And if she does get out of the hospital, would I go back to Nanaimo? And if I do, when will I see you again? And what about while we're waiting to hear from her? What about school? It's almost September. We have to start thinking about that."

He took the grass from his mouth and tossed it aside. "You know what's going to happen now? I'm going to go in and make us a good, hot cup of tea. And after that, who knows? There are some things only time will tell."

∼

Kit walked down the driveway. She didn't expect to find any mail in the mailbox for her today; there hadn't been anything in several weeks. But, still, she made herself swing the empty milk bottle as she walked, feeling the crispness of the air against her bare arms. The maple leaves were just turning yellow at the edges. School would be starting soon. Her stomach twinged with a combination of excitement and nervousness. She'd be going back to her old school, the one she'd gone to years ago, before she'd moved to Nanaimo. She would see some of her old friends again. They would become friends all over again.

Then, as she rounded the last turn in the driveway, she saw a stooped old man at the mailbox across the road. His hair was wispy white and he was leaning on a cane. It was him! Crazy old Mr. McCauley. She stopped mid-stride. Maybe he wouldn't see her. But he turned towards her and shaded his eyes against the sun. He raised his hand in greeting. "Morning," he called.

"Morning." She regarded him warily.

"You Jack Avery's girl?"

"Yes, sir."

He pushed himself straighter and studied her. "Last time I saw you, you were no more than a wee tyke."

He seemed normal enough, not at all the way she had imagined him. "I just came back this summer," she said. "I'm Kit."

"Kit…," he repeated, nodding his head. "I remember you. And your mother. Lovely woman."

"She's in the hospital now."

"Ah…I'm sorry to hear that. You give her my regards, will you?"

"I will."

"What's that father of yours been up to these days?"

Was he just being polite? It seemed to Kit that he was watching her carefully, waiting for an answer. "Oh…this and that," she said evasively.

"A little more this than that…eh?" He gave a chortling laugh.

Was he implying he knew about her father's rum-running activities? Kit didn't know how to reply so she laughed along nervously.

"Well, you have yourself a fine day, hear?" He waved and began to make his way up the path.

Kit watched his wobbly retreat through the trees. She wasn't sure what to make of him. How much did he know about her father's activities, after all? Maybe everything. Maybe nothing. He was certainly a frail old man. Probably lonely, too. A thought began to form in her mind. Perhaps all those stories about him stalking the woods at night, rifle in hand, were simply that...stories. She had been told those stories so she wouldn't want to go out after dark...so she wouldn't see what was really happening in the dead of night. How easily she'd believed them.

Then she noticed the mailbox. The red flag was raised. She rushed over, deposited the empty milk bottle at the base of the mailbox and opened the squeaky metal door flap. There were two letters, both in her mother's handwriting! One was addressed to her father. The other was thick and bulky, more of a small package than a letter. It was addressed to her.

She tore it open. Inside, something soft and white and woolly. She pulled out a pair of socks. She could tell from the stitches they'd been knit by hand.

Then she unfolded the letter.

August 20, 1924

Dear Kitty,

I'm sorry I haven't written for so long. I had these socks finished and ready to send quite some time ago (I hope they fit; I did my best guessing the size) but then I began to feel quite a bit weaker. I had a poor spell that lasted several weeks—a high fever and terrible sweats. I couldn't leave my bed. The doctor said it was the natural course of the illness. I was too weak to do much of anything, even hold a pen and write.

I thought about you every day no matter how sick I felt. I kept your letters under my pillow. Through those days and nights when I felt the worst, I kept thinking how I'd let everyone down—you most of all. I haven't been able to be much of a mother to you. I'm sorry about that. And I'm sorry you weren't allowed to visit me when you came to the hospital. When I read that in your letter, I knew how disappointed you must have been.

The fever finally broke one night and since then I have been getting better by the day. I still get tired easily but I can tell I am getting stronger. My appetite has returned. I do not cough nearly as much and I am able to sleep through the night. For the past few days I have been able to go to the sun porch again in the afternoons. I'm even thinking of getting out my painting case one of these days and making a start on a picture. It's the first time since I've been sick that I've felt up to it.

The doctor is very pleased with my progress. He says that I have a strong constitution and because I am relatively young and was so healthy before I got sick, I have been able to make a good recovery. He says if I continue to improve I can have visitors as early as next week. Isn't that wonderful? I am going to ask them to make an exception to the rule of not allowing children to visit. Let's keep our fingers crossed that you'll be able to come. Maybe in a few months I will be well enough to leave the hospital. Even then, the doctor says it will take a long time to get completely strong and healthy again. I'll need a good place to recover and quite a bit of help, I'm afraid. You must be patient, my dear one. I do not know what the future will hold but we shall see.

Believe me, Kitty, I am determined to get better. People do recover from this illness. My friend, Ada, is being discharged from the hospital tomorrow. She looks the picture of health. I am so happy for her but I will miss her cheery disposition. She promises to visit me every time she comes back for a checkup with the doctor. And she says when she picks out her wedding dress she will bring it to the hospital to show me.

I expect you must have sprouted like a weed this summer. Let's keep our fingers crossed that by this time next week you will be able to visit. I can hardly wait to see you, and it would be very nice to see your father again as well.

All my love,

Mum

P.S. I was just thinking now as I closed this letter—do you know the thing I miss most of all at the moment? The smell of your hair when you hug me.

Kit clasped the socks and the letters to her chest with one hand, grabbed the bottle of milk the milkman had left with the other hand, and ran back towards the house. Halfway back she stopped and had to reread the letter just to make sure she hadn't misunderstood. Yes, there were the words written in her mother's beautiful script. It was true. Her mother was going to be strong and healthy again.

She pounded up the steps to the house, calling as she went, "Dad. Dad. There's a letter from Mum! She's getting better. We might be able to see her next week."

He came out into the sunshine and took both letters carefully, almost as if they might break. Then he took a deep breath. He read the letter addressed to Kit first and then opened the one addressed to him. Kit studied his face as he read. His eyes flicked back and forth across the page. His mouth parted slightly, as if he were about to speak, and then closed again.

"Well?" Kit said when he had finished reading. "What does yours say?"

He folded it up and put it in his pocket. "Much the same as yours."

"It's good news, isn't it? That she's getting better?"

"It sure is."

"We can invite her here, can't we?" Kit rushed to say. She knew it was a bold question but at that moment she felt buoyant and happy, as if a lucky star was shining on her. She wanted everything to work out. "We could tell her that when she's well enough to leave the hospital she can come to the farm. That we'll look after her."

He was staring out across the fields, towards the water.

"Dad? Can't we invite her here?"

He was still gazing into the distance.

"Dad?"

He turned to look at her, his eyes gradually focusing on her face. There was an expression on his face she couldn't read. "I'm going to have to think about that," he said finally.

~

Two days later Kit's father still had not answered the question. Kit had to bite her tongue to stop herself from bringing the subject up again. That afternoon he told her he was going into town to take care of some business. It was the first time since he'd injured his arm that he was able to drive the car on his own.

A few hours later, Kit decided to rake out the ashes from the ash box in the bottom of the wood stove. It was a dirty job but it had to be done. She was just about to carry the pail of ashes outside when she heard the car return. Her father came into the house and down the hall to the kitchen door. "You know, Kit," he said, "if we're going to invite your mother to the farm while she gets better we're going to have to finish that well."

Kit almost let the pail slip from her hand. She stared at him for a second and then a huge grin broke out across her face. "You really mean it? We can ask her to stay?"

Her father grinned back.

She set the pail down, rushed across the kitchen and threw her arms around him. "Thank you, Dad! Thank you."

He laughed and hugged her back. Then he held her at arm's length. "Kit, now don't go getting too excited." There was a serious expression on his face now. "I know I haven't been the best father…I owe you this. I owe it to your mother, too. But I want you to understand this…The truth is…well, the truth is…I can't promise I'm going to change my ways. Do you think you can live with that?"

Kit nodded slowly.

"All right, then." His smile returned. "I suppose we should tidy up the farm a bit. Maybe get the grass cut. And we've got to get that well finished. Can't have your mum staying here without water, can we?"

Kit started to shake her head, but stopped. "But how can we finish the well by ourselves? The rocks are huge down there now…I can barely budge them. And your arm is only starting to get better." The thought of the unfinished work made her slump down on a kitchen chair. She continued on. "We don't even know if we'll ever find water…and if we do, you said the whole well has to be lined with bricks and mortar. Then the cover has to be made and…and…"

"I've been thinking about that too," he said. "And I've arranged a couple of men to come out and give us a hand.

They'll have that well finished in no time. You wait and see."

Kit sensed an uneasiness in his voice as he said this—a certain wariness so slight, she almost let it pass. She narrowed her eyes as she studied him. There was something he wasn't telling her. "Is that what you were doing in town just now?"

"Yes."

"Who are these men?" But even as she asked the question, a suspicion began to stir in the back of her mind. "They're some of Mr. Olmstead's men, aren't they?" she ventured.

She was hoping he would deny her accusation. But he offered her a sad, half-hearted smile instead.

Her heart sank. So, she'd been right. The suspicion continued to turn and shape itself in her mind. "Mr. Olmstead and Mr. Randall have been wanting you to come and work with them," she said slowly, "and you've made a deal with them, haven't you?"

He shifted uncomfortably and shot her a quick look. In that short moment, before he glanced away, Kit was able to read his expression. He was taken aback, she realized, surprised at her cleverness in uncovering the truth. She had surprised herself as well. And she wasn't finished yet.

"You're going to work for them if they help you finish the well," she said, finally.

Silence built in the room. Now that it had been said, Kit began to feel a little dizzy. Then her father sighed heavily and said, "Kit, I'm not going to lie to you. I'm doing what I think is best. But it's my business. Let's leave it at that."

～

A week later, Kit turned the crank on the windlass and the bucket came up into view. It was full to the brim with water. She looked up at her father and grinned. "It works! We have water again."

Her father clapped her on the back. "It's going to be a good well, all right. The water's clear and there's plenty of it. And did you notice? It doesn't smell like sulphur."

It was true. There was not so much as a whiff of rotten eggs. Kit dipped her hand into the bucket and slurped the cold water. "It tastes good, too," she said. "As good as any water I've ever had."

Kit carried the bucket into the house and filled the wash basin in the bathroom. She looked up and saw her face in the mirror. How could she have ever doubted Caleb? He'd been right all along about finding water. If only she could tell him that now.

She leaned in closer to her reflection and stared straight into her eyes. *Caleb? Wherever you are, I hope you're all right.* She did not speak aloud but each word rang, bright and clear as bells, inside her head. The brown and gold flecks in her eyes seemed to swirl; for a single, magical moment, they became unglued, fluid, free, shifting like a kaleidoscope—and then the moment passed. The coloured flecks settled into place again. An illusion, perhaps—but then again, maybe not.

She pulled back and smiled calmly at herself. And somehow she knew Caleb would be all right.

Kit cupped her hands into the water and splashed it on her face. Beautiful, fresh, cold water. Delightful. Water dripped, glistening, from her chin.

But had water ever come at such a price? Her father had been caught up in rum-running again so they could have this water. Kit pushed the troubling thought from her mind. She was not going to let anything spoil this moment. She grabbed the soap and worked it into a lather. She was going to put on a freshly pressed dress. She would pick a bouquet of roses from the garden. And then they would drive into town to see her mother.

~

The car bumped over the newly cut grass. The yard had been tidied and there was a fresh coat of paint on the front steps. They started down the rutted driveway, building up speed as they went. Kit glanced across at her father. He was at the wheel, hair slicked neatly back and smelling of aftershave. She looked down at the flowers she held in her lap; the petals trembling with every bump in the road, matching the excited way she felt—full of delicious jitters. She was finally going to see her mother. The skirt of her dress was spread carefully underneath her so it wouldn't wrinkle. Her new socks were turned neatly to form a cuff.

The car was going fast as it rounded the curve in the drive. Then, halfway around, they came face to face with another car. Brakes squealed. They stopped just in time. Kit leaned forward, peering through the windshield. It was a police car. She heard her father curse softly under his breath.

Two policemen got out of the car. They approached in an unhurried manner, checking the licence plate and then eyeballing Kit's father.

"Are you Jack Avery?" one of them asked.

"Yes. Is there a problem?"

"We've had some reports of certain activity at this address. We'd just like to check things out."

Kit saw her father clench the steering wheel tightly. "What kind of reports?" he said.

"Deliveries being made to this property, nighttime activity with a boat. Things of that nature."

"Who made these reports?"

"I can't give you that information. Let's just say things have been noticed. Now…" He indicated the driveway back towards the house. "I'm going to have to ask you to back your vehicle up."

"Very well," Kit's father said, his mouth set grimly. He stepped on the reverse pedal and twisted around to see as he backed the car up. "I bet it was that McCauley that tipped them off," he muttered. "That old busybody."

Kit swallowed hard. "They can't send you to jail, can they?"

"Not if I can help it."

"But I thought you said you weren't breaking any laws in Canada."

He parked the car in front of the house, staring straight ahead as if he hadn't heard her.

"Dad?"

He turned to face her. "It's complicated, Kit. Making alcohol, selling it, exporting it…it all has to be done according to law. If it's not…well…" He shrugged and glanced towards the police car pulling up beside them. "Don't say anything, you hear me, Kit? Let me do all the talking."

She nodded. Everything had started off so well that morning and now it was going all wrong. She began to feel a heavy tightness across her chest, a sense of foreboding, making it hard for her to breathe.

The policemen got out of their car. "Mr. Avery, we'd like to have a look at your boat."

Kit's father inclined his head. "I'd be happy to oblige you if I could, but I'm sorry to say I've lost my boat. It hit a reef and capsized. You're welcome to come down to the wharf though." He led the way across the field to the bank overlooking the wharf.

The two police officers walked down the ramp and looked at the wharf from different angles. One of them took out a notepad and began writing notes. Then they climbed the ramp again.

"Now, Mr. Avery, can you show us the barn?"

Kit thought she was going to faint. She knew very well what they'd find in the barn. Once they opened the door, her father's secret would be revealed. There would be no hope for him then.

"There's nothing to see in the barn," her father said.

"We'd like to have a look around all the same."

Kit followed the men at a distance as they recrossed the field and stopped in front of the barn door. Her father was fumbling with the keys.

"Why do you keep it locked up?" she heard one of the officers ask.

"It's an old building. It's starting to rot. I don't want anyone going inside and getting hurt." He pulled the padlock open.

Kit could feel her arms and legs trembling. She realized that she was still clutching the flowers. They were shaking even more than they had been in the car.

Kit's father pulled the door open and stepped back.

The barn was empty. Kit blinked her eyes to be certain. There was nothing there. The stacks of burlapped cases had vanished.

The policemen went inside and poked around. The one

with the notepad made a few more notes.

"Is there anything else I can show you?" Kit's father asked.

"No. That will be all, Mr. Avery. Thank you."

~

Kit and her father watched the tail end of the police car disappear through the trees down the driveway.

"What happened to all the cases of liquor in the barn?" Kit asked.

"Funny how things work out," he laughed. "I gave it away to the Olmstead boys. We worked out a deal. That was their payment for helping us finish the well and tidy up the farm. They came by late last night, loaded everything up and took it away."

Kit looked up at him sharply. "So you gave them the liquor instead of agreeing to work for them?"

"That's exactly what I mean. We're all squared up now."

"And you're through? You're getting out of the business for good? That's that, then?"

"Well…" He flashed his screen-idol grin. There was a twinkle in his eye. "You might say that…"

He took her hand and squeezed it.

~

When Kit entered the sun porch of the Pavilion, she thought she was seeing an angel—a radiant vision with sunlight wreathing the head in a halo. Was it her mother? Kit felt a flicker of uncertainty. Even though the woman before her had her mother's hair, her mother's smile, somehow she looked different. Smaller. She was sitting in a wheelchair. Although it was a warm day she was wrapped in a blanket.

Her hands were folded in her lap and her wrists were as thin as reeds. Kit hesitated. This woman could not be her mother.

Kit's father had already crossed the sun porch and was at the woman's side. He looked down into her face and a warm, gentle smile passed between them.

Then the woman in the wheelchair turned back to the doorway where Kit stood. Their eyes met and in that instant all Kit's uncertainty vanished. Of course it was her mother. Of course. Of course. And Kit was rushing across the sun porch. She felt her mother's arms encircling her, drawing her in, felt the way her body curved in around her. Her mother was nuzzling her hair, breathing it in. They did not speak right away. There would be plenty of time for that later. At that moment words were not necessary.

AFTERWORD

Between 1920 and 1933 the Volstead Act in the United States strictly prohibited the production, selling and consumption of alcohol. It was a widely unpopular law. Many people in the United States considered this so-called Prohibition to be a violation of their rights.

North of the border, in most provinces of Canada, including British Columbia, alcohol was legal during this time. It was in good supply and easily available. Not surprisingly, a black market liquor trade soon developed between the two countries, alcohol flowing from Canada, a country of big supply, to the United States, a country of big demand. Rum-runners risked being ambushed by border patrols, the Coast Guard, police and pirates—all in the hopes of turning a huge profit.

The West Coast of Canada and the United States, with its myriad isolated islands and miles of convoluted coastline, has always been difficult for authorities to patrol—and so a perfect setting for smuggling. In southern British Columbia, especially in Victoria, the Saanich Peninsula and Vancouver, the rum-running industry thrived. But although black market activity was rampant, and there were whispers of daring adventures and midnight chases, a code of secrecy existed among the rum-runners. Even years later, all but a few remained tight-lipped about their involvement.

Roy Olmstead was the most notorious rum-runner on the West Coast. His smuggling business brought two hundred cases of Canadian liquor into Seattle every day, grossing about US$200,000 a month. In the fall of 1924 the authorities began to close in on Mr. Olmstead, watching his activities closely and collecting evidence through wiretapping his telephone. Roy Olmstead was eventually convicted and went to jail. (All other characters in *Chasing the Moon* are fictitious.)

Although U.S. Prohibition—and rum-running—ended in 1933, the dangerous and secret world of smuggling still exists. What is being smuggled now, however, is not alcohol but drugs and illegal immigrants, creating challenging problems for authorities on both sides of the Canada–U.S. border. You can be certain that, as most people lie sleeping in their beds at night, somewhere a boat is slipping from its moorings, racing across dark water and chasing the moon.

PENNY CHAMBERLAIN loves hearing stories about real-life adventures. In her work as a physiotherapist she has met many people with fascinating tales to tell. One that she will always remember came from an elderly man who confessed to having been a rum-runner in the 1920s. Inspired by the encounter, Penny learned everything she could about the daring lives of rum-runners, then began writing *Chasing the Moon*.

Penny was born in Nanaimo, British Columbia, and now lives in Victoria with her husband, Adrian, and their daughter, Katie. She loves children's literature and her favourite pastime is reading and writing children's books.

Chasing the Moon is Penny's second book. Her first book, *The Olden Days Locket*, is also juvenile historical fiction. *The Olden Days Locket* was nominated for a Saskatchewan Young Readers' Choice Diamond Award, a Red Cedar Book Award and a Chocolate Lily Award.